The shot that blev
millisecond of daylight. I radioed the board and advised them of shots fired, officers involved, and gave them the address. The emergency services operator asked me to repeat and confirm the address. I had my mic open when Scoots shot Washington. She said, "Oh my God." I shouted out the Dodge window for Hooper to bring the bolt cutters.

After the Bent Dick dust up, Bush had found a clean white shirt. It stood out like a railroad semaphore in my headlights as I skidded into the alley. Hooper's car blocked my way. He had bailed out and was pursuing the wounded burglar as fast as forty years of enchiladas and degeneracy would allow. Washington was on a direct collision course with Bush. Bush raised his left hand like the Statue of Liberty, pointed his revolver at Washington, and shouted, "Halt, federal officer". Of course, Washington, eternity whispering in his ear, didn't hear. He crashed headlong into Bush, the pair landing in a dusty heap at mid alley. For the third time in a single day, Bush had been knocked on his ass by a fleeing, impaired citizen. Washing shuddered and died.

In the dim light, Scoots, incredibly active for a man missing a foot, climbed onto the roof of the Ford pickup, then onto the roof of the camper, then over the fence. He ran east, toward Hooper, on foot, and Bush, on his butt in the dust.

"Bull, the shooter is in the alley with you. He's gotta shotgun and he's behind you." I shouted.

DRAGON MARKS EIGHT

A NIGHTS ON FIRE NOVEL

BY GARY CLIFTON

CHAPTER 1: ARMAGEDDON

The first call hit the Central Alarm Office at 2:26 A.M.

"Dallas 9-1-1. What is your emergency."

"This is Percy Morgan at 4781 Brookshore. House across the street is on fire and there's a woman in the front yard screaming her children are trapped. For God's sake send help, quick."

"We're on the way sir. Can you hold the line, please?" A clock on the operator's console logged the call at 2:27 A.M. and automatically "toned" Station 57, on Audelia Road, a mile from the Brookshore location, to gear up and respond.

Investigation would soon disclose Billie Jack Givens had guzzled a quart of Jack Daniels before he crashed on the den sofa that night. Had he lived until daybreak, he might well have puked himself to death.

Billie Jack ran a brassiere factory. A rounder in spades, he'd always been a lucky, good ol' Texas boy: thirty-four and never married, outwardly a successful business man, more cash than he could cram in a sack, but financially frugal.

It seemed Billie had bedded half the gals in Dallas. Then he met Linda Marie, a flashy blonde divorcee with two active, happy go lucky boys, who had tried her hand at a brief stint of topless dancing in a dive on Northwest Highway. Jack, predictably, had fallen in lust, then a form of love, and married his new beauty.

A brassiere factory; a small operation in a run-down storefront, on Industrial Boulevard? Anyone with a pocket calculator could quickly figure it out. No way in seven kinds of reason could *Leemis Fashions*, cranking out ladies' necessities, using part time employees, generate the kind of cash required to support Billie Jack's lifestyle.

Billie Jack Givens, addicted to topless bars, moved in a circle of characters from the shadow world of the dark underside of Dallas. His lifestyle inexorably brought him into contact with plenty of friends in low places. The IRS would never see the true source of a whole other world of income he filtered through his tax return.

But on this fateful night, quiet footsteps entered the room and approached the sleeping Billie Jack. He was so drunk, breathing itself was tentative. Waking up wasn't an option. Gasoline sloshing around the carpet from a spouted can didn't make him stir. His survival instincts were receiving a final exam—a last chance to live. Trapped in life's trick box, Billie Jack Givens was about to flunk.

Fictional TV depictions of fire setting are just that: fiction. The arsonist spends several minutes spreading gasoline around, casually strolls to the door, then turns and tosses in a match. Reality does not allow that. Liquid gasoline will not burn. Oxidizing fumes drive a gasoline engine by a series of explosions within the carburetor.

The carburetor effect is identical when unconfined gasoline is dumped inside a closed structure or residence— the fumes quickly fill the room, then the entire interior of the house from floor to ceiling. With the slightest spark, fumes explode in total, breathing every speck of oxygen, and causing devastating damage. Amateurs pouring gasoline often learn this lesson too late. Death and massive burns are the price for carelessness.

Flames leave no air to breathe, searing heat to avoid, and a solid curtain of smoke to blind anyone still surviving. In seconds, temperatures reach 1000 degrees at ceiling level. A survivor of the blast lying on a bed finds, when they spring upright, the temperature increases exponentially with distance from the floor—the hair bursts into flames first, then the figure becomes a torch.

The door closed. A match was tossed back in. The killer, somehow standing just so, miraculously escaped the initial explosion.

The blast was more whoosh than a sharp report and barely

perceptible outside Billie Jack's house in the wee hours. The sliding glass kitchen patio door, frame and all, blew twenty feet, falling inches short of the swimming pool. Neighbors would report Billy Jack's Doberman only barked after the blast and after the sound of glass breaking and a woman screaming hysterically. Then the alarm expanded as many dogs around the quiet neighborhood erupted in a symphony of frightened, barking animals. The sequence would play heavily on the eventual conclusion.

Now good ol' Billie Jack was going down—or more correctly up—in flames on the den floor. Reflex brought him to his feet, a human torch roasting at a thousand degrees. He managed to inhale two, perhaps three breaths of searing flame, each hours of death agony to the dying Billie Jack. His throat seared shut, he collapsed on the carpet in a writhing glob. Incapacitated in two seconds, he was dead in twenty.

Death came quickly, hovering silently in possession of what remained of the flaming heap. Although the victim died in seconds, each was an eternity. Life would relinquish its hold on the sleeper's body as it had found it at birth—helplessly coiled into the fetal position. It was almost always the way we found the fire dead.

Down the hall, brief screams of children! By the time Billie Jack fell, explosion and flame had already breathed the last tiny molecule of oxygen in the house. Escape would be a matter of deadly luck and proximity to a door or window. The small voices quickly grew quiet—dead quiet. The animal sense of survival had failed again. Death, already hovering in the den, needed only to drift on soft gray smoke down the hallway to gather the harvest.

When neighbor Percy Morgan's first call came into the Central Alarm Office, hellfire and damnation would soon follow. Incredible as it might seem, thirty-seven seconds after being roused from sleep, pulling on gear, hustling to their equipment, the firefighters were up and running, literally.

The average response time by the Dallas Fire Department from first call received by the switchboard to first unit at the scene over a twelve-month period is about less than five minutes. Each second becomes an hour when loved ones are burning alive before you.

Response time is holy writing to the firefighter. Time is life—literally. When firefighters fail, the dead, the maimed, the burned, and the lost possessions are their crosses to bear. Firefighter nights were spent with bunker trousers inserted in fire boots, an attempt to gain seconds when they "bunk out" for night alarms. The old two-story fire stations were gradually being replaced by modern, single level structures where firefighters sleep on the same floor as their apparatus.

The brass, sliding poles lent well to firefighting lore, but far more time is required for a fire crew to descend in turn than for a crew to rush to their equipment. Drivers are required to know every street, every detour, every traffic signal in their district. There is no exception. District fire houses are notified of each construction site or any other area of possible congestion. Geography is deadly serious in the firefighting business.

With the shrieking clamor of hell itself, the crew from Station 57 plunged into the night. They came with all the practiced speed humanly possible, the emergency equipment wailing its song of despair. Men and machines could respond no faster. The seconds that seemed like hours would be all the time the fire needed on this night.

Each firefighter would carry personal burdens of guilt for days afterwards. Routes would be studied, restudied, then restudied. The response records would be rechecked until the fire cards became worn and greasy. Each man would anguish over the response time for many hours, then many days. *If we could have only gotten there a little quicker...maybe only a half-minute sooner.*

But, the outcome wouldn't have been significantly different if the whole company had been parked in the front of the house with hose lines on the ground when the match was dropped. Gasoline and death are a stacked deck against the firefighter's stopwatch and a 2 1/2-inch hose line. They had lost the race before the first call reached the switchboard.

Firefighters found flames raging a hundred feet into the

night air. They were encouraged to see that the blonde in blue jeans and cowboy boots screaming in the front yard had survived. That she was fully dressed would never enter their minds.

CHAPTER 2: The Constable Stands Ready

The dream wasn't a home run just yet, but I was rounding third base. The chesty blonde in a see-through nightgown drifted, ghostlike toward the bed. Then this damned buzzing crashed through a wall and she disappeared in a misty cloud of lingerie.

Yeah, yeah, I'd tossed a few beers, then I followed this sweet young thing I'd met at *Adair's Saloon.* She'd had her way with me before I drove home, only about a sheet and a half to the wind, to my not so luxurious Spring Valley Road apartment. I'd managed at least an hour's sleep when telephone Hell invaded my bedroom at 3:40 A.M. Damn, in those pre-cellular days, if only I'd slept over with the chick from Adair's. I picked up the receiver but forgot to say anything.

"Kobok? You there?" It was Detective Bull Hooper, Dallas Police Homicide.

"Yeah, Kobok here." I heaved myself upright on the side of the bed.

My name is Stephen Kobok. I'd been ATF agent 15 years that summer. To avoid any semblance of a national police force, the federal government had allowed several agencies to morph into bureaucratic realities. ATF, then part of the U.S. Treasury Department, was the same job Eliot Ness had made famous in the *Untouchables.* Ness had spent considerable time mowing down mafiosos with Thompson sub machine guns fifty years earlier. In the mid-eighties, we were more concerned with lengthy reports and avoiding being transferred somewhere with no zip code. And we weren't famous.

I'd never been exactly the paragon of Ivy League mold of many feds. But ATF had this special cubby-hole reserved for agents who tended to be a tad scruffy or inclined to forget the rules from time to time. Guys on the Arson and Bomb Squad did not need to appear as if they just stepped out of a *Sears* display window. Climbing through burn debris and bodies mixed together did not require a shiny exterior.

Hooper growled, "Dallas Fire just reported at least three dead in a residence fire in Lakewood. Jes' following DPD instructions to call ATF on any suspected Molotov cocktail firebombing or arson-homicides. No Molotov here. I'm thinkin' this might just be a simple brutal murder."

"Simple?"

"District fire captain says at least five gallons of gasoline dumped on a victim in the den. And Kobok? Two dead kids. Get dressed and I'll call that goofy trainee agent you been stuck with."

"Okay, Bull, thanks." Squad room banter had it that Hooper had been a Dallas cop since before color TV. Nearing mandatory retirement, he was big, tough, and identifiable from a hundred yards by the thin rim of gray hair rimming his head above the ears and a cigar stub in a corner of his mouth. The upper 90% of his bald pate could blind the unwary with deflected rays of sunshine. Hooper was a legend among the Dallas criminal element as an extremely poor candidate to piss off.

"Kobok, the district chief on the scene says they found Blood Lord biker colors at the scene. I'm wonderin' if there's a chance this deal might be related to that biker war we been investigating?"

I wasn't shocked. The thought of the scene was bad enough, but I could hack it. The thought of doing so with the monster headache that had a choke hold on my brain was another story.

"Investigating" outlaw bikers was a stretch. The Blood Lords and the Diablos, two outlaw biker gangs had been killing each other as rapidly as possible for the past couple of weeks. ATF and the Dallas P.D. had watched, but little investigation was involved.

Biker clubs are usually formed by upstanding citizens who enjoy riding motorcycles. Upstanding indicates they're employed and can afford a Harley. The outlaw gangs are in a minority and are often close with the KKK or at least wallow in a KKK-like environment. Often on stolen bikes, they were heavily in crime, particularly narcotics trafficking and regularly sent their "ol Ladies" out to engage in prostitution.

We'd spent considerable time, sorting bodies in the ongoing Diablos/Blood Lords fracas. An outlaw biker's colors, hard earned by being vicious and dysfunctional, are holy—not to be lost or misplaced for any reason. They were worn reverently as a badge of honor, even scabby honor. We hadn't seen Beeman in several days. I figured he was dead and buried somewhere to have become separated from his colors. Otherwise, no way this filthy, biker-sacred rag would be beneath a bed in affluent Lakewood...unless he burned the place down.

I found a bedside notepad. "Damned if I know much from this distance, Bull. Gimme an address."

"It's 4780 Brookshore Drive. I'm callin' whats his name." He hung up. He meant he was going to summon rookie ATF agent Randall Bush to the scene. I was too hungover to care.

I grabbed a quick shower, brushed over my close-cropped hair, and snapped my *Smith and Wesson*, 357 magnum service revolver and badge on my belt. As I stepped outside my apartment, the muggy, predawn August Dallas heat hit me in the chops like a giant wet blanket. Priorities were to first find a large 7-11 decaffeinated and Brookshore Drive, hopefully in that order.

With a world class hangover, I herded my "take home" vehicle, a five-year-old Dodge, toward the far east neighborhood of Dallas called Lakewood. Wee hour traffic was light. Lakewood, scattered over several square miles of refurbished mansions and upper class palatial homes, was home to an army of yuppies and successful people. It seemed a very unusual neighborhood to draw Homicide and the Feds to an arson fire murder.

I've said it before. Dallas! City decay has ground away at the image over the years since then. But at that time, the very sound of Dallas resonated as the good life. The luxury capital of the world, with pampered blondes trapped by massive traffic jams in their Mercedes' on the LBJ Freeway. Masses of gleaming, glass walled skyscrapers lining freeways. The home of America's Team, the *Dallas Cowboys,* thrust Dallas as the hopes of unemployed masses far and wide. Dallas, however, like all things mortal, was far less than perfect—far less.

But who could have forecast in the early morning humid heat what exact tentacles of human endeavor could wend through the tiniest cracks to reach impossible conclusions? Pandemonium, violence, and horror had just exploded into Lakewood society in spades. Life in the fast lane is always a lottery and I was headed dead on into uncharted waters at warp speed.

Well before cellular telephones, we still relied on radios and payphones. "Sixteen-ten to thirteen- thirteen" the two-way radio barked. It was the rookie trainee Hooper had mentioned on the telephone.

"Go ahead Randall."

"Kobok, is Lakewood that area east of Gaston Avenue?"

"About three miles east of downtown and north of Gaston. Don't you have a *Mapsco*?"

"Yeah, but I'm not used to it yet."

"You're a Dallas native, Randall."

"Yes, but I've never had to drive up Gaston Avenue."

Randall Bush was a recent graduate of a prestigious East Coast law school. Squad room talk agreed the kid was just biding his time with ATF until his Texas bar exam was approved, and he could go into private practice. But he's passed the ATF entrance exam with ease and his father, a prominent Dallas psychiatrist had enough pull to land the kid in Dallas. Normal policy dictated that new hires be assigned a "reasonable" distance from their place of origin. As I understood it, his years on the east coast were inserted as his hometown. Hence lawyer Bush still lived in his parent's mansion in far North Dallas.

"Lock the doors and keep your pistol handy, Randall. Drive fast and maybe all the bad guys will be too drunk or stoned to get you this time of morning."

Come to think of it, I thought, a kid from mansion-town probably never had been on Gaston Avenue. Gaston ran from downtown to East Dallas, along steady rows of used car lots, vacant store fronts, liquor stores, numerous hookers, an occasional wino passed out on the sidewalk, and general decline. Most of the residents wouldn't have been there either if they'd had a nice fifteen-or twenty-bathroom, gated entry mansion up north.

"Okay, partner. They didn't tell me when I took this job I'd have to get up in the middle of the night."

"Okay, Randall."

Bush wasn't a bad kid, or a snob. He was just as green as a new banana—a newcomer in a bizarre, alternate part of society where most never tread. Unfortunately for the kid, he was about to take a dunking in one of the most bizarre and sickening morasses of inhumanity I'd ever seen.

CHAPTER 3: PURGATORY

Even with a blistering, possibly fatal headache, the devastated remains of 4780 Brookshore were easy enough to find. The residence was in the midst of the glut of parked emergency equipment with flashing lights and emergency personnel clustered around. Stuffed in a row of brick homes, only the walls remained of this single-story version. Before the fire, the house had sat amidst well kept, similar, mostly two-story brick homes, in a typical ultra-affluent residential neighborhood. The absence of a front driveway meant that a rear entry garage would be accessible from an alley running behind the house.

I'd seen a buttload of fires. Pitched roof fires usually burn through the highest point, leaving various ruins, dependent on the intensity of the fire. With this entire roof consumed, the conclusion was obvious. The Fire Department had rolled up on a very hot fire.

I parked a block down and dug my fire-boots out of the Dodge's trunk. As I threaded through the vehicles, yellow tape, gathering news people, and neighbors roused by the noise, the odor of gasoline hung heavily on the damp pre-dawn air. Hooper had suggested five gallons, which guaranteed enough heat to eat that roof.

W.A. Roberts, a Dallas Fire Department District Chief, emerged through the hole where a front door had stood not long before and stepped out into the yard. The scene was eerily illuminated by the flickering light atop a small generator chugging away on the front sidewalk, aided by flashing emergency lights at curbside. The flickering effect aggravated my delicate condition.

"Hey, Kobok, welcome to Purgatory." His thin smile was

barely visible above his brushy mustache and beneath his helmet in the limited light. Husky, nearing fifty, his wife of nearly thirty years had died in a car accident a year before. I'd been an honorary pallbearer.

"Hey, W.A. Only Purgatory?"

"Yep. Hell comes later."

"Survivors?"

"Wife, Linda Marie Givens bailed out a bedroom window. We found her hysterical in a heap on the front yard." Soot stained water dripped off the edges of his helmet onto his heavy bunker coat. In the flickering light he looked like the Marlboro man.

I was about to learn he was spot on in his identification of Purgatory.

I looked up at him. "Bailed?"

"Smashed a bedroom window and escaped after the initial explosion. Fumes hadn't penetrated heavily enough to scorch her with the bedroom door closed. Cut her arms. We transported her to Baylor, Gaston Avenue." His gravelly voice grated like a bar-top blender.

I nodded. "We'll need to talk to her. Hooper's on the way out."

"Hey, I gotta extra bunker coat in my wagon if you want to save your shirt."

"Too hot, dude, but thanks. This rag is expendable, but not my lovely body."

He grinned through the flickering pre-dawn light and motioned with his flashlight for me to follow him back through the door hole. I followed him through the kicked-in front door laying intact within the doorframe, flat on the entry way floor.

A young firefighter pushed past us and vomited just outside the door. I wonder why not just barf in the God-awful mess inside.

In another minute, Randall Bush, almost an attorney at law, stepped inside, wearing the dark blue jacket bearing the logo "Police, Federal Agent" across the back. To preserve his high dollar, silk shirt, he was willing to endure the sticky, nearly unbreathable heat in the air by wearing the jacket. Visible in the semi-dark, he wore an expensive pair of hunting boots on his feet. Apparently, Bush had upgraded the standard issue "cheapos" the government issued us.

"Hey, Randall."

"Kobok, my government junker quit. Parked a half block down."

Bull Hooper was right behind him, sloshing along in an old pair of galoshes he kept around for digging up dead bodies. Both treaded carefully, like they expected to step on a land mine. A nail would have been more likely.

Hooper, husky, but a head shorter than me and twenty years older, his bald head exposed to water and soot dripping from the few remaining rafters overhead, was chewing on his ever-present cigar stub. I wondered if he slept with one clamped in his teeth. Old but gold as the cop lexicon went, he retained a reputation for being quick to kick the ass of most any mope that pressed their luck.

"Hey Bull," Roberts said. "dunno this young fella…?"

"Randall Bush, W.A.," I said. "Fresh out of the ATF academy."

"Nice to meet you, Randall." Roberts shook Bush's hand. "Hell of a case to break in with."

"I'll do my best, sir. I've assisted Special Agent Kobok in several fire investigations."

I glanced at the kid. He'd never seen anything within a mile and a half of what he was about to encounter. But, nobody had forced him to take the job.

Hooper flash-lighted the blackened, charred heap of what an hour before had been Billie Jack Givens. Billie Jack was now a blob of grease and fat amidst sofa springs in a room where anything flammable had been obliterated. Bush gagged but retained his stomach contents.

Interior walls were damaged, but still upright. What remained was fully open to the pre-dawn sky above. A charred, five-gallon gasoline can lay near the blob. With a toe of his galosh, Hooper nudged a soot covered Jack Daniels bottle laying intact in the debris, then looked up at me.

"Careless smoking while fondling a gasoline can after drinking a quart of whiskey?" I swallowed hard to avoid losing my coffee.

"Yeah, or the suicide of the century." Hooper tossed his cigar stub into corner debris and lit another nasty stogie. He exhaled a batch of toxic smoke, the smell distinctive, but not nearly as nasty as the God-awful odor already flooding the room.

Bush gagged again. It didn't appear this morning was going to work out well for him.

"Whada we know about this guy?" I studied the mess.

Chief Roberts tugged his notebook back out. "Uh...runs a corset and brassiere factory down on Industrial, *Leemis Fashions*."

I asked, "Could a brassiere factory support this house and a family?"

"Damned if I know," Hooper said. "But what better support than a bra?"

I conceded that I was fairly well educated in the function of brassieres but had no idea of what they cost.

"You said three vics, W.A.?" I asked.

Roberts looked at his notebook in the dim light. "Wife escaped. Two kids—boys, dead down the hall there." He pointed, holding up two fingers. "This is number three." He pointed to the mess on the floor.

Life produces a number of smells unique to themselves. Burned human flesh, saturated with gasoline, is in that category. The smell went well with my ringing ear headache.

"Boy, this guy is sure as hell dead," Hooper remarked, in a cop speak attempt to soften the horror. Cops get hardened to the misfortune of others, but it's an acquired skill. What the straight world often confuses for tough indifference, is more often an attempt to prevent violence-induced insanity.

Hooper's point was on the mark to some degree. It was impossible to identify the mess on the floor as even human, let alone a male human. A forensic pathologist would have to perform an autopsy to determine sex and identity. We only assumed it was a "him" because he was found on the den in Billie Jack Given's house and all other occupants were accounted for.

I stared at the lump on the floor. Modern Americans, morbidly drawn to violence, glorified, but camouflaged by the soft lenses of television and movieland, rarely ever actually see the horrible reality of a violent death. Usually, if misfortune does arrange for a firsthand view, the citizen faints on the spot. TV victims lie down and die neatly in a style far removed from the fate of the remains on that floor. Real ones do not.

Society smooths the problem by hiring people to sweep up the debris of death and skillfully restore the shattered on their journey through morgue, undertaker, and graveyard. The bereaved and the uninformed skip the middle steps, showing up at services to view the final, outwardly orderly conclusion. Only a marker and the spot on the ground are visited, not the decaying remains that lie below. Of course, Billie Jack Givens was non-restorable, if it proved to be him on the floor. The best he could have hoped for was that if we could scoop enough up the morgue could work their magic.

If circumstances involved a courtroom procedure, it is held among well-dressed people in clean underwear and clean surroundings. Trial judges seldom allow death photos into evidence: prejudices the jury, the defense lawyers contend. The memory of the deceased is all too often a loving photo, taken at a proper time. The truth is, death, at least in the form we usually saw, is a hell of a mess.

The form on the floor was a not-yet-systemized, blackened, horrible atrocity that resembled nothing human. Hooper could crack all the jokes he wanted. It suited me just fine.

I stooped over the can. "We gotta cap for this can?"

W.A. said, "We found a cap in the garage and none close to the body."

"No other cap, so...?" Hooper asked.

"This guy got barbequed with his own unleaded," I straightened back up. "Y'all notice the sliding patio door is laying out there with the stick-lock still in the door channel? Door was locked, and the blast blew it out intact."

"That ain't all." Hooper shined his light toward the rear. "This house is older. No direct access from the house to garage where this can appears to have been stored. To get from kitchen to garage required opening the sliding door, crossing the patio, then entering the garage through the side pedestrian door. "

I studied the layout. "Also odd in that the master bedroom

opens directly off the den where ol' Billie Jack now rests. To get to the other bedrooms down the hall, a second door to the hallway also opens off the den. For mama to get from the master bedroom to her kid's room, she had to walk through the den."

"That significant?" Bush asked.

"Dunno yet, Randall."

Roberts added, "Only two outside doors to the whole house. The kitchen sliding door with the stick in the track, and the front, locked with a key. First responders hadda kick it in...and the back gate was padlocked. Took it down with an axe. Wife said an intruder was in the house. Maybe that's who left the biker colors we found beneath he bed."

"An intruder?" I repeated.

"Yeah," W.A. said. "But apparently a week or two ago."

"Smokescreen?" Hooper asked.

He intended no pun, and his observation was razor sharp.

Hooper said, "Guess we can rule out electrical short or suicide."

I said, "Definitely not electric. I get this image of Billie Jack drinking a quart of Jack, then staggering to the garage to retrieve the family gas can, then dousing himself and lighting a match. Think we can rule out suicide, too."

Herman Jones, the night field agent for the Southwest Institute of Forensic Science walked in, puffing his pipe like the *Little Locomotive That Could*. Herman was the cleanup man who picked up the slop that humans created and carted them to the morgue. He shined his light on the remains at room center. "Can I have this one, now?"

"Yeah, Herman," I said. "Two more on deck." We were soon to see in living soot and horror, the chasm between Purgatory and Hell.

CHAPTER 4: SPECIALIZED EVIDENCE

Roberts led the three of us into what had been the master bedroom, directly off the den. The room, although minus a ceiling and roof, was still relatively intact. Had the wife dallied here more than a few seconds, smoke and carbon monoxide would have been fatal. She obviously had escaped very quickly. A broken window and blood on the sill pointed out her route to survival.

Roberts knelt, shined his light beneath the smoke, water, and soot damaged bed. Hooper pulled out the filthy, sleeveless denim jacket, water soaked from extinguishing the fire.

"Hot damn," Hooper nearly lost his cigar. He held the jacket aloft. A cloth logo sewn across the back blared in red: *"Blood Lords"*. He pointed to the name scribbled in magic marker inside the collar: *"Sonny"*. Repeating the name several times he exclaimed, "Sonny? If that ain't by God Sonny Beeman, I'll kiss Kobok's toe."

Hooper and I had arrested Beeman a year before for beating one of the biker gang girls to death, then dismembering her with a chain saw. The case wouldn't fly after two key witnesses disappeared,

"Yup," I said. "What kinda screwed up situation had to occur to transport a trophy from a sorry dirtbag like Beeman beneath the bed of a gasoline-destroyed mansion this far off his flight pattern."

Hooper exhaled cigar smoke. "We've seen stranger combinations. And we don't know Beeman's daily schedule. Maybe he was the lawn boy."

He bent and retrieved a soot covered woman's purse from beneath the head of the bed.

"What's ya' got, Bull?" I flashlighted the find.

"Linda Marie Given's purse. At least her driver's license is in it. He handed me the license and I put it in my pocket.

"Witnesses, suspects, gossip?" I asked.

Roberts said thoughtfully, "Wife was in the front yard when we rolled up. Neighbor across the street said she and her husband there," he gestured back toward the remains of Billy Jack, "had dish throwing fights often. Lady next door said Linda had told her she had breast cancer, but Billie Jack wouldn't pay for medical treatment."

I said, "That's pretty extreme."

Bush piped up. "Josef Mengele."

We all looked at him. Roberts' expression was as if Bush had just spoken Mandarin.

Bush saw he'd made a dumb comment. "Josef Mengele, the Angel of Death. You know, Hitler's henchman who conducted medical experiments on concentration camp inmates."

Hooper blew a huge smoke of cloud. "Rook, I have reliable information that Billie Jack played the harmonica in the Dallas Symphony Orchestra. Mengele? Good God."

"Detective, I attended the Dallas Symphonic a few weekends ago. They have no harmonica section."

I said, "Randall, I believe we're looking for suspects a little closer to Texas. Besides, Mengele died in Brazil in the late seventies."

"How did you know that?"

"Read it in your job app." I didn't tell him I'd just watched a documentary on T.V.

Bush stood, astonished. Funny, Bush was just as handsome astonished as he was when eating an apple. Twenty-fiveish, probably six feet two, his closely cropped blond hair went well with boyish freckles. An outstanding high school quarterback, his sturdy build suggested a regimen of weights and regular exercise. He did not look like a cop.

Hooper exhaled again and said, "Like I said, uniforms been knockin' on doors. As y'all well know, some won't answer the door at night for cops or anybody else. But a couple folks down the block say two greasy dudes sitting in an old pre-seventies model, blue Ford F150 pickup for a couple hours until the house blew, drinkin' beer. The descriptions sound like biker types. Kinda fits with Beeman's colors under Linda's bed."

"Beer cans. Prints?" I asked.

"No cans, no nothin' and not a soul called the switchboard or had enough sense to get the tag number. Tell me you're surprised?"

"Biker types, huh?" I asked. "Maybe Beeman and one of his buddies robbed, then torched the place. Anything else?"

Hooper exhaled a cloud of poison. "One lady said that yesterday afternoon, Billie Jack had a hell of an argument in the front yard with a guy she described as big as the side of a house. Thick glasses, drivin' an older model blue F150. Could be connected to the two guys parked down the street before the fire, also in an older blue F150? Maybe another biker settin' up a burglary?"

I said, "Maybe he was with Beeman, watchin' the house before the fire? We need some mugshots. But our biker files don't show anybody that fits that description. Maybe they brought Godzilla out of the cryogenics vault to end the biker war of all wars."

Hooper shrugged. "Not yet. I'll have patrol officers do a canvass during better hours to get much more. I doubt anyone can ID Beeman...or the other guy on account a' being parked in the dark."

I scribbled in my notebook. "Maybe the neighbor could ID the big guy who argued with Billie Jack. We gotta find him first and get a photo. What else do we know?"

"Doberman didn't bark," Roberts said.

"Doberman?" I looked up, surprised.

"Forgot to tell y'all about him. We gave him a tranquillizer dart," Roberts said. "Carried the animal to the shelter."

Hooper looked at his notebook. "Mr. Morton, neighbor across who was first caller, told me about the dog when I first arrived. The damned thing apparently barked at anything or everything at the slightest provocation. Vicious and a neighborhood pain in the ass. They're sayin' this time it never made a peep until he heard a muffled explosion, then crashing glass a second later."

I said, "First the gasoline fumes blew the kitchen door

and other glass outward. Breaking patio door glass would have been the first thing neighbors...and dogs would have heard. A combination of glass from the explosion and the wife smashing the bedroom window to escape would have been almost simultaneous. Master bedroom closed woulda kept the first blast from breaking the bedroom windows for her. Also probably saved her life."

Hooper scratched his ear. "From what the neighbor over there says, hard to figure anybody but a family member could of gotten the can outta the garage. Dog was inside the back yard with the gate locked. From what I hear, it woulda ate anybody else's ass who crossed between the sliding door and the garage side door."

I said, "So we're lookin' at a scenario where somebody climbed the back fence, avoided the dog, found the gas can in a dark garage, got inside and doused Billy Jack with gasoline, didn't wake him up, then exited, either locking the front door with a key or sliding the stick back in the floor channel of the patio door...and didn't immolate himself. We're lookin' for Superman."

Hooper nodded. Bush still appeared impressed by my history lesson. I hoped he didn't ask too many historical questions.

I said, "Or, like we said, an occupant of the house. We need to see what the wife has to say."

Hooper said, "And the dog didn't bark until the fumes blew and the wife busted out a bedroom window. Maybe this intruder had a key?" His weathered face twisted in thought.

"Maybe Sonny Beeman with a key?" I added.

CHAPTER 5: HELL

I ratcheted up my dead kid face. "Kid victims?"

"Gotta walk back through the den," Roberts pointed. "It's bad."

Hooper tore a Kleenex from his pocket into small pieces and we all plugged our noses as best we could.

Roberts looked at his notes. "Near as I can tell, the boys shared a bedroom. Billie Jack seems to have used the third bedroom as a home office. Fourth bedroom was used for storage.

Actual flames had not reached the bodies although they had been roasted black as the fire consumed the roof overhead. The heat would have been in excess of eight hundred degrees at floor level, possibly 1000 to 1300 degrees at ceiling height.

The larger, obviously older boy lay across the other, an apparent attempt to shield his younger brother. Remnants of pajamas clung to both in small patches; strips of flesh peeled away from both bodies. They were about the same age as my friend Anne's son, Tad. The kid on top was burned more than the one beneath.

I studied the pathetic, distorted little faces. Texas law required that an investigating officer be able to confirm that the body of a victim of violence was the same victim for whom a defendant was being tried in the courtroom. We were a stretch from developing a defendant, but I made certain I could say in court that I had confirmed from photos and word of relatives that I could identify the devastated bodies on the floor of 4780 Brookstone.

Without warning, *God, where were you...how could you,* came to mind for not the first time. Then the usual surge of guilt...a weakness I usually kicked out the back door. I'd vowed to quench any such thoughts. As always, I'd eat this carnage and share it with no one, not that anybody wanted to hear about it... or even gave enough of a damn to care.

Nobody's give a damn factor was lower than mine. Like Hooper, I had more bodies behind me than Dracula and the Wolf Man combined. I'd given up on attending Mass years ago.

Randall Bush barely made it back to the hallway before he heaved on the debris littered floor. He leaned on the doorjamb for a minute or so. "Sorry, Kobok."

"No problem, rook. In a little bit, I might use the same spot. If you need to step out in the fresh air, we'd all understand."

"No," he said with spunk. "I'm staying."

Flashlight in the crook of his arm, Roberts opened his notepad. "Jason and Trey Givens, twelve and...uh, ten..."

I looked up. "Givens? Step father...?"

"Step father adopted them." Roberts said.

No time to falter or show emotion, the big boy rules didn't allow that. But the scene was horrifying and there was no cushion, no shoulder, not for me. I swallowed my misgivings, bit my lower lip, and swore to run my foot up somebody's ass over this. I liked that phrase.

Roberts, other duties pressing, stepped out. We spent a half hour tossing the room by flashlight as dawn began to ease a little light into the scene. The room was water and soot saturated but appeared basically intact. Mementos—a peewee baseball trophy, soggy schoolbooks—were sad vestiges of young lives short-circuited. A smoke blackened *Dallas Cowboys* pennant hung from a wall. Water weakened pressed board shelves leaned off center against one wall.

I wiped sweat from my face with a sleeve until it became too saturated to use. The carnage, the dead kids, the nauseating smell was not going to run its foot up *my* ass.

A small wet desk stood in a corner. I went through the drawers and pulled a bound diary with the name "Jason Givens" inked on the front. The pages were filled with journal entries, naming several animal-characters, each entry accompanied at page bottom by a number. "Snake marks two, Monkey marks three, Tiger marks four, Dragon marks four" filled the bottom of the first page.

That page was dated several weeks earlier. Some pages had no entries or dates and often days passed between entries. A crude drawing of the four characters, plus several others was scribbled inside the front cover. Several scribbled-on sheets of paper were folded into the journal. They appeared to be score sheets, similar to gin rummy.

The last entry dated the day before the fatal fire read: "Tiger marks one, Snake marks three, Monkey marks four, Dragon marks eight". The words "Dragon marks eight" had been circled many times until the pen had partially penetrated the page. I studied the symbols and slipped the journal into my folder.

Three photographs survived in musty frames on a dresser. Two boys had to be the dead kids on the floor behind me. A second captured a couple—an attractive blonde and a stocky man with bushy mustache about Billy Jack Given's age. A third was of all four family members. All smiled out from beneath the celluloid, trapped for eternity in freeze frame. I slipped all three from the frames and stuffed them in my pocket beside the diary. The boys' photos would help in any courtroom identification that might develop. I don't know why I took the adults' pictures.

"Whatcha got?" Hooper asked.

"Family photos...and some kinda kid's diary or journal... in code. There's a funny looking gadget here. Looks like a ball with the edges cut like a ten or so sided diamond. Probably not significant, but I'll have the lab geniuses look at it. They can lay aside their comic books long enough to decipher this thing." I patted my pocket.

Bush came back into the room of horror. "Can I see it?"

I pulled the odd shaped sphere out and handed it to him.

He examined it by flashlight. "Dodecahedron."

"What?"

"It's a twelve-sided dice or some kind of game part called a dodecahedron, pronounced *dough'-deck-a-hee-dron.*"

"Sounds like pig Latin to describe the early part of a barroom brawl, Randall." I dropped it back into my pocket.

Hooper said, "We need to sweat hell outta Mrs, Givens and find that damned scumbag, Beeman...and two guys who sat up the street in a pickup."

I raised an eyebrow. "Probably in that order, Bull."

We were finished in that room. Time to learn the next episode in the downward spiral of human degradation.

CHAPTER 6: MATERNAL INSTINCT

We walked back into the den. Herman Jones, the logo across his jacket declaring "Medical Examiner" was poking at Billie Jack's blob with a chrome plated tire iron. The body hissed steam when touched. A skinny man, encumbered with coke bottle lens glasses and puffing contentedly on his pipe, Herman, if met in a dark alley, would have scared the hell out of Adolf Hitler. Lab techs had arrived in force and were systematically going through the room. Bush barfed again. Some got on his hand made boots. Christ, I had a headache.

We stepped out onto the front sidewalk. The gathering dawn humidity, heavy with smoky, foul air, was roses in Spring after being inside that horrible place. A black Honda sat at curbside, undamaged by the fire.

"Linda Givens'." Hooper caught me looking at it. "Locked and I'd love to look inside, but we sure got no grounds for a search warrant." He scratched an ear. "Billie Jack's brand-new pickup was parked in the rear driveway, totaled by fire.

"We need to toss Beeman," I said. "He's gotta be a prime suspect. We can try for the Blood Lord house, but I can't believe he'd be around there."

Hooper said, "Guys, we need to talk to Linda, the magic escape artist before we start on bikers. You guys go by Baylor, interview her, and I'll go fill in my Captain and start a preliminary report."

Hooper headed downtown. Bush and I changed footwear. I donned my Justin Lizard boots and he pulled on a pair of shoes which had to cost a month's pay. No chance I'd inquire and show my ignorance.

The bulk of public emergency cases were automatically

hauled to Parkland Hospital. Parkland shared the same real estate as the Southwest Institute of Forensic Sciences which, in turn, held the ever-popular gathering spot for the unfortunate, the morgue.

But, the procedure is not etched in stone, even though in theory, Parkland is a taxpayer supported institution wherein the patient paid only "what they can afford." Baylor Hospital in East Dallas and Methodist Hospital in the Oak Cliff are definitely not inexpensive. Geography and urgency often dictated that injured or seriously ill patients be taken there. Emergency crews had hauled Linda to Parkland's Baptist brother, Baylor.

Parking near Baylor was a full-time challenge. Think squeezing a golf ball into a Coke bottle.

The hotel across from Baylor had a dual purpose. The run-down facility rented an occasional room to someone needing to stay near the hospital. It also housed a federal prison "half way house" for inmates in limbo from being locked up to transitioning back into society. A federal gold badge would buy free parking in the rear hotel parking lot—saved a few bucks and a lot of time fighting the parking spot wars.

I drove Bush and I down Gaston Avenue. His high mileage, take-home car, which had overheated coming to the Brookston address and was DOA at curbside down the block from the Given's residence. Rather than fool with it in the heat and feeling the need to pursue the case, I opted for the office to send out a tow truck. We'd need to go by the federal building, check Bush out another vehicle, and knock out a preliminary myself. However, Linda Marie was right on the way.

Bush, trying to be discreet, gave the Dodge interior a once over. "God, Kobok, don't they ever routinely clean these cars. There's a beer can on the rear floorboard."

"Is it empty?"

"Looks like it."

"Then we'll toss it out next time we pass a dumpster."

The crush of in-bound early morning rush traffic had much in common with evolution. The drive, which should have taken twenty minutes expanded to forty, allowing a daylight inspection of the stretch I had driven two hours earlier. The area could easily be featured in "shining examples" of urban decay.

"Bush, when I retire, I'm gonna move down here. Maybe open a massage parlor."

"No foolin'?"

"No foolin'." I didn't elaborate so as to give Bush's intellectually superior mind something to ponder.

He rode in silence, deep in thought. I suppose massage parlors were a mind-full.

I wheeled the old Dodge into the rear parking lot of the half, half-way house hotel. Bush retrieved the empty beer can and a pair of fast food sacks from the rear floorboard and tossed them into a dumpster.

As predicted, I flashed my badge at the desk clerk. She was black, thirty, with horn rimmed glasses. "You're deputized to shoot anyone who messes with that antique Dodge," I said.

She laughed without commenting, undoubtedly already having heard every possible quip, sob story, or other line available to mankind.

Bush and I danced across heavy morning Gaston Avenue traffic. A lady in white, probably not a nurse, who looked mean enough to repel vampires, directed us to Linda Marie Givens' room.

"Curious to see what this lady has to say," I said. She was about to show she was no lady at all.

Baylor Hospital, sprawling two blocks along Gaston Avenue, was just gearing up for the day. Linda Marie Givens, her right arm heavily bandaged and elevated with an overhead sling, her bleached blonde hair matted and stringy, studied the pair of us with tear reddened, but unusually hard, blue eyes. She was street-flashy attractive, but loss of a family tends to alter appearances.

I stated the usual, "We're federal officers, assigned to investigate the fire in your residence. We're sorry for your loss, Mrs. Givens."

"Sorry? Are you two nitwits supposed to find who murdered my children? That sorry ass, Billie Jack was no big loss, but my God, my kids..." She dissolved in tears.

We waited several minutes while she regained composure.

"Has the Fire Department Chaplain been by to see you, Mrs. Givens?"

"Yeah, lotta damned good that does."

I stood there, enjoying the hangover induced squealing in my ears. How the hell did the police and fire Departments get somebody to do that job? Death notifications were bad enough. To try to match them up with a religious spiel was beyond comprehension.

"Did you and your husband go out last night Mrs. Givens?"

"Not together. About seven, Billie Jack drove to a liquor store to get a quart of Jack Daniels."

The empty Jack Daniels bottle beside Billie Jack's remains flashed to mind.

"Did he drink the whole quart?"

"Yeah, that illegal?"

"What time did you go to bed?"

"Me? About eleven. Billie Jack had passed out on the sofa by ten or sooner."

"What did you do before you went to bed?"

"Read *The Ladies Home Journal*. Billie Jack sat at the kitchen table, then on the den sofa, and got drunk on his ass. I was drawing water for a bath when the house blew up."

"Firefighters and neighbors report you were in the front yard, dressed in blue jeans and western boots."

"Uh, I hadn't undressed yet."

Bush piped up. "Did either you or your husband regularly sleep on the sofa, Mrs. Givens?"

"Our sleeping arrangement are none of your business, kid."

I said, "It's a reasonable question, ma'am. Your husband was found dead near where the den sofa sat."

"Awright, dammit. We was on the outs and didn't always sleep together. Billie Jack Givens was too busy chasin' low life broads to take care of family business."

"Outs?" I asked. "What was the problem?"

"I have breast cancer. Billie Jack wouldn't up the cash so I could see a doctor."

"No hospitalization?" I scribbled in my notes. "Did your husband have any life insurance?"

"Uh…I dunno." I read lie in her answer.

"He said the company health policy wouldn't cover it, the prick."

"Ma'am, we understand your sons…Jason and Trey were your children from a previous marriage. Any reason your ex would have reason…?"

"He's as useless as last week's garbage. Doesn't even send the boys a birthday card. But he's too much of a wimp to come 'round the house."

"Where is he?"

"Florida, remarried, and still worthless. His name is Jason, too. Jason Francis."

"Enemies? Somebody mad at your husband?" I asked. "He seems to be the principal target."

"Billy Jack hired stripper sluts to work in that brassiere factory and liked to play grab-ass in his office with 'um. Two or three were from that strip joint on Industrial Boulevard just up the street from our business. A lot of them were hooked up with bikers. Billie Jack and one of the bikers got into some kinda argument over one of the girls. They called her "Beaver" for God's sake if that tells you anything."

"Would that be Sonny Beeman?"

"Never heard of him." Body language said the contrary. My gut said, Linda Marie did, in fact know the dirtbag whose biker colors had been found beneath her bed.

"Did your husband have a uh, specific girlfriend."

"Girlfriends, dude. He had quite a love life. That's why we weren't sleeping together. I didn't wanna catch something penicillin wouldn't cure."

"Some dude called the house twice, making threats," Linda said.

"Over this girl called Beaver?"

"Christ, man, I don't really know. Damn well coulda been. Billie Jack also hung around a joint on Northwest Highway…the uh, Purple Parrot."

I asked. "How did the perp who set the fire get into your house?"

"Stick wasn't in the rear sliding glass, as well as I recall.

Somebody came in that door, started the fire, then dropped the stick in the channel as they left...I suppose. Hell, you're the cops. You tell me."

I asked, "You told the fire department an intruder had been involved. Describe him, please?"

"Er, uh, I only heard...I didn't see nobody. Sucker broke in two weeks ago. Stole some of Billie Jack's business checks and my driver's license."

I asked, "How'd they get in."

"Old dumbass Billie Jack left the stick out of the sliding patio door."

I studied Linda closely. I had the grieving wife's Texas driver's license in my pocket, retrieved from the crime scene.

"So you have no driver's license?"

"Yes, I do. I went by the DPS Office and requested a duplicate."

"Did somebody have a key to the front door?" I asked, picturing the two men neighbors had reported parked down the street before the explosion. "Fire Department says a vicious dog kept them out of the back yard."

"Nobody I know of had a key." Her eyes hardened. "By the time the fire department finally arrived, the dog was excited. He wouldn't have attacked a stranger before the fire."

"Is that a fact? The dog was tame?" Bush said.

"Yes, junior. It's a fact."

I said, "The gasoline used appears to be from your garage. Did you have a can of gasoline?

"Yeah, Billie Jack had some for mowing. Can was in the garage...uh, the side garage door wasn't locked."

I said, "The rear overhead door was locked from the inside."

"Yeah, but the side door between the garage and kitchen was not."

"Which," I thought, *"meant that somebody had to get by the dog to carry the gas can from the garage to the kitchen."*

"Mrs. Givens?" I asked. "Your son, Jason kept a journal which contained some sort of code perhaps...symbols of creatures like snakes and rabbits. Beside the journal was a single, metal dice with maybe a dozen sides...or maybe they could be called positions. It was about the size of a golf ball, and on each separate surface, an image of one of the characters in the journal was engraved. Looked old...the dice that is. Folded in the journal were several sheets of paper which appeared to be scoresheets. That mean anything to you?"

"Billie Jack's father was in the navy. Went all over the world. That's probably why Billie Jack was so irresponsible. The kids dug that dice thing out of some his old stuff Billie Jack kept from his father's locker. They were playing with it, but I didn't pay any attention."

I asked, "Has...did Billie Jack have an assistant manager who can look after the brassiere factory in his absence"

"Yeah, Billie Jack's brother, Norvil Givens is part owner. He just left. Surprised you didn't pass the dumb bastard in the hallway." Suddenly, I realized I didn't believe anything she said.

I asked, "Did you ever see Sonny Beeman socially?"

"No." The hard eyes said "liar." She just said she didn't know Beeman.

"No way he would have a key to your front door?"

"No damned way."

"How advanced is your breast cancer, Mrs. Givens?" I asked.

"None of your damned business."

"Any reason a Blood Lord biker's jacket would be under your bed, ma'am?"

"Oh, for Christ's sake. I thought feds were smarter. I got no damned idea how biker colors would be in my bedroom unless you jackasses planted them."

"Mrs. Givens, your husband's life insurance?" I asked again, fishing for motive.

"I...I don't really know. God, I hope so." Many years of hearing lies said her answer was exactly that. Things were already looking bad for Linda Marie.

As we elevatored down, Bush observed, "You know dad gummed well you can't drop a stick in a sliding door channel from outside. This just has to be an inside deal...and that hateful woman in there is my first choice."

"You did hear her use the term "colors."

"Yeah, you're right. Didn't catch that."

"Randall, Sonny Beeman wouldn't have enough sense to know what the stick was for, let alone be able to drop it into the channel with the door closed."

CHAPTER 7: Gold Strike

We stepped off the elevator into an early morning very crowded lobby. A prim lady in white, with silver glasses hurried from the reception desk to head us off.

"Uh, are you two gentlemen the federal men who just visited Linda Marie Givens?"

"Yes, ma'am," we replied in near unison.

I assumed Linda had called downstairs with a complaint. When she said, "Mr. Robbins, the hospital chief of security would like a word," it appeared Linda was definitely the catalyst. "Room 117, down that hall." She pointed.

The security director, a husky man of forty with a mole on his nose stood and greeted us.

"Kobok, how ya' been."

"Pauli Regetti," I replied. "Good to see ya'." Pauli had been an investigator in auto theft with the Dallas P.D. before he'd been forced into retirement the year before with a bad back.

He moved to a large safe in the corner and pulled out a small metal box. He flipped open the lid and dumped a set of car keys, about a coffee mug of gold jewelry, and a money clip on the counter.

"Kobok, this stuff was in Linda Givens' jeans pockets when she was admitted this morning. Y'all gotta take custody. Holdin' this kinda weight is way outta of the hospital's responsibility."

"That gold real, Pauli?"

"Kobok, I worked in a pawn shop a while after I got dumped by the P.D. That whole pile is gold. Prolly worth six-eight grand."

The car keys went to a late model Honda and the money clip bore the initials: "B.J.G." I counted. The clip held $243 in cash.

Pauli asked anxiously, "Can y'all take it off my hands, Kobok?"

I signed off on the security form, dumped the contents into a large envelope Pauli provided and started out the door.

Pauli said, "What do you think's goin' on, Kobok?"

"Linda Marie Givens was fixin' to take a bath with her jewelry, her car keys, and Billie Jack's cash. Seems normal as hell to me."

As we walked back to the car, I said, "DPS will have a record if she did, in fact, apply for a lost driver's license. I don't believe she did. She's lying out her ass. Odd thing to lie about."

"I can check that when we get back to the office, Kobok. If she didn't apply for a duplicate, we could show there was no intruder to steal the license to begin with. This looks like clear intent by Mrs. Givens to escape the premises with certain valuable property as they said in law school."

"Yeah, but did she mean to kill the boys, too?"

"God, Kobok, what a world."

Our group clerk, Patricia Boudreaux, called Tootie, called me on the two-way. "Thirteen-thirteen, you on the air?"

"You're up early," I replied.

"Kiss off," she said sleepily. Hell, maybe she'd been on an all-nighter.

"Morton, a neighbor in whatever y'all are workin' on called. Something about a pickup parked down from the Givens home. Blue Ford, old, first four digits of Texas License: 'NLR-1'." Bull Hooper had obviously given my office number to the witness who called in the first alarm. Good on him.

Bush said, "I can fiddle with the computer, Kobok. Betcha I can find that pickup, as well as whether DPS issued her a new license."

I swung the Dodge into the GSA garage. Bush and I walked the block to the Earl Cabell Federal Building. No, I had never looked up who Mr. Cabell was.

Tootie, looked over her old glasses at me. Black, beautiful, and the smartest person in the group, she could type three hundred miles per hour.

"Dammit, Kobok, you need to try callin' in every week or so."

"Got it, kid. By the way, Bush's car is dead. We need a wrecker to tow it to the contract garage. It's parked in the 4800 block of Brookshore. You got the tag number in your book."

"Damn, dude. Y'all coulda handled that."

"The garage needs the tow fee. Haven't you heard, the economy is in the toilet." We had a General Services Administration a short block away with a full staff of mechanics. For some reason, ATF used a contract repair shop several miles away.

"So's your mind, Kobok," she said to Randall. "Bush, you have the chance to get the hell outta here. Please don't stick around and be a clone of Kobok." She smiled.

"Got some evidence here, Tootie." I waved the manila envelope. I sat at my desk and bagged the three items from the hospital security safe in three separate baggies, then filled out an evidence tag and wired it to each bag. I tossed the bag on Tootie's desk. She was also the evidence custodian.

Until four months earlier, the Arson and Bomb Squad had been headed by a certifiably crazy supervisor named H.D. James, translated by squad room banter as "Howdy Doody James." He'd been medically retired four months earlier and was currently committed to the Terrell State Hospital. I'd hoped he was locked safely in a rubber room, but like poor Mr. Earl Cabell's history, I had never checked.

In a manner of speaking, I always wondered how a cretin like yours truly could be held to a standard which a loony like Howdy could never achieve. I often looked in the mirror in awe.

The incumbent squad supervisor was Cummins Klaster. A native of the southeastern U.S., exact location unknown, he'd been transferred down from Washington. Around forty and marshmallow soft, Cummins was a five-foot eight, bundle of deskbound soft tissue and neurotic insecurity. It appeared to me that his flabby condition might have constricted his brain. Paranoid, not the sharpest tool in the shed, and prone to early onset panic, Cummins struck me as a typical government selection of candidates to oversee men who carried guns and spent all day trying to lock somebody up for a heinous crime. He'd been on the job eleven years. How he had managed to run a mile before breakfast in the academy was one of those unexplainable wonders of the world.

He wore his hair in the agency approved, preppy comb over, except his receding hairline only allowed about half success. On about the third day he was in the office, he called me in and said, "Kobok, I'm new, but I can see you're the true leader in the squad room."

"Holy Hell, Cummins, I dunno if that's a compliment or a threat. I'll do my damnedest not to lead an insurrection."

"See that you don't," he said as petulantly as a six-year-old denied ice cream.

He soon earned the name "Short Cummins." Not a bad fit. He wasn't a flaming nut like Howdy, his predecessor. He was an indecisive, milk toast numb-nuts.

The agency had dropped the old "no potential" standard wherein an agent had to make several successful prosecution cases in a year or end up in Miami. A federal judge had ruled that such quotas were a violation of somebody's rights and hence the new dog and pony show was imposed.

Miami had been the battlefront of a shooting war the past four or five years, where dopers felt the lengthy coastline was intended as a welcome mat for drug smuggling. Our sister agency, the Drug Enforcement Administration had beefed up manpower, equipment, and methods. With combined efforts from U.S. Customs and local cops, smuggler's cajones had been squeezed pretty severely. Among other innovations, drug smugglers had begun hiding amidst the constant flow of illegal aliens seeking U.S. assistance and sanctuary. ATF had decided Detroit, Butte Montana, or Beirut, not necessarily in that order were now punishment stations.

I'd made my "quota" the year before with the help of Bull Hooper when we broke up an East Texas drug and gun running ring. At present, none of us knew exactly what the hell was next.

I had just gotten started drafting a preliminary report of the Givens murder when Bush, a desk away, erupted like a nine shot roman candle. "Beaver works at the *Fireplug,* Topless joint on Industrial."

"That's just down the block from Billie Jack Given's brassiere factory. Makes it handy to hire strippers to make underwear. I'll call Hooper and see if we can arrange a little visit to that Blood Lords hangout tonight."

But first, a little exposure to the only place in creation worse than the horror in the Givens' boys' bedroom.

CHAPTER 8: THE REVERSE SIDE OF MEDICAL PRACTICE

Doctor Lynn O'Hara, a pathologist with the Southwest Institute of Forensic Sciences called to alter my "get over the hangover". "Kobok, autopsies are scheduled for all three Givens victims at ten o'clock. I called Hooper. He said he'd be here and told me you're on the case, too. When you come, be sure to bring that cute lawyer-kid I saw you with the other day down at the courthouse."

I wondered how she knew he was a lawyer. She and I had been closer at one time, much closer. She was about eight years Bush's senior.

The Institute, jammed behind the sprawling Parkland Hospital complex, housed the morgue and a full range of forensic activity from firearms examination, to fingerprint analysis. Thousands of people drive by Parkland daily. Few even have the slightest inkling of the house of horrors nestled in the two-story building hidden behind.

Short Cummins wasn't around. I tossed the report in his in-basket and Bush left him a note, saying his car was toast in the 4800 block of Brookshore. By the time Short Cummins saw the notice, Tootie would have taken care of it, anyway.

"Bush, I have to witness autopsies of the three victims this morning. As you probably already know, Texas law requires that at least one investigating officer witness the post mortem exam. No problem if you don't want to go along. When burn victims, particularly child burn victims, are being butchered, the procedure can be pretty hairy."

I might have well poured water on a copperhead.

He said as we walked in the heat back to the GSA garage.

"Kobok, I signed on to do the job. You don't think I can measure up?"

"No, Randall. Just think of your silk shirt and necktie."

"What?"

"C'mon, kid, I'll drive."

"We're federal agents. What does state law have to do with it?"

"Thought you went to law school. We're still in Texas and if we ever make this Givens fire into a criminal case, it will probably have to be filed in state court. But even if it's filed federal, the victim identification requirement still stands."

"Oh, yeah. A house fire. It might not have the Federal Nexis, so we file it in state court."

He was referencing the rule of law that declared the feds only had total jurisdiction in cases which involved interstate commerce. We were ordered to assist local cops by investigating homicides by arson. We had to prove that interstate connection before they would be accepted in the Federal Court System. Otherwise, we went to the Dallas County District Attorney who represented state law.

"See, kid. Law school did teach you a thing or two."

Heat simmered off the asphalt as I squeezed the Dodge behind a dumpster beneath a "No Parking". As I led Bush up the stairs to the main entrance, I felt like a prison guard leading a condemned man to the gallows. I punched in the door code to the basement morgue and stepped into the next world. Hooper had not yet arrived. He was apparently being fashionably late for the gory main event.

As it was still early in the day, a dozen or so Teflon gurneys, each bearing a naked body, were still tumbled parked across the room. Two pathologists, each with an assistant called a "deiner", worked over separate gurneys next to a line of stainless-steel sinks along one wall. Soon, all gurneys would be parked in the cooler, the forensic butchery complete. Our three fire devastated victims were readily identifiable about halfway across the room.

O'Hara looked up and waved us over. Pathologists wear rubber aprons over their green lab smocks—the easier to avoid saturation with gore. O'Hara looked demurely sexy in her lab costume, her face covered by a surgical mask, blood and body fluid dripping from the end of a large knife she held. I guess since I'd seen the whole show while sipping wine on her sofa, I was entitled to a moment of lust. Lynn O'Hara was one fine looking lady, and especially accomplished at playing doctor on her sofa. Lustful thought be damned, my headache kept on keeping on.

She called out, "We're closing this one up here, Kobock. Coffee over there in the office." She gestured with the blood-soaked knife.

Bush, already showing slightly green, said, "I, uh, don't drink coffee."

She said through her mask, "Not a bad idea. It's probably strong enough to use as tire paint."

Bush did take the invitation to retreat to a small, glass windowed office in a corner.

Mounds of body parts in and out of clear plastic bags were stashed along a row of sinks along one wall. All awaited sealing or bagging and eventual refrigeration by staff. The stench of formaldehyde and other chemicals plus released bowel contents mixed with bodies which had lain undiscovered for varying periods of time was probably more indescribable than the burned remains of Billie Jack Givens on his den floor. The combination of rotten flesh, and bodily discharges of both man and dog were similar.

I stepped over to O'Hara. Standing over an elderly man with his abdomen gaping open from the standard pathology "Y" incision, she held a dark purplish glob in her hand which I recognized as a heart. Laying the organ on the sink drainboard, she quickly sliced it several times vertically, like a baker hand-slicing a loaf of bread. With each cut, my heart gave a slight tremor or sympathetic shock. As she laid back slices with the knife, she said tenderly, "Oh, the poor soul, arteries so blocked he hasn't been able to take three steps without getting light headed in years."

On the gurney behind her, lay the naked corpse of a slender white man about thirty. With scraggly, unkempt yellow hair, his body was covered with at least a hundred tiny black dots, each oozing minute traces of black, coagulated blood. The wounds were easily identifiable to any police officer as shotgun pellets having found homes. A half inch hole in the center of his forehead meant that he had been finished off with a large-caliber slug to the head. Bloody mush spread in a circle beneath his head was evidence the bullet had entered small and exited much larger.

His sightless eyes were fixed in death on the brilliant light above. The scene created an incredible urge to look upward more closely to see what was there to hold the gaze of eyes that no longer could see.

"Hey, Doc. You're about to stumble into the buggy of the guy behind you." I gestured to the victim with the shotgun wounds.

"Dammit, Kobok, my name is Lynn." She turned and read the tag wired to the victim's left big toe. "Dope dealer, run outta luck." She turned back to her elderly patient.

"Ex dope dealer, Doc."

"Lynn, dammit."

"Oh, sorry, Lynn. Stop waving that knife. I'm terrified."

Her deiner, Richard Garner chuckled. "Crap, Kobok, if she wants to cut your ass, no sense trying to resist. Doc O'Hara is mighty fast with an eight-inch blade."

I'd been around the morgue enough to know Richard very well. Fiftyish, balding, with Walmart half glasses, Fred had just uttered the first attempt at humor that I'd heard out of him. He was, in a word "goofy"—the sort who never caught a joke, always seemed a step out of step, and an intense loner.

I considered saying, "If her knifework is remarkable, you should see her buck nekked on her sofa." Instead, I said, "Damn straight, Richard."

O'Hara tossed the bread sliced heart back into the old man's hollow chest cavity and said, "Let's close it up, Richard. Gotta get started on Kobok's crispy critters."

As Richard stuffed parts from a pile on the sink board into the old man's cadaver, she motioned me aside. Behind her, Fred began stitching up the "Y" incision with a sack needle, using stitches an inch across and two inches apart.

"Dude, you look like hell," she pulled off her surgical mask.

"A little sleep would become you. Especially if you were dozing at my place."

"Deal, Doc...er, Lynn." I was still stuck on playing doctor. "Right now, I'm up to my ass in this God-awful atrocity on those three gurneys. After all these years, I still let dead kids kick my ass."

"Got suspects?"

"Wife looks first in line. Hung up with outlaw bikers some way. The blob there was her husband. Ran a brassiere factory down on Industrial boulevard. Hired strippers to sew, which can be synonymous with some sorry biker dudes in the mix."

"Hey, tough guy, you of all people gotta know you can't let this crap get to you."

"I'll live, Lynn. But only after I drop by your place for a glass of merlot. On second thought, I'd bring beer."

"Okay, then." She pulled her mask back on and turned to Richard. "Park Mr. Goldrich in the cooler and wheel over..." She turned back to me. "Which one first?"

"The blob. I might self-destruct if we do the kids first."

"Comin' right up, Kobock." Richard started across the room, wheeling the old man.

He wheeled Billie Jack Given's remains against the sink. In forensic exams, the diener does most of the cut-work, while the pathologist examines the parts the deiner extracts. Using a small circular saw with a knife edge blade, Fred cut the upper third of what remained of Billie Jack's cranium off. He held a clear plastic shield in front of him. The process normally resulted in considerable blood splatter as evidenced by the nasty mess on the ceiling. Any liquid in Billie Jack's head was long fried solid. No gore existed. O'Hara reached out and deftly fielded the subtracted shell, tossing it on a sink board.

With an ugly knife, he cut through the dura matter, the tough plastic like membrane that encloses many parts of a human body, then pried out the brain with a silver pry-bar. The brain popped free with a sound like a wet towel hitting a concrete floor. He handed it to O'Hara who turned it in her hands like she was examining a cabbage in the super market. "Unremarkable," she repeated a word I heard used by other pathologists. She meant it was not damaged.

Bush crept up, stopping ten feet away.

"Randall, You don't gotta watch," I warned. "Take my word for it. Get used to this gradually." I figured that by the time "gradually" arrived, Bush would be locked into a prestigious downtown Dallas law firm.

"I can hack it, Kobok."

Bull Hooper strolled in. "Hell fire yes, kid, you can get used to it. Step on up."

O'Hara studied the handsome young man. "Guys, that's bullshit. Bush, take a chair."

Richard stepped away and drug a chair over. Bush stood resolutely, then moved closer.

"Better sit, Randall," I said.

He took a step closer.

Richard made quick work of the remains of Billie Jack. O'Hara had examined a pile of removed organs, including the trachea Fred had sliced and pried out. The human body doesn't surrender its parts easily. She turned to Hooper, Bush, and I. "COD is thermal burns and suffocation from inhaling several breaths of flammable liquid induced flame. Close him up, Richard."

Richard tossed body innards into the cavity, willy-nillly. Bush now very green, started to the floor. Hooper and I caught him about halfway. He was still able to walk with our assistance. We each shouldered one of his arms and managed to get him out the door, up the elevator, and onto a sofa in the reception area. Hooper found a restroom, dampened several paper towels and laid them on the fallen rookie's forehead.

At this point, one of those intangibles that often interdicts well-meant plans appeared. Dr. Lynn O'Hara had an office on the first floor. I had seen her administrative assistant, Kelly, several times at a distance. Her image, however, was indelibly imprinted on my simple mind.

Kelly, hearing us in the hallway, appeared, preceded ten feet by the tantalizing odor of lilacs. About 25, in a short skirt and form fitting knit blouse which highlighted an ample chest line, she approached on lovely legs that went all the way to the floor.

"Oh, my," she imitated Little Red Riding Hood. "You fellas go back to whatever you need to do. I'll get some ice and a better cloth for his head. We see this happen often. Dr. Kelly can fix it."

She finished the comment staring me directly in the eyes. She had the appearance of a TV star and the "look" was purely predatory. Good God was this keeper trying to make meaningful contact? If she was, she'd certainly succeeded. I wondered if I might faint. Bush had the only sofa.

I tore myself away and followed Hooper back to the basement morgue. O'Hara was at the corner desk, scribbling in a file folder, signing off on Billie Jack Given's post mortem exam.

Hooper spoke up. "Kobok, I gotta be in court at eleven. Can you cover the two kids' examinations?"

"Yeah. If you can resurrect Bush and drop him at the federal building. He's gotta check out another car. His wheels are out on Brookshore, deader than good manners."

"Okay," the big man replied. "I ain't responsible if he dies." He smiled and stuffed a fresh stogie in his mouth. He strode across to the elevator and disappeared.

O'Hara looked up. "Okay, Tarzan, when can I expect you to drop by my place?"

"Uh, not tonight, Lynn. We gotta try to roust a biker. He'll probably be at a puke joint on Industrial if you'd like to come along. You'd be very popular in a biker bar. Rain check for you and me, maybe? Soon?"

She looked at me, expression funeral serious. "Kobok, I broke it off with you last time because you had the loyalty of a garden slug. I do not nor did not want a marry-up deal. Just being high on the lust-list would do."

I thought of Anne. Aside from being attached to her kid, neither of us felt our relationship was permanent. Lynn O'Hara had much in common with a Kamikaze in the bedroom—or sofa.

"Okay, Lynn. I'll call you."

The forensic workup on the two boys went quickly. They were basically collateral damage from the intentional murder of Billie Jack. If we ever managed to get to trial, their deaths might not be charged in the same proceeding as Billie Jack.

The prosecution would save them for a second trial in case the verdict went against us in the Billie Jack trial. It was standard procedure.

"Maybe we could do a trial run at lunch today," O'Hara tossed her mask and rubber apron on the office desk. "I need a half hour to clean up the report. Go check on Bush and I'll be up in a few."

"Lynn, I've been out here to witness two bikers' autopsies last week. As I recollect, a guy named Richard Sharf, nicknamed "Gut" was wearing biker colors. Do y'all keep stuff like that? I'd like to get the thing into our evidence vault."

Gut was a close buddy of Sonny Beeman. I hadn't seen him around, but he did need to sit down and tell us what he knew about Beeman and Linda Givens.

"Boxed up in records, fourth floor storage. Kelly can help you." She bent back over her folders.

And with that, the Devil's playground reared its ugly head. Well, not exactly ugly, but certainly beyond the guardrail of normal expectation.

CHAPTER 9: TEMPTATION

When I stepped out of the elevator, Bush was long gone. Hooper had apparently revived him enough to carry him downtown. I stuck my head into O'Hara's office. Kelly sat at a small desk, typing at warp speed, and emitting the fragrance of the Dallas Botanical Gardens. I'd noticed her before, but had overcome the urge to make a fool of myself.

"Yes, sir?" She looked up with large blue eyes. "You're Mr. Kobock, right?"

"Yes ma'am. Thanks for nursing Bush back to life. I assume he left with Hooper, or is he on a gurney downstairs?"

"Oh, fudge." She giggled. "He'll be fine. I've seen plenty of old timers on that sofa out there."

"Old timers? I know the feeling."

"Shush yourself, you are a very sexy man. Tough, rugged, ready. How can I help you, Kobok?"

"Last week, y'all autopsied a biker named Richard Scharf. Dr. O'Hara didn't have the file number. Says the physical evidence is in a box in fourth floor storage and that you could find it?"

"Oh, yeah, okay." She tapped her computer and jotted a number on a post-it note. "Kobok, that place scares the be-Jesus outta me. Suppose you could go along?" She studied me with the deep blue eyes.

Yeah, yeah, I know the drill. IAD would know I wasn't naïve when I ventured up there. But what the hell, the kid did appear genuinely frightened and boy she smelled good. I'd been in that fourth-floor junk room. Wall to ceiling cardboard boxes crammed with records, plus row after row of sealed cans containing bloody clothes and other reminders of horrors going back several years. The place carried the faint smell of decay and blood. It was, in fact, spooky.

Kelly brought a passkey. I followed her impressive backside down the poorly lighted fourth floor hallway. She let us in. That she locked the door behind her seemed normal enough for a frightened young lady.

Shelved boxes and cans were arranged numerically, and we quickly found the metal can bearing the correct number. I set it on the floor and resumed looking for the corresponding file box. After several minutes, Kelly spotted it, about three feet above my reach.

She circled the rows of shelves and said, "Somebody's borrowed the ladder again. We'll have to go find it."

I stood in blank stupidity.

"Can you lift me up?" She stretched up her arms, causing a tantalizing uplift in her chest line.

I knelt on a knee and formed a step with my hands supported by the other knee. She rested a red spike heel in my hands and the long legs lifted majestically upward until the hem of the short skirt reached the critical boundary. She fumbled with the box, then, delightfully feminine, lost her balance and came tumbling down. We hit the floor, Kobok, sexy blond, and about fifty file folders, in that order, bottom to top.

I've told the Priest about this, since. I know it counts against you in Hell, anyway. But it just sort of happened by Divine chance. Her face landed close to mine. Her smell was irresistible. Mouths only needed inches to meet and she tasted like apple pie. She had that old warm blouse off in seconds and in a few more, totally nude, she was grappling—that's right—grappling with my fly.

"My God, that's hard," she gasped huskily.

"Yeah," I rasped. "It's a standard issue, .357, model 66, Smith and Wesson Service revolver."

She tore at my belt, or at least it seemed so at the time. Convinced that her frenzy was only a female-chauvinistic explosion of animal greed, I knew it was useless to resist. Great Scott, I was being used on the floor of the fourth-floor storage room of the morgue. Powerless, I had no choice but to surrender to her carnal advance. She pinned me to the floor with her beautiful, blond nudity. I was helpless. Later, the Priest would be skeptical.

Then, a key in the door. She sprang off me like a caged tiger in her frantic search for clothing. Thrust aside like last year's Thanksgiving turkey, I lay, semi nude on the floor. The door swung open, catching us in full view of the intruder, both of us scrambling for clothes.

"Holy shit," I gasped, grasping for trousers and pistol.

"Holy shit," Kelly gasped, struggling to get the tight blouse over a whole bunch of human flesh.

"Holy shit," Richard gasped. Dr. O'Hara had either sent him to get the goods on me or on some other errand.

Richard stumbled out of sight. I frantically pulled on my pants and other vital pieces of polyester. Kelly did a reverse Gypsy Rose Lee in fifteen seconds. She actually got re-dressed quicker than she had disrobed.

"Jesus Christ, Lynn O'Hara will kill me right here on the spot." I pulled my belt tight.

Kelly straightened her hair. I sensed she was about to scream "rape."

"Gee whiz, dude, chill," she said casually. She stepped to the door and peeked down the hall. "I'll take the elevator. You use the back stair. Maybe we can make it another time." Her spike heels clacked down the hall. This was not Kelly's first trip to the storage area.

I spent a few precious moments of invaluable escape time reassembling the Scharf file. Files under arm and tin can in one hand, I descended as surreptitiously as possible down the back stairs. What if O'Hara carried a pistol beneath her apron? What if she just gutted me with one of those huge knives? I reached the main floor, fantasizing about the gate to hell.

"What did you do?" demanded the red eyed gatekeeper.

"Got raped on the fourth floor of the morgue," I said, partially aloud.

Great God, I nearly collided with O'Hara coming out of the ladies room.

"What did you just say, Kobok? What the hell's wrong with

you? You're sweating like you just finished a marathon."

Holy mother, she had me. She'd use the knife. I braced. Hell loomed behind a rubber apron. Maybe I could rush by her, flee the building and request a transfer to Butte, effective the next day. Maybe she'd let me live another day—perhaps just another hour.

"I, uh, have been in that stuffy store room, then walked down the back stairs, Doc, er, uh Lynn."

"Well, I'm ready for lunch."

Behind her Kelly slipped into her office. She had her skirt on backward and red heels on the wrong feet.

O'Hara said, "Kobok, before we go, your faint friend, Bush called. He says, the pool doesn't have another car until tomorrow. We need to swing by the federal building and pick him up. He's recovered enough to go to lunch with us."

"Okay, Doc, uh, Lynn, I gotta put this stuff in my car. Where do you wanna eat."

Richard hadn't snitched. God had to love Richard.

"I'd like to try this French place on McKinney Avenue."

"Okay." I would have eaten elephant on toast by that time.

"You know, Kobok, you oughta know better."

Oh God, Richard had burned me to the ground after all.

"What?"

"Be sure you sign that evidence out before we leave."

The smell of Kelly's perfume drifted down the hall. Richard was a stud. Life was fantastic. Time for sustenance and libation.

CHAPTER 10: Puttin' on the Ritz

Bush was standing on the Jackson Street side when we picked him up. Funny about the affluent. They're programmed not to sweat. In his silk blazer, imported shoes, and striped necktie, he appeared immune from the God-awful heat. Normal humans would have been soaked from perspiration. Bush could have been posing in a Fifth Avenue window display.

O'Hara spotted him and said, predictably, "What a fine-looking young man. Incredible that he seems to have recovered from his morgue-shock in an hour or so."

"Yup."

Bush slid into the back seat. "Good morning Dr. O'Hara. Sorry I didn't measure up this morning."

She smiled. "Randy, like I said, we've had plenty of old timers lose their stomach during a forensic procedure. You'll get used to it."

He won't be around long enough, I thought. "Bush, they give you any idea when you can find another car?"

"Tomorrow. Can you give me a lift home today?"

"You mean tonight. We're gonna have to have a look inside that biker joint on Industrial. The uh…"

"Fireplug," Bush replied.

O'Hara said quickly, "You mean the devil's den of iniquity."

Having seen Lynn O'Hara in private after a glass of wine, I stifled a smile. Her show beat the hell out of anything found in any low rent topless joint.

"Enough, Kobok," she admonished.

I eyed Bush in the rear-view mirror. The exchange seemed to pass over his head.

"Your system recovered enough that you're up for lunch?" I asked.

"Sure. We having pizza?"

"No, Lynn has a place on McKinney Avenue she likes. Don't recall the name." I would have preferred grease and enchiladas.

"The Le Horneen," O'Hara said in a tone reminiscent of Scarlett of the same last name.

"Oh, excellent choice," Bush said, like he'd just opened his Christmas stocking. "I went there with a date a couple of weeks ago."

The restaurant name, to me seemed more appropriate as the "Lay Horney" for several reasons. Although I didn't want to let a valet parking slug get the keys to my government vehicle, I also secretly didn't feel like paying the guy. I parked in an end-zone, tossed my "U.S. Treasury Department, ATF" sign on the dash. We suffered the fifty-foot walk in the blazing heat to the Lay Horney.

We passed beneath a canvas canopy, walking on a dark green outdoor carpet. A guy who appeared to have been on a ten-day bender stood just inside glass doors, dressed in a brass buttoned, knee length dark green coat at two sizes too large. In dim light, he would have been a knock off for Napoleon's cook. Had he not been under at least partial cover of air conditioning, the heat radiating inside the canopy/plastic carpet would have been fatal in less than ten minutes. He pulled the door inward with a sort of flourish.

"Mademoiselle, monsieurs, welcome to the Le Horneen," he greeted in an accent as phony as a tin Rolex. With another flourish, he motioned us forward to a second guy in a jacket equally as goofy, only it was maroon. Did a maroon coat outrank the green coat guys in Napoleon's army. He wore a name tag which read, "Maitre d' Jean-Pierre".

"Un tabell for three," he said in counterfeit.

"Hey, Jake, how the hell you doin'," I said to the very un-French Frenchman.

O'Hara and Bush both turned and glared at me as if I'd just grown a tomato from my forehead. A fat lady cashier, riding a stool behind an entry counter appeared ready to bolt for the door at the intrusion of such a crass, crude commoner.

"Hey, hell, Kobok, didn't recognize you."

He had not noticed me because he'd homed in on O'Hara's ass which looked like a glittering jewel out of that apron and smock get up she usually wore. That's probably how he managed to get himself sent to the joint for tossing a Molotov in his dope dealers Lincoln four years ago. As I recollected, he had four to do before parole at the Federal Correctional Center in Texarkana, Texas. That had occurred no more than two years ago.

"When did you get out, Jake? Thought you had to serve more...?"

"Early parole. Federal judge decided we had too many inmates. Turned some of 'um loose. Don't worry, I got permission from my parole officer to work in a joint that sells booze. Gotta talk like a damned fruitcake but beats being in the joint."

"Glad you're out, Jake. Stay off the shit and maybe you can make it."

Bush and O'Hara both stared at us, mouths agape. I guess neither one had ever seen an east Dallas scumbag screw-up before. In O'Hara's case, at least not a live one.

"Kobok, you still on the bricks. Figured you'd be a wheel in Washington by now."

"Been there, Jake, done that. Don't want any more." I had never actually lived in D.C., but had spent enough time up there to know not to want to go back.

"Damn, Kobok, I never met nobody who'd lived in Washington before." He pointed to the pudgy cashier. "This is my ol' lady, Agnes."

I nodded to Agnes, who was equally transfixed, expecting me to 'cuff her homey and drag him out the door.'

I glanced at the growing line behind us waiting to have seats and worms or whatever they served. "Uh, maybe we oughta sit down, Jake. Gotta table sorta in the back?"

He led us to a table overlooking a little garden out back, helped O'Hara with her chair, continued to admire her backside, and placed a menu in front of each of us.

A drop-dead Dracula clone brought a wine list which I

deftly handed to Bush. He ran a finger down the list, then turned the menu to ask O'Hara's opinion, then ordered. I asked for a beer. After increasingly disapproving stares from Dracula, O'Hara, and Bush in that order, ol' Drac retrieved his wine list and disappeared.

The black and white menus were in French, or Greek for all the hell I could tell. We received a ration of translation from a very non-French waiter, who had to have the menu memorized because he sure as hell couldn't read it. I turned to O'Hara who explained every item on the menu.

"They teach French in medical school, Lynn?"

"High school." She smiled, demurely.

I ordered what she guaranteed to be a French chicken sandwich. I joked. "Damn, Doc, I mean Lynn, I've known some spring chickens but never a French one." The line dropped like a metal rooster and I dummied up.

Bush and O'Hara ordered something in French and the waiter evaporated just as Dracula brought the wine and my beer. He held the bottle and glass away from him like it was coated with anthrax. Probably jealous because he couldn't drink it.

"Well, Kobok," Bush said as Dracula walked away again. "How do we stand on suspects in our case on Brookshore?"

I glanced around and said softly, "Randall, it is not a 'case' until we bust somebody's ass. It's not good to speculate and get your mind closed up on facts. If I was to guess, I'd say the little wife, some damn way in cahoots with Sonny Beeman or some of his pals would be prime suspects. You saw her reaction when I asked her about life insurance. There may be other factors and I'm not fully convinced she's the killer."

O'Hara sipped wine with a dainty touch quite different from the effort required to carve up human beings. "My God, Kobok, surely she would have gotten her sons out first?"

"Maybe she made the old mistake of torching Billie Jack with the idea that afterward she'd break out the boys' bedroom window and rescue them. Amateur arsonists often underestimate the characteristics of fire, especially a gasoline fire. Gasoline is not charcoal fluid—much hotter fire. The fire spreads too hot too fast and breaking out a common household window is not easy unless you bring a hammer. However, if she dumped five gallons of high octane on him in the den, then tossed a match, she should have gotten burned all to hell. If she is good for it, she someway managed to toss in a match with the master bedroom door just closed enough to avoid giving her some major flash burns...or worse."

"That's remarkable," Bush said. "How do you know all...?"

"Didn't go to law school, Randall."

The waiter brought our food. I ordered another beer.

O'Hara looked at me reproachfully. "Kobok, you're a candidate for liver failure. Sure you're not drinking too much?"

"No, I drink just the right amount." I grinned.

O'Hara and Bush ate plates full of gray stuff with yellow stuff poured over it. Maybe one was yellow with gray poured, because I downed my chicken delight without looking directly into their plates. It was apparent that whatever the combination, the goo they were eating would be easily converted by the body before elimination.

The waitress brought us a pastry dessert which wouldn't have covered a poodle's paw. He handed me the check which was about equal to a day's pay. When we reached the well-fed cashier, I flashed my Visa. She said, "On the house, Mr. Kobok. Jake says you treated him like a gentleman when you busted him."

I dropped a twenty on her counter and Napoleon's cook held the door as we blended outside into the heat. By the way, twenty bucks was humongous in 1985.

Bush spoke first. "Kobok, should we be taking a gratuity, especially from a guy you sent up?"

O'Hara nodded like a high school librarian.

"Folks, for old Jake and his ol' lady, to handle a tab like that, Jake, and probably her too, are dealing again. What Jake just thought was a bribe, is my cue to tip the dope-cops to where he is. He'll probably be back in the joint sooner or later. Sorry Jake, but you always were a dip."

"Kobok," Lynn said. "That's sort of disingenuous. You said you were glad he was out."

"Sale Gere, Doc." I guessed that was French for "Stay outta the dope business."

"I suppose you're right." She slid in on the hot vinyl seat.

"Lynn, we need toxicology on Billie Jack ASAP." I patted her shoulder.

"Maybe tomorrow," she slipped on sunglasses. "You gonna snitch on me for accelerating the process."

"No, I had other plans for you in mind."

Bush coughed at the implication from the back seat. He was probably ill from the crap he had just consumed at the Lay Horney. Damn fool should have opted for McDonald's.

"Call me," O'Hara said as she stepped out on the Institute parking lot.

"Or you call me as soon as we get lab results on the Givens' clan."

I watched her sway up the steps. "Bush, she's got the running gears of Jane Mansfield."

"Who?"

"Doctor O'Hara."

"No, I mean who is Jane Mansfield?"

We drove back to the federal building. This time Short Cummins was present.

"Cummins, we're gonna roust a topless joint on Industrial tonight. Need to interview a dancer and a biker named Beeman. He's in the computer."

"Search warrant?"

"No search involved. Just interviews."

"Need help? Need me to go along?"

"No and no, but you're welcome if you'd like. Probably won't be any activity until ten or so. Those people are nocturnal, like rats. They're mostly still in bed this time of day."

"Don't get Bush hurt."

Bush standing beside me looked at me expectantly.

"Witnessed his first autopsy today."

"How'd he do."

"Kicked ass. No problem." I thought of Kelly, impromptu nurse, her red heels and the rest.

I called Hooper and alerted him to the upcoming evening's

activity. He said he'd enlist as many patrol officers as we needed and meet us at the *Kickstand* coffee shop a half mile from the Fireplug at 9:30.

Bush and my badge got us into the heavily gated neighborhood near Central Expressway and Walnut Hill Lane. I made certain the goon on the gate would still be on duty later in the evening. Bush climbed out at his father's mansion overlooking a made lake with several spewing fountains.

"Wear old clothes, tonight, Randall."

"Don't have any," he grinned boyishly as he slammed the Dodge door.

After whizzing 9 miles in only fifty-one minutes, I spotted Tad, my current squeeze's son, bouncing a tennis ball off the side of my apartment complex's wall. He scooted inside, came back with two gloves and a baseball, and we played catch until all the moisture in my body had drained. Anne came out on her balcony in shorts and a bikini top. Holy hell, she looked like Ann Margaret.

"Got time for a little pasta and a couple of beers," she called down invitingly.

"Gotta work tonight. Might be home by midnight. Rain check? How late is too late?"

"If the front door light is on, I'm on."

I went inside, downed three beers and took a much-needed nap. This evening might involve some hands-on action.

I'd carried the Sharf file up to my apartment. "Gut" Sharf, a Blood Lord, had been shot 7 times while exiting the Purple Parrot Topless Club on Northwest Highway, at 1:07 A.M. two weeks earlier. His companion, Wilson Wagers, "Sonny" Beeman had been uninjured. I recalled something being said that Beeman and Sharf had tangled over the same chick. Later, I'd learn that "chick" was a world away from what I had expected.

CHAPTER 11: Beaver in the Flesh

When I retrieved Bush from mansion-land, he was waiting by the guardhouse of the gated community. We met Hooper at the Kickstand at just before nine. The radical change in environments had to cause Bush sticker shock. In a few minutes, the whole universe would change.

"Kobok, I already talked to the district sergeant. He'll have two uniforms meet us at that closed down gas station across from the Fireplug joint at 9:30. That enough manpower?"

I ordered a grease burger and coffee. "Yeah, by ten the place should be jumpin'. Forty or so customers, all Blood Lords, all stoned and drunk. We can handle that."

Hooper rolled his cigar. "How do you wanna play it?"

"Normal, we walk in, be nice, find this "Beaver" chick who I believe is Sonny Beeman's ol' lady. We set the bait, Beeman won't be far away."

Bush asked over his coke, "Don't we need a search warrant?"

"Naw. ATF can inspect any licensed liquor place during regular hours any time. We aren't gonna inspect squat. We just want Beaver and Beeman. If any ass-kicking is necessary, you don't get involved, Bush. I'd bet a buck they won't make any trouble, but if they do, we'll handle it." I pointed my forehead at Hooper.

Hooper laughed. "As many Blood Lords and Diablos that have bought the farm in this stupid shooting the past couple weeks, I'm surprised there's forty of them dumb enough to cluster up in one place. Don't think they'll put up any fight. If they do, we'll do whatever we gotta do." His grin meant ol' Bull Hooper might kick somebody's ass.

"Why does anyone want to be in an outlaw biker gang, anyway?" Bush asked.

"Deathwish, kid, plus being eat up with the dumb ass." I washed down the last of my burger with stale coffee. Health food is invigorating when preparing to visit a fine place of unusually earthy entertainment.

The two drafted uniforms were sitting in a marked squad car in the designated closed service station at 9:30 sharp. Over the hood of my Dodge, we strategized. The screeching of the Fireplug jukebox had to be rattling windows a block away. A dozen motorcycles and an equal number of battered pickups and cars were parked outside.

"Hooper, Bush and I will go in the front door. Uniforms take the side door, enter, and help if a brawl starts, although I doubt it will. We got no warrant and it's a public place. So, we can't keep anyone from running out either door. Anybody who runs probably has warrants outstanding. Matter of fact so does most everyone in there. I hate to say it, but we need info, not arrests. We can come back another night, ID every sucker in there, and have the paddy wagon full in ten minutes. And don't shoot nobody."

Bush said uneasily, "Sure we don't need more help? These are bad asses."

Hooper lit a fresh cigar. "Bush, you'll learn soon enough, these turds are afraid of us, not the other way around. At least by-god they better be. If I hafta break some goon's damned neck, watch and learn."

"Remember, it's not arrests we want. We need to talk to a stripper named "Beaver" and a dirtbag called Sonny Beeman if he's in here. Everyone ready?"

Inside, the blasting music was accented by a packed house and marijuana smoke nearly too thick to see through. Hooper had been right in assessing the naked stupidity of the glut of Blood Lords, all engaged in a murderous melee with the Diablos. Gathering up in close quarters so vulnerable to a drive-by shooting was dumb, dumb, double-dumb.

About thirty-five tattooed outlaw bikers, all of whom appeared to have avoided soap for at least a year, stood around the circular bar extending into the room, gawking upward at a skinny, tattooed, naked girl in cowboy boots clomping around on top to screeching music. The reek of body odor was defeating the nearly unbreathable smoke and marijuana smell in the "choke me out here" contest.

Hooper shouted above the din into my ear, "A whole damned room load of punks who've hit rock bottom and still keep digging."

The effect of total silence when Hooper found and unplugged the juke box was, as they say, deafening. The familiar sound of solid objects clunking on the floor meant that numerous armed bikers had tossed their pistols and probably several stashes of some form of dope.

As suspected, about a half-dozen greasy men fled out the two doors. A solid wall of hostile faces held their places. By brief flashlight inspection, we spotted no one who resembled Sonny Beeman's mug photo enough to grab him. We'd try to ferret him out, using Beaver the stripper as bait.

Hooper mounted the bar/stage via a stair at the rear and walked down the surface, kicking several drinks out of his way. His husky hulk standing above the crowd bore an amazing resemblance to a lowland gorilla. Hooper, however, was tougher than any ape.

"Greetings fellow Americans," he roared. "The police are here to serve and protect. Tonight's rules are this: We ain't lookin' for no nickel and dime dope cases nor do we intend to clear out the place and seize all them damned pistols and crap I'm hearin' hit the floor. However, anyone gets unruly, we got fifty SWAT guys just down the block who are gonna enter, break some stuff, and everyone in here gets to give your friendly urine specimen…and then we kick a few asses as we provide a courtesy ride to the Sterrett Center."

Dead silence gripped the place.

Hooper continued. "Outstanding. Citizen cooperation is the backbone of a civilized society."

The sullen silence remained. The crowd may have been collectively stone deaf from the music. He stepped back down the stairs to face the bartender, a tall, slender man of about thirty-five with a scraggly goatee, a pot belly, and gold glasses.

He demanded, "Whut the hell do y'all want?"

Hooper leaned close to his face. "Beaver. I wanna marry her."

"Never heard of her."

Hooper grabbed the man by both lapels of his sweaty shirt and lifted him several inches off the floor. "Say again, dipshit?" That the shirt didn't disintegrate was impressive.

"Oh hell, you mean Beaver. Why dincha say so. She's in the dressing room right beyond the stairs, there." Hooper dropped him. "What's the problem, officers?" His voice had risen several octaves.

"We'll ask the questions, dude," I said. His glasses had nearly slid off his nose.

"Okay, guys, cool down."

If he thought Hooper was hot, they'd never met.

The door read "Ladies", but in view of the hard fact there were no ladies within miles, Hooper led the way in. I squeezed by a glut of bikers and followed, motioning Bush to follow."

"Ladies only, Kobok."

"We'll adjust, Randall."

The little room stunk of sweat, cheap perfume, cigarette smoke, marijuana, and decay. About six girls in various stages of dress stood around. EPA would have declared a national disaster. Fortunately for my stomach, nobody was using the commodes..

Hooper boomed, "Beaver stays. Anybody don't want a piss test get out now."

Nobody moved.

"Okay, Bush, bring in the re-agent kit. Now Beaver, raise a hand, or it's down to the Sterrett Center for all of you."

"I'm Beaver," said a dark haired, drug dissipated girl sprawled on a small sofa that had been wedged into the room. Nude except for a red G-string, her legs sprawled apart lewdly, she had a tattoo of the rear half of a mouse running north creating the illusion the upper half had disappeared into the vital area.

Hooper repeated. "Everyone out."

"I'm nekked!" pleaded a skinny blond.

"So's everyone beneath clothes, Lady, " I said. "Put on a shirt or something."

The crowd exited in a wad behind a symphony of profanity, struggling to all get out at once. The odor of them remained.

"Beaver, we need to have a little talk.." I said.

She slouched, legs still spread, a tattoo of a cat prominent on her bare left breast. About twenty, goin on fifty, she said, "No charge to y'all, officers." Her voice slurred by drugs and booze, she gestured to Bush. "Sweetie Pie first."

"Uh, Jeez," Bush stammered.

Hooper delivered Beaver a zinger. "Damn, girl, cross your legs, I gotta weak stomach."

Beaver never moved.

On the time-tested adage of not letting an untried rookie hear things he might not understand, I said, "Bush, why don't you go back out into the bar and see if those two uniformed officers need any help?"

Bush stepped through the door, closing it carefully.

I said. "Beaver, you don't produce some photo ID, it's only half a mile to the Sterrett Center."

"For whut, for Christ's sake?"

"Conspiracy to commit hybachery."

"Hy what?"

"It means we'll find a reason. We just need to know what the hell your name is, young lady."

"Jesus, dude, chill. I's Deborah Jean Brown."

"Photo ID? How about a valid Texas Driver's License?"

"I ain't got no license."

"Ya gotta have a picture ID to work in this joint. Get it out, now." I pulled handcuffs from my rear waist. Yeah, that was harsh treatment, but I was fresh from the burned devastation of the Givens family.

"Hey, baby, if you wanna play kinky with them handcuffs, I don't mind if your buddies stay and watch. I left my whip at home. You wearin' a belt you can use?"

I waved the cuffs. "No chance, kid. I'd have to charge you fifty bucks like any other chick."

She smiled slightly, but just enough to reveal yellowed teeth. Meth was already consuming her. She reached up and pulled a shoulder-bag from a hook above the sofa. The shoulder-bag signaled that, in all probability she was into prostitution on the side. All who carried such a bag were not hookers, but all hookers were armed with a shoulder-bag. I wondered if she danced, sewed brassieres, and sold her body on the street, she was probably a hell of a worker. The "go fast" result of shooting speed supplies considerable energy—for a while. Sky rockets burn out pretty fast.

As she reached in the bag, Hooper rested his hand on his pistol. Stranger things had happened.

I took the bag away from her and dumped the contents on the sofa beside her. From a small wallet, I pulled a laminated Texas ID card. Similar in appearance to a Texas Driver's License, it was the magic pass for those who have lost their right to drive one way or another. The photo on the card matched the dissipated young woman sitting comfortably 99% nude in front of Hooper and me. The Card bore the name "Deborah Jean Brown", with an address in Pleasant Grove. It was not the address of the Blood Lord headquarters.

"Who lives at this address?"

She sighed. "My mother, Francis Smith."

"We check that and it's not mama, you get a federal charge: False Statement to a Federal Officer."

"Christ, homeboy, it's good ol' mom. Go check if you can catch her sober enough to remember her name."

Hooper jotted down the info from the card and said, "Lemme walk out to the car radio and check for warrants." He stepped out.

Beaver said, "I'm using the name Deborah Jean Beeman now, asshole."

"Sonny Beeman is your old man?" I asked.

"Yeah, and yer gonna regret fuckin' with me, dude. He finds out you hassled me, you need to go hide at the station house."

"We're from the federal building, sis, but Sonny shouldn't have any trouble finding me. Matter of fact, I need to talk to Sonny. He's an old friend." I didn't tell her Hooper and I had busted him on a murder charge earlier. Hey, that's sort of like being a friend.

"He's gonna fuck you up. Whadya think about that."

"I'm too scared to think."

Hooper walked back in and whispered in my ear. "No warrants or other wanted in the name Deborah Jean Brown or Beeman. We run her in and print her, I'll bet AFIS will get a hit."

He was suggesting that if we jailed and fingerprinted her, the FBI computer would match her to a violation of some sort under a different name.

So, I turned and lied like hell. "Beaver, looks like you're wanted for murder in Utah. Get some duds on and you can call a lawyer...or badass Beeman, from jail. Looks like it's a death penalty case. No problem, you'll be in Utah by morning where the weather is much cooler." I turned to Hooper. "How do they execute in Utah? Firing Squad?"

"Yeah, I saw a film of a Utah execution once," Hooper said. "Only one of the shooters has a bullet, the rest blanks. The guy with the live round missed and shot the dude in the eye. Jesus, what a mess."

Eyeball shots must weigh heavily on toked out biker chicks.

"Jesus!" Beaver wailed. "I ain't never been in no damned Utah. Don't even know where that is. What am I gonna do?"

"Tell us how to find Beeman."

"I tell you, do I still hafta go to Utah?"

"Naw, we're federal agents. We can get the charges dismissed. Probably mistaken identity anyway."

"Sonny went to San Antonio. Somethin' about a damn motorcycle. He's comin' here tonight when he gets back."

"What time?"

"Hell, I dunno. Later is all I know."

"Did you work for Billie Jack Givens up the street at Leemis?"

"Yeah, couple days a week."

"Billie Jack and Beeman get into it someway?"

"Uh...not really." I read lie.

"Did Beeman know Billie Jack, or come around Leemis?"

"Yeah, to pick up my paycheck."

"Did you screw Billie Jack?"

"Uh, no." another lie.

"Did Beeman make it with Billie Jack's wife?"

"Hey, dude, Sonny's a big ol' full grown dude. What he does ain't my bidness." She gave the normal biker chick reply which I translated to "yes".

"Tell me about Richard Scharf?"

"Who?"

"Gut."

"Oh yeah. Some Diablo sumbitch shot him fulla holes. Damn near got Sonny, but they ain't tough enough to do Sonny Beeman."

"You sleep with Gut?"

"That punk ain't never got none o' this." She pointed to her crotch. I thought I might follow Bush's morgue act and barf.

"Who was Gut's ol' lady?"

"Uh, D.D."

"Stripper:"

"Yeah, nice tits."

"She work for this joint and Billie Jack both?"

"She danced at the Purple Parrot on Northwest Highway, but yeah she worked for Billie Jack, too."

"Where is she?

"I'm thinkin' when Gut bought it, she went back to Scoots. His leg is fucked up, but he's hung like a mule. 'Sides, she was with Scoots first. Him and Gut had some words when she went over to Gut."

"Scoots. Orville Wilson Garcia."

"Huh?"

"Scoots. His name is Orville Wilson Garcia."

"Whutever, dude."

"What's D.D.'s name?"

"Charlene sumpthin'. Dunno her last name."

Could Gut's murder be Beeman's doing? Sonny might have killed him, hiding under the confusion of the ongoing biker war. Scoots was Beeman's buddy. Did he kill over a woman?

Hooper and I left Beaver in shellshock on her sofa, still in G-string and tattooed skin. We motioned the two uniforms to follow and made for the front door. Bush was engaged in animated conversation with three pudgy, filthy bikers. I poked him on the shoulder.

"Problem, dude?"

"Oh, no. We're just having a conversation about lawyers. This is Red Fred." He pointed to a big man with a full red beard and head of hair. "He went to a year of law school. Wants to hire me if I go into private practice."

I ignored Red Fred and the other two. "Randall, best remember right now you're an employee the U.S. Treasury Department—ATF."

"Yeah, I understand, Kobok, gosh. We were just talking."

We pushed through the crowd. As the door closed behind us, the screeching music exploded anew.

CHAPTER 12: BAD ASSES

We sent the two uniforms on their way. Hooper, Bush, and I met a block down and conferred, using my Dodge hood again.

I said, "Hooper, we got this. I know you're off the clock. Get some sleep. Me and Bush can wait here. Sonny Beeman is gonna show up as sure as sunup."

He said, "May be sunup before he shows."

I looked at my watch. "The Fireplug closes at 1:30. It's past eleven. Beaver makes a few bucks tonight, he'll show to claim it. Soon, I'd bet." It seemed I was going to miss curfew at Anne's apartment.

"Don't forget Beeman's gotta outstanding traffic warrant. Nickel and dime, but you can lock him up."

"Okay, Bull." Hooper was twenty years older than me and a half head shorter, but the feeling that his mainspring was eternal was unavoidable.

Hooper drove off in his old GMC pickup. I drove Bush and I back to the closed service station across from the Fireplug.

"What was the social gathering with you and the bikers, Randall?"

"Like I said, that big one, called himself 'Red Fred'. Said he went a year to law school. He and both others said they wanted to be able to get in touch if I passed the bar and went into private practice. Another guy there…uh 'Animal…, uh, McGurk, wanted to have his picture taken with me to send to his mother. Said she was doing life for murder in Mississippi and hoped to raise her morale." He studied me from the passenger seat in the semi-dark, apparently waiting for approval.

"I already gave you my sermon about who you work for. No

need for further inquiry." He was just fortifying my suspicion that he'd be gone when he got licensed and found a lawfirm position. "But Randall, Red Fred, real name Cletus Roscoe is on parole for murder and Animal, true name Felix McGurk is suspected of at least two murders."

"Darn."

"Did you think lawyerin' would bring you clients from Sunday school?"

"I saw Bent Dick in that crowd you were entertaining."

"He said his name was Bent Dick. Does that mean his pecker is…?"

"Naw, Sullivan was on parole for like…burglary. He stole a motorcycle, a Honda. What kinda badass outlaw biker drives a Honda? Cops got after him, and he drove the Honda under a city bus at about 85 miles per. Didn't kill him, but it left his neck turned about a third of the way to the left."

"How could he function?"

"Sideways. He's all screwed up. Gotta make a partial turn to do anything. Dunno how he eats. Carefully, I guess."

"He was clean cut. Didn't look like a biker."

"That's cuz he lives with his mother down in Pleasant Grove. She's meaner than the whole damned Blood Lords/ Diablo crowds combined. Makes him shave. Been in the joint for murder. No idea how she paroled out."

"My goodness."

At just before midnight, a battered Cutlass with a driver and at least one passenger drove slowly by. My battered, dark blue Dodge was unnoticeable in the dark. They didn't see us. They circled back and parked a half block down. Both men got out, picture book images of outlaw bikers, in the limited street light.

To get to the Fireplug, they had to walk right past us. I didn't recognize the driver, but the passenger was Sonny Beeman, fat, ugly, dirty, with shoulder length, dirty blond hair and a full matching beard. I stepped out into their path. Both hesitated for good reason. We could have been Diablos. Their macho, plus probably a snoot full of dope, made them feel invincible.

"Hey, Sonny, it's me, your pal Kobok." Bush stepped around the Dodge from the passenger side.

Beeman, who had retreated a step, said, "Keeeerist, Kobok. What the hell I did?"

"Sonny, if either one of you is carryin' heat, Bush here is gonna have to shoot both of you."

"Hey, man, chill," Beeman exclaimed.

I said to the companion, a skinny rat-faced specimen with shoulder length black hair. "Got ID?" Then I recognized him. "Hey, Rat" He was Harry "Rat" Gentry, several times convicted of assault and God only knew what else.

Rat stiffened. "Think you can take it from me?"

"Go ahead and shoot his ass, Bush." Bush, obviously confused, actually placed a hand on his magnum. I trusted he had enough sense not to shoot the man. It happened, he didn't need to.

"Hey, hey, shit." Rat threw up his hands like an old Gene Autry movie. Beeman didn't speak but also raised both hands to shoulder height.

Beeman said, "Kobok, we don't want no trouble with the feds. What the hell y'all want?"

I said. "Rat, we got no business with you. Move on and no harm will come to you." Smarter than he looked by a factor of ten, he dropped his arms and moved toward the Fireplug.

"Rat, stay smart. You come back outta that outhouse with a bunch of guys, Bush is still duty bound to shoot some of you. And he's a deadly shot, just out of the academy." I had no idea whether Bush could hit the building across the street, but neither did Rat. He hurried away.

We needed to get clear of the area before Rat enlisted help.

"Sonny, you're under arrest. Cuff him, Bush."

"Man, this is piss!" Beeman objected. "Busted? For what." He bowed up as if to fight.

"Sonny, Sonny, you gotta recall the last time, I kicked your ass. This time, ol' Bush is gonna shoot you out here in this dark street. Nobody's gonna give a damn."

Bush stood, doe eyed, but Beeman put both hand behind his waist.

We had him cuffed in the back seat and were halfway down the block before I saw in the rear-view mirror, several bikers spill out of the Fireplug door.

To enter Sterrett by car, we pulled close to the outside door, which opened immediately. A guard was watching via camera. We pulled in against a second overhead door and the outer door closed, trapping us. "Show credentials to the camera," the guard said via a speaker. I flashed my credentials and the second door opened. I found a parking slot.

Bush sat in wonderment. "Darn, Kobok, I've never done this before."

I got out and helped the handcuffed prisoner out. "Randall, just try to make sure you're never the one in handcuffs." I dug my folder out of the trunk.

We checked our pistols in the little lock boxes outside Central Intake, taking the key with us. We seated Beeman in a small interview room just inside the first barred door. In the bright light I studied Beeman. If Linda Marie Givens was sleeping with this sleazy character, she just damn well might have been capable of murdering her husband. She at least needed an ophthalmologist. Sonny Beeman was one ugly bird. But he was also probably mixed up in Billie Jack and the boys' murders.

I motioned for Bush to remove the handcuffs. Beeman turned and rested his beefy, heavily tattooed arms on the small metal table. "Whut the hell, Kobok?

Feds doin' a traffic pinch. What a crock."

"Sonny, I heard you were atop the Diablos hit list. Hellfire, man, I wanted to get you off the street for your own safety. It's a welfare deal."

"Bullshit, you don't care about my welfare."

"When did you drive to San Antone?"

"Early this morning. Left around four when I got done with business. How'd you know…?"

"How well do you know Billie Jack Givens?"

"The brassiere guy?"

"Yeah."

"My ol' lady and some other skanks I know work there."

"You know anybody who drives an old, blue F150 Ford pickup?"

"Yeah, about ten people, I guess."

"It would be the same old F150 you and another guy were driving when you sat in front of Billie Jack's house last night."

"Whoa, I was in the Fireplug last night 'til they closed. Then took a chick out to the Blood Lord house, got some, then me and Rat drove to San Antone."

"Around four, you said."

"Yeah. What the hell?"

"And Rat will swear on his mama's grave that's the whole truth, nothing but, etc?"

"Yup. We tried to buy a brother's bike down there in San Antone but couldn't make a deal. Had a few beers, drove back. Then y'all got your ass in the act."

I'd have wagered if "steal" was inserted for "buy" we'd be closer to the truth. "Gimme the guy's name, address, telephone, and his pants size."

He rattled off a name and other info. I scribbled in my folder.

"Who was the second guy waiting in line?"

"No way."

"Dude, another witness might help you avoid a murder rap, 'cuz that's where we're headed."

"Scoots, man, but I ain't upping where he's staying."

I recalled from my files that Blood Lord Orville Wilson Garcia, called "Scoots" because of a bad foot had murdered a Diablo in front of a witness. Not only was he a dead man walking with the Diablos, a Capital Murder warrant for his arrest made him open season to every cop in the territory.

"So Scoots was at the Blood Lord House last night. How did he get there? Maybe in an old dark blue F150?"

The cold eyes gave just enough flicker to disclose I'd hit home. Scoots was probably parked, watching the Givens house before the fire. Beeman was probably with him. But why, exactly? To participate in a murder? More likely waiting on Linda to come out and play. Maybe she came out, did her number, and then both torched Billie Jack?

"Scoots is a long-time burglar. He help you defeat the door locks to get inside to gas up Billie Jack?"

"Wasn't there, dunno whut Scoots drives." Both again were lies. Chances were good Beeman had been within a two-minute walk from the Given's house when Billie Jack and the boys got it.

"Witness reported a very big, very agitated man in an argument with Billie Jack in his front yard a couple days before the fire. That you driving Scoot's truck?"

"If I wanted to beef with Billie Jack, I'da gone to his office. Never really been to his house."

I leaned forward. "Then how the hell did your Blood Lord colors get beneath Linda Marie Given's bed?"

His mouth agape, he blurted, "Y'all planted them. I ain't never been…"

"You screw Billie Jack's wife?"

"That illegal?"

Bush said, "It sure would be if it's hooked on the end of an arson murder."

Beeman looked across the table as if Bush had just sung the first stanza of *Sound of Music*. "Whut?"

"Yes or no?" I asked.

"Um, no comment."

"Better cop to getting a little of Linda, dude. Beats the murder rap I got in my back pocket."

"Awright, awright. I went by the Brassiere place to pick up Beaver's pay. The bitch, Linda, was there and she gimme the eye. I remembered her. She danced at a joint on Northwest Highway a couple years earlier. Had them sewed on boobs, except the doc had screwed it up. She had nice knockers, but one is slightly off. You know, man, Chinese tits like one hung low?"

"What club on Northwest Highway?"

"Purple Parrot."

"We hear Billie Jack hung around that place? Did he own some or all of it?"

"Naw, I don't think so. Linda worked there before I met her."

I knew the owner of the Parrott, Dimitri Bastovic, who'd drifted down from Chicago years earlier. Tough, three hundred pounds and reportedly mob connected, he'd earned the reputation for being ruthless and about half nuts. I'd handled a car bombing on the parking lot of the Parrott a year or so earlier. Nobody injured, and the case remained unsolved. Dimitri had probably murdered the perpetrator.

"Linda have breast cancer?"

"Naw, but she was on Billie Jack's ass all the time to get cash to straighten up her boob job. I told the bitch she looked jes' fine nekked."

"Why were you and Billie Jack in a hassle?"

"We wadn't."

"Crap. We know Beaver works or did work for him at the brassiere place. I figure he was gettin' some of her and you objected."

"Man, you're wrong as hell. I didn't object to Billie Jack takin' Beaver in his office for a quickie. Christ, Kobok, she's a good earner. Whut the hell else are women good for. I was pissed because he paid her for a tumble on the desk and not me."

"You sayin' you screwed Billie Jack?"

"No, hell, no, man. I didn't care if he got some. I jes' wanted the damned money he paid her for services rendered, you dig? It wasn't no damned hassle. I jes' tol' him where the money was supposed to go."

"That chick you were balling last night? Was that Beaver?"

"Yeah, my ol' lady. And a couple of brothers was waitin' in line."

"But you murdered Billie Jack before you left Dallas this morning…after you and some other mope sat parked in that old F150 for a couple hours down the block from his house? Maybe you and Scoots sitting out front waitin' for Linda to come out and pony up some lovin.'

"Got tired of waiting, she let you in, and y'all gassed Billie Jack?"

He leaned backward, hands out front protectively. "Hey, hell man, whoa. Slow down here. I ain't had no reason to kill Billie Jack. Christ, I barely knew the dude."

"You doused him with gasoline and burned him to a cinder. In the process you killed both his boys."

"Bullshit. Is Billie Jack really dead…and the boys. Jesus. Who…why?"

"I was kinda figuring you in the mix somehow, Sonny."

I tossed three photos I'd kept from the morgue on the table.

All three were shots of Billie Jack and the boys at the stage of autopsy where the body cavity was spread wide and devoid of organs."

"Kobok, if Sonny Beeman is gonna kill a sumbitch, he don't need no match. And if you think I'd do a kid, you're way the hell outta line."

"Especially if the victim is a woman. The kids were collateral damage, Beeman. Billie Jack was the target."

"I ain't never hit a woman in my life, dammit. I ain't saying nothin' else, Kobok. I wanna lawyer."

Never hit a woman? At the gravity of such a lie, I braced for Heavenly Lightning to Divinely penetrate the concrete and steel fortress, strike Beeman dead, and finish me with the leftover juice.

Bush saved us all by dropping another irrelevant zinger. "You should talk to Red Fred. He went to law school, and his rates have to be cheaper than an established lawyer."

Beeman glared at Bush. "Who the hell is this guy? He a lawyer or one of y'all?"

"One of us who's a lawyer."

Beeman stared across the table. "Kid, were you really gonna shoot me up there on Industrial a while ago."

"Shoot or kill?" Bush replied in a voice similar to requesting pepperoni instead of sausage. "Mr. Beeman, they taught us in the academy to shoot into the center body mass. Shoot and kill are the same thing under those circumstances."

"Holy Hell," Beeman gasped.

"One more chance, Sonny. The buddy who was standing in line to get at Beaver? A name might save you a murder rap. Would that be your gimpy buddy, Scoots?"

He smiled slightly and shook his head. He might give up Scoots, or whoever was in line, assuming there was anyone, when we busted him for capital murder. Until confronted with the three-needle cocktail, he wouldn't spill. Until such time, I would proceed on the assumption the second guy in line was Scoots. They'd probably murdered Billie Jack and the boys, then drove to the Blood Lord House, slept with Beaver, then what? I made a note to make ATF San Antonio checked his alibi.

"Sonny, is D.D. still with Scoots?"

"Dunno. She was, but I ain't seen her like in the last week."

When we booked him in, he serenaded us with a symphony of profanity far more advanced than any subject taught in law school.

"Mr. Beeman, you'd be more respected if you didn't swear so much," Bush admonished.

The man on the gate of Bush's mansion-heavy community was not the same guy I'd dealt with earlier. Bush got out, spoke to him, and he raised the gate.

"Pick you up at seven in the A.M., Randall," I said as he stepped onto the cobblestone circle drive of his parent's place.

"My God, Kobok, it's nearly one A.M." He glanced at his Rolex. "God, I'll have to be up by five."

"Me, too." I drove away. The gate jerkoff raised the gate when he saw me coming. I figured he had orders to discard as many beat up vehicles like the Dodge whenever possible.

Anne's front door light was on when I swung in from Spring Valley at 1:24 A.M. I figured she'd dozed and left the light on unintentionally, so I went straight to my place. In one minute my phone rang.

"You gone blind. The light's on." I grabbed three beers from my fridge and beat it straight across the courtyard. I worked three cold ones around a full dose of Anne and collapsed on her bed at about three.

It had been a 24-hour day, with more to come. Hell, no telling what the women would look like in Butte, Montana if I couldn't clear the Givens murders.

I'd later learn that approximately 100 bullets had been fired into the Diablo house near the city limits of Garland, a Dallas suburb during the night. Casualties were limited to minor wounds caused by flying splinters and broken glass. But the Blood Lord-Diablo war was still alive and well.

CHAPTER 13: BANK BIDNESS

Bush was leaning on the gate guard's open window ledge, dressed to the nines—maybe the tens, if that's possible.

He glanced at his Rolex as he slid into the passenger seat. "You're ten minutes early."

"Imagine that, Randall."

We beat Short Cummins to the office by the same margin, ten minutes. He wandered in wearing his usual odd assortment of white socks and mismatched green coats and trousers, with a pink tie. Bush and I were sitting at desks which were head to head. I had been roughing out chapter two of the Givens preliminary report. Bush was on the telephone, trying to milk the partial license number the neighbor had given for the large man who Billie Jack had argued with before the fire. Cummins strolled over.

"Progress on the Givens case?" He took a plastic chair beside my desk.

I gave him a brief summary of the previous day, leaving out the nightcap trip to Anne's apartment.

"Wife is still the best suspect, hey?"

"Yes, but there's always the chance, she had some help, like Beeman. Or, maybe Beeman did it. We got a way to go, Cummins, 'cuz there's always the chance she's innocent.

Bush slammed down the phone and burst, "F 150, 1970 model, Texas license number beginning N-L-R-1. Only two F150's older than 1970 with the first three numbers NLR in this area. One is registered to an 80-year-old female up in Grayson County. The second is registered to Bruce Clarence Ligon, age 32, lives in an apartment on Beacon Street in East Dallas. Got priors for disorderly conduct, drunk in public, and get this, arson. All sentences probated except he spent thirty days for observation in the Terrell State Hospital."

"Arson of what?," Short Cummins asked.

"Doesn't say. Released from Terrell two months ago."

"Randall, but that's good work. Soon as I get a corner on this report, let's go see if we can find Brice."

Then, Bull Hooper short-circuited the inquiry about Bruce. My desk phone buzzed. "Bull Hooper on 3," Tootie said.

I flipped on the speaker phone. "Kobok, bad news, worse news, and some good, but first have you heard about shots fired into the Diablo house last night."

"Nope. Casualty count?"

"Minor wounds. All will survive."

"Is that the good or bad news?"

"Neither, that's just a statistical footnote."

"Gimme the bad first, Bull." Short Cummins sat raptly on his plastic chair. He'd possibly never heard bad news.

Hooper said, "Sonny Beeman bonded out at 6:32 this morning. He was in on a capias warrant. The huge sum of $124.57 was paid in cash which satisfies the fine, costs, and penalties."

A capias warrant is issued when the defendant is assessed a penalty by the court, then fails to pay. Paying the whole bill set Beeman free.

"That doesn't sound so bad, Bull."

"It was Linda Marie Givens who appeared at the bond window and bailed that loser out. Whatcha make of that?"

"She told Bush and me she didn't know Beeman. How'd you learn...?"

"Clerk on the night desk called me. Old friend. Knew we were up to our asses in that biker war."

"Fortifies why Beeman's Blood Lord colors were under Linda's bed and why he's now a much better murder suspect. Thought she was in Baylor?"

"Released yesterday evening...about the time we were tossing the Fireplug. She had cash."

"What do you mean?

"That's part of the good news. The president of the Lakewood

Tradecrest Bank called in here a while ago. Seems his bank received a check for payment for $76,000 from Billie jack Given's business account yesterday afternoon. The check, bearing Billie Jack's signature, which the bank calls a forgery was written on Billie Jack's business account check, but deposited in Ajax Savings and Loan up on Ross Avenue. The Ajax account is Linda Marie's. He thinks Ajax screwed up and let Linda write a few checks to cash."

"Why didn't she just go to Billie Jacks' bank and write a check to cash?"

"Because she's not a signer on Billie Jack's account. The bank guy said a couple of months ago, Linda did exactly that. Drew a large sum in cash from Billie Jack's business account. Billie Jack came in the bank, raised hell, and canceled Linda as a signer. Linda couldn't go to Billie Jack's bank and make a withdrawal. She had to try to make a deposit in her own account with Billie Jacks' forged signature."

"She actually get any money?"

"Dunno. Banker hinted she did. We'll have to go to the S & L. She woulda had to write checks on her own account to get any money."

"So, she took a huge bite out of his account, knowing, he'd find out, then he conveniently went up in flames the same night she'd written the check. Sounds like motive to me."

"Seventy-six grand nearly cleaned the account out. That pretty good incentive, especially if she knew Billie Jack was gonna be all up in her ass the next day or so."

"Hooper, she told us an intruder stole her driver's license and some checks outta Billie Jack's checkbook. She was laying the foundation for this little deal."

"Can you pick me up out in front of my building. Otherwise I gotta go check out a car."

"On the way. Bank open this early?"

"Dunno, but the bank guy called me. He's there, at least."

"Hey, before you walk down to the street, can you call the Intelligence Unit and see what they have on The Purple Parrott and Dimitri Bastovic, the owner?" In the eighties, we did not have computerized files either in ATF or the local police departments.

"Yeah, sure."

I explained the deal to Bush and Short Cummins. "Bush, you're gonna have to flesh out the Givens report. Don't forget to include the stuff we picked up at the hospital."

"I'll check it," Cummins said.

"Bush, also you need to call ATF, San Antonio and see if they can confirm Sonny Beeman's alibi. And hold on to that info from the partial license plate on the old Ford parked at the Given's place before the fire. And Bush?"

"Yes," he looked up from the pad he was scribbling on.

"Call DPS, Austin and see if Linda Marie Givens applied for a duplicate driver's license to replace the one the 'intruder' stole from their house."

"Okay, Kobok."

"Keep me posted." I walked to a row of file cabinets, pulled the file on the car bombing at the Purple Parrot and walked in the sizzling sun to the GSA garage.

Hooper's husky form, standing hatless and fogging a nasty stogy on the Commerce Street side of the Police and Courts Building was difficult not to see. He was leaning on the concrete entryway down which Jack Ruby had walked, just over twenty years earlier, to put Lee Harvey Oswald in his grave. Hooper had been in the group grope when Ruby had pulled the trigger, but never landed in the news.

I handed him the Purple Parrot file and looked across the seat in question. "Intell Unit?"

"Talked to a friend over there. He says Bastovic is mob connected, but didn't you work a bombing out there? You oughta know that Russian bastard is nuts. My guy said, the mad Russian is heavily into importing girls from middle European countries and forcing them into prostitution. We've had a couple of Jane Doe homicides who we figured belonged to Bastovic, but good luck. Not only no witnesses, but no ID of the victims."

Since the bombing on the Parrott lot had resulted in no death or injury, Homicide had not been called out.

"We need to have a talk with Dimitri and just to screw with him, line up every damned stripper and sweat them, too."

"Okay with me. But I got court tomorrow. Maybe you and Bush..."

"Okay, but the strippers are gonna get Bush all upset."

"Hell, Kobok, they get me upset."

A tall, balding man of fifty unlocked the front door to the Lakewood Tradecrest Bank. "Fred Bilderback, bank president," he greeted. We showed ID and shook hands. He locked the door behind us. I'd never been in an empty bank before.

"Thank you for calling, sir," I said.

We sat across from him in an office sufficiently drab to be a prop in a sleep clinic. He tossed a folder on his desk. "I'm supposed to ask you fellas for a subpoena. After we see exactly what y'all need, can you be sure and get me one to cover my ass?"

We both nodded.

"Sorry we didn't catch this sooner, gents. Clerk in bookkeeping lives out toward Lakewood and had read of the disaster in the Given's home. Then she sees this large check written on Billie Jack Given's account and deposited in Mrs. Given's S & L not far from here. There are samples of Mr. Given's signature in there. You can see no attempt was made to copy his handwriting. Appears to me Mrs. Givens is trying to steal $76,000 from her husband's business account by a very poor forgery. Since he just died in what the papers call an arson fire, I thought y'all would want to know."

Hooper asked, "You said something on the phone about a previous incident?"

"Riot is more descriptive, Officer. Couple of months back, same deal, except we paid the draft from Mrs. Givens' S & L. Eight thousand, which we ponied up and took the loss. We tried to file charges, but Mr. Givens said he'd handle it...wouldn't file a complaint. Mr. Givens came in shouting and had us remove her as a signer on his account."

"You ever meet Mrs. Givens, Mr. Bilderback?" I asked.

"I vaguely recall her being in here. Flashy blonde, chesty, too much makeup and perfume. Don't recall ever talking to her, but I do remember her boobs and swishy butt. Hadda couple of nice-looking boys with her. She talked to those kids like they were galley slaves."

I thumbed through the stack of canceled checks in the folder. Most were for wages at Leemis Fashions. I jotted down the names. Several checks were for routine business expense: utility bills, janitor service. Near the bottom was a check for $50 payable to Dr. Alexander Tolbert, M.D., with offices on Walnut Hill Lane which had been returned uncashed.

I asked, "What's this, Mr. Bilderback?"

"Dunno. That was written while Linda Givens was still a signer on the account. She wrote the check. Came back in an envelope with no return address and the notation 'Return to sender' written across the back. Crazier things have happened, and we just routinely filed it."

Then, a larger curiosity. A check had been written for $900 payable to Thomas Grant Insurance Agency in Garland, a Dallas suburb.

"Hooper, does the signature on this check match the writing of the forged $76,000 against Billie Jack's account, or is my eyesight seeing what it wants to see?"

"Sure does." He slid the check over to Bilderback.

"Looks so to me," Bilderback nodded. "Another forgery"?

I asked, "Mr. Bilderback, you ever hear any talk from the Givens' about Linda having cancer?"

He shook his head and lit a pipe. "No and if any of my staff had heard, I'm sure they would have told me."

I asked, "Can we get a machine copy of Billie Jack's known signature and a copy of that forged check, plus a copy of the 900-dollar check to the insurance guy?"

He nodded and walked over to a copying machine with the file.

I borrowed his yellow pages. Dr. Tolbert had an enlarged ad, clearly advertising his specialty of corrective and cosmetic surgery. No mention of cancer was included.

Bilderback handed me the copies I'd requested. We thanked the angular banker and walked toward the Dodge in the heat. "Hooper, Linda was trying to wrangle the dough to realign her boobs. Beeman told Bush and me she'd had a boob job which gave some idea of size but not dimension."

"Dimension?"

"Beeman said they got one higher than the other or something like that. She needed a "correctomy", and I think seventy-six large should have done the trick."

Ajax Savings and Loan was tucked between a sub sandwich restaurant and a tanning salon in a well-worn strip shopping center, just down from a large Sears store. The manager, a close clone of the Bride of Frankenstein began uncooperatively. "We can't divulge customer info without a subpoena. Come back later."

Hooper, who was unlikely to be appointed PR point man for the Dallas Police Department, took over. "Ma'am, we're working on a triple homicide which involved two juvenile victims. Your institution had been used as a transit for a check, forged on the adult victim's account and used to defraud another bank. So, while we go get that subpoena, you can come on downtown and sit on your butt in Homicide while we talk to the judge. That way, we can get your statement out of the way, so you don't get indicted for conspiracy." He grinned and leaned forward. "Does that clarify the situation…ma'am?"

Clarify it did. The file reflected the account was held solely by Linda Marie Givens. The seventy-six thousand check, forged on Billie Jack's account, had, in fact, been deposited earlier on the day before the night he was killed. We could have handwriting experts compare the signature, but it was plain, Linda was caught trying to steal from her husband's account. The forged signature of Billie Jack Givens, a machine copy of the one Bilderback had just given us, appeared to the naked eye to closely resemble Linda's handwriting.

The S & L barracuda routinely made copies of all checks deposited. The now cooperative lady ran us a copy of the copy of Linda's counterfeit check, which was a duplicate of the copy Mr. Bilderback had provided. Evidentiarily speaking, Linda was in a bind.

The S&L record also showed Linda had managed to write a check to cash for $2000, based on the forged deposit from Billie Jack's account. The money allowed her to bail Beeman out of jail. But why?

As we walked back to the Dodge, Hooper said, "By damn,

Kobok, if nothin' else, we can haul her in for bank fraud. She looks dirty as hell in the murders of her husband and kids."

"Yeah, but I still have doubts, Bull. I suppose she could have meant to get the boys out a front window and couldn't. But I still have a problem with setting the fire with the kids in harm's way."

"Still a murder…..Billie Jack."

"Doesn't that check to Thomas Grant, insurance man, make you wonder what kind of insurance Linda purchased?"

"Yeah... we need to talk to the insurance agent."

I radioed Tootie for messages. "Kobok, Detective Hooper's lieutenant called. They need him at a homicide scene on Greenville Avenue." Hooper jotted down the address.

"Can you drop me there, Kobok, it's not far? Probably an armed robbery gone sideways."

"Did your lieutenant agree to giving us any manpower for the biker rally this Sunday?"

"Naw, he says to just go set up surveillance, take photos up the whazoo, and see what happens."

The Blood Lords, with the forethought of a horsefly, had scheduled a rally, which is a sort of group grope wherein bikers gather with their old ladies, get drunk, stoned, and out of control, then usually end up in an inhouse brawl. Think Sunday picnic among zombies. This event was particularly volatile because the Diablos would probably arrive in force and kill a few people as a continuance of the ongoing biker war.

"They're using that old abandoned drive-in theatre out south. Guy owns it gave 'um permission," Hooper said. "Betcha there's at least three homicides. We need the whole SWAT bunch out there, not just me 'n you."

"We can bully Bush into going. You get any overtime?"

"Hell no."

Federal agents received a 25% "premium pay" salary boost to cover nights and Sundays. It rarely covered the hours, but it beat nothing.

"Maybe we can talk to Short Cummins and see if he'll order up a few ATF agents for Sunday's delight."

CHAPTER 14: THE DEN OF INIQUITY REDUX

I let Hooper out among the glut of emergency vehicles parked around a convenience store on Greenville. Crosstown traffic was mid-morning congested, but I made the Southwest Institute of Forensic Sciences in a half hour. I squeezed the Dodge behind a dumpster, told Tootie by radio I'd be out at the morgue, and elevatored to the third floor. Andy Barr, handwriting expert took a quick look.

"Kobok, the signer on the seventy-six-thousand-dollar check was not Billie Jack Givens. Dunno if we can prove who actually did the forgery but is sure looks like the wife's handwriting. I'll do a proper exam and have a report ready in a day or so."

I handed over the journal with the funny drawing, the dice thing, and the score sheets. "Can you see if you can decipher this."

He nodded and was studying the 12-sided gizmo as I walked out.

While in the building, I decided to elevator to the basement morgue and touch base with Doc O'Hara in the Givens case. She and Richard were bent over the corpse of a grossly obese woman no older than forty. O'Hara was writing on a clipboard. Richard had just finished stuffing the gaping abdomen with body parts and was stitching the opening back together with his sack needle.

Richard looked up at me, expressionless. It appeared he was conflicted as to whether to snitch off the Kobok—Kelly scene he'd witnessed. If he hadn't by now, maybe he wouldn't.

"Hey, Turkey." O'Hara peered over her gold half glasses. She head-motioned me away a few steps and handed me a post-it note. "My telephone number. Call me or I'll disclose all your shortcomings to the news media."

"Short comings" was strangely close to my current supervisor's handle. Had to be my imagination. I slipped the paper into my pocket.

"I had just that in mind, Doc. Did we wear out your sofa? Just up to my armpits in the Givens case right now."

"Sofa is ready and willing. Me too."

"I'll call…soon."

"Billie Jack's wife still the main suspect?"

"Yeah, and probably her biker lover. The Givens' test results tell us anything?"

"Billie Jack's blood alcohol count was .21. Too drunk to have heard the house collapse. Like I said, he was burned alive. Breathed pure flame three or four times before his throat seared shut. Both boys died of smoke inhalation. Thermal burns were post mortem."

"Can I get a copy of the report?"

"Kelly, I think you know her, is my assistant. She's in my office on the main floor typing reports. I would assume she has the Given's paperwork finished. Just go up and introduce yourself. I've got two more procedures." She gestured at two nude cadavers on gurneys nearby

"Uh, okay, Doc…er, Lynn. I think I know which one she is." Was that a lie that counted in the tally for Hell? What male visitor didn't know who Kelly was?

I stuck my head into O'Hara's office. Kelly was nowhere in sight. The computer was on and a small radio on her desk was playing Willie Nelson. Then she burst in the door at a warm up pace for the marathon. Dressed in white slacks, a red silk blouse, and red, spike heels which appeared identical to the ones she wore the day before. She bent, displaying a lovely backside, picked up the foot treadle for her dictating machine, and squeezed. The room filled with the smell of lilacs…or maybe it was roses. I was rapidly becoming incoherent.

"Damn, damn, double damn, sorry damned equipment. It's new. I must have blown a fuse."

Based on the previous day's experience, my fuses were at the max, too. "Uh, Kelly, don't they have a maintenance guy on duty?"

"The dork called in sick this morning. Guess I'm gonna have to call an electrician."

"Doc O'Hara says you might have the Givens paperwork ready?"

She pointed to the computer. "That's what I was working on. God knows now when I'll get it finished." Her lower lip curled slightly outward, hinting at oncoming tears. The effect was stupefying.

"What can I do to help, kid?," said the fly to the spider.

"I was just in the electrical closet. Can't tell crap from Crayola about which is which."

No, by grab, I didn't fully grasp her evil intent...well, maybe I just sort of ignored it. In seconds, I was in the electrical closet down the hall. It was surprisingly large. When Kelly punched the door lock button, I realized I was vulnerable to her nefarious advances. Well, you know, when a man is overcome with lilac... or rose intoxication, he just can't always be held accountable for his lapse in moral fiber.

"Here it is, Kelly." I tapped the breaker labeled "119-O'Hara". "It's not thrown. You outta have full power at your desk."

"I have fuller power as we speak," she said behind me.

I turned. Kelly's clothes were in a pile on the concrete floor. She was still wearing the red spike heels. My God, a vision right out of a porn movie. Then she had me. I was powerless. Smothering me with wet kisses while tearing—well maybe just sort of tearing—at my clothes. As she pulled me to the floor, her hundred pounds or so multiplied by ten. In seconds I was atop her, lost in degeneracy.

In a few seconds more, the sound of a key turning in the door lock had the effect of a lightning strike. I sprang to my feet, clutched my pants in front, and when the door swung open, was busily inspecting the electrical breaker box. Kelly, snatched up her clothing and being slender in stature, cleverly secreted her bare self in a slight offset in the closet wall.

"Jesus mother," exclaimed Richard as he stood, mouth agape, in an apparent stupor. "Jesus mother," he declared over and over several times before staggering out of sight down the hall.

For the second time, Kelly was redressed, restored and returning to her office in less time than I could zip my fly. I heard O'Hara, a health nut who always took the stairs, laugh in the stairwell nearby. Inundated in paranoia, I ducked into Kelly's office just as O'Hara made the main floor and stepped into the office she shared with Kelly.

O'Hara stared hard at me. "Why are you still here, Kobok?" she said sternly. Great God, Richard had had enough! He'd dropped that dime.

I gave O'Hara an up and down. Did she have one of those ten-inch knives hid in her apron? I'd survived one close call, but this time the jig was up. I considered crashing out the outside window overlooking the parking lot. I gathered, ready to launch.

O'Hara said, "Kelly must not have the Given's report finished."

Kelly said, "My dictation machine is not working. I can't transcribe the tape."

O'Hara knelt and peered beneath Kelly's desk. "It's unplugged, silly." She reached down and plugged the machine into the wall outlet. Then she said, "I was looking for Richard. Sent him up to get a screwdriver from the electrical closet and he never came back. He hasn't been himself the past couple days." At that she turned and walked away, searching it appeared, for Richard.

My heart skipped a beat when she stuck her head around the doorjamb. "Call me," she mouthed silently.

Kelly knocked out the report, printed me a copy and I started for the outside door. Kelly's telephone rang. "It's for you." She handed me the receiver.

Bush said, "I'm done with the Givens status report. They've assigned me another car. If you can meet me at that detail shop on Central at Henderson, I'll have this thing cleaned up. Then I can accompany you while they clean it."

"Bush, we don't normally pay out of pocket to clean up pool cars."

"It's filthy. I have paper towels to sit on until I get it in for cleaning."

"Be there in twenty minutes, Randall. It's time to see your friendly doctor."

"My father's a doctor and he's not very friendly."

CHAPTER 15: THE PLOT SICKENS

We stopped at Denny's for lunch. Heavy Hilda, the waitress was as big as Bulgaria. She fell in love with Bush. After several futile attempts at cozying up were ignored by the mighty young lawyer, she finally brought us some food.

I had a cheeseburger and coffee. Bush picked at a salad. Looking at my meal, he remarked, "Those cheeseburgers should be called 'deathburgers' considering the grease and cholesterol they dump in your system."

"Deathburgers. Got it, Randall."

Dr. Alexander Tolbert's nip and tuck clinic was integrated into a jumble of medical buildings across Walnut Hill Lane from the sprawling Presbyterian Hospital Complex. The parking lot was packed, requiring us to walk a city block in man killing heat. A wall of three determined ladies in white nurses' attire advised us Dr. Tolbert was in surgery and that if we had no appointment, we were out of luck.

Bush whispered, "Surgery here means he's in back somewhere. Doctors like this one don't use the hospital Operating Room across the street. They have their own facility."

Armed with the knowledge that the good doc was on the premises, I advised his three blocking backs that we were federal officers looking into a murder in which he was probably a witness. All appeared horrified.

Bush and I had barely settled into chairs amidst several ladies, all past fifty, all displaying facial bandages of different levels of complexity. One of the nurse-guards advised us the doctor could spare five minutes. The doctor was sixtyish, plumpish, with about a year's hair left. We both flashed credentials and took seats across from his cluttered desk.

"Murder," the doctor said in an east coast accent. "What…?"

"Doctor," I said. "We're investigating the arson/murder of Billie Jack Givens who was burned alive in the den of his home in Lakewood the night before last. His two sons, ages 12 and 10 were also killed."

"What are you asking, officer?" He leaned forward, increasing his chins by ten.

"Mr. Given's checking account shows he paid a fee to your office. His wife is reported to have had breast augmentation surgery which somehow didn't work out as she pleased."

"You're saying I screwed up a boob job. Never had a complaint in thirty years. I've handled a lot of boobs." He smiled.

"We doubt you did the original surgery but believe there's a good chance she came to you for corrective surgery."

Bush spoke. "Or at least corrective consultation, sir."

"I can't discuss patient information," he said, predictably.

I tossed the autopsy table photos of all three victims on his desk."

"Jesus. You sure it's murder? Not an accident?"

I nodded. "At least the father, Billie Jack Givens. The boys could have just been in the wrong place."

"I still can't…"

"Mrs. Givens, uh, Linda Marie, claims she has breast cancer and that her husband would't pay for medical care."

"Well, she would have seen an oncologist."

"We believe the cancer story is possible cover to justify her need for money to readjust cosmetic breast surgery."

He turned to a computer. "I never treated her."

"Stripper? Maybe hangs out with this big mean looking guy."

I tossed Sonny Beeman's photo and a copy of Linda Marie's on the desk and collected the autopsy photos.

"Oh, yeah. Never really my patient. No examination whatsoever. She gave a phony name…t flashy blonde who came in here with this jerk. He actually threatened to break my fingers, so I couldn't operate unless I examined her breasts. She pulled off her shirt right there in that chair you're in. She had really beautiful breasts. I told her the slight discrepancy could easily be made worse by another surgery. Explained breast tissue is vulnerable to negative reaction any time it goes under the knife, particularly a second time."

"Did you report...?"

"Threatened to and ordered them to take a hike."

"Like I said, Mr. Given's bank record shows he sent you a check."

He screwed up his face. "Hell, I'd forgotten. She insisted on paying me a small fee. Wrote out a check, still minus her shirt. I had the staff send the check back to the bank it was written on."

I studied the doc's face. "Doctor, will your canon of ethics allow you to testify to exactly what you just told us? That Linda Givens showed up with the man you identified, asked for corrective breast surgery and the man threatened you?"

He studied his desktop. "Well, since she was never a patient and that bozo really did make threats, I suppose I could testify to that. Not to my assessment of her boobs, but the rest, certainly."

"Could you testify there was no evidence of cancer?"

"Yeah, I suppose so. I'd need to talk with my attorney, but I think it would be okay. She's definitely not my patient and never has been."

We made the long foot-trek back to the Dodge. The vinyl seats could easily have fried an egg. They had a similar effect on my backside. After several minutes, the A/C took some of the edge off, but by that time my butt was at least sunny side up.

"Randall, Doc Tolbert looks to me like a man who ate too many deathburgers."

"Not too many, yet, but the end is a definite short term prediction."

"You ever been to a brassiere factory?" I doubted Bush had ever seen a brassiere in its natural habitat, let alone during the manufacturing process. I'd personally seen the first situation, but not the second.

"Well." He looked across the seat at me as serious as a first-time sky-diver. "Can't say that I have, but I did visit the lingerie department at Macy's once to buy my mother a robe for Christmas."

CHAPTER 16: UNMENTIONABLES IN VOLUME

The drive down Central Expressway, Mockingbird Lane, and Harry Hines Boulevard took nearly forty minutes in early afternoon traffic. When we passed the Parkland Hospital Complex which hid the Southwest Institute and its morgue from Harry Hines, I asked Bush if he wanted to stop for a quick autopsy seminar.

My attempt at dark humor bombed. He instantly blanched a shade of light green. I didn't mention Kelly, the piranha girl who worked for Dr. O'Hara.

Leemis Fashions was tucked into a shabby storefront two blocks north of the Fireplug Topless Club. A poorly done sign: "Leemis Fashions" above the front door confirmed we were in the right place.

A worn, thirtyish secretary with too much lipstick greeted us like warm dishwater. We flashed badges.

"We need to speak to Norvil Givens, please," I said.

Norvil came to the sound of his name, without waiting to be summoned. He was forty, fat, balding, with rimless glasses that appeared to continuously slide down his nose. He nervously punched his eyewear up to a more comfortable position with a knuckle. He had less hair than Hooper.

"You're here about Billie Jack and the kids?"

"Yessir," we both replied.

"I jes' come from the funeral home. Services are tomorrow." His eyes were reddened from tears.

"When and where?"

"Uh, one o'clock at *Spillman-Preston*. Burial is in their cemetery right on the premises. About cleaned out the till around here to get up enough cash to pay for a triple funeral."

I'd be certain to attend. Odd who shows up at funerals. "We're very sorry for your loss, sir."

He said, "Kids weren't really his. I guess you already…?"

"Yes, sir." I nodded.

We talked in a little office with two small desks, two desk chairs and a black sofa facing the desks which I'd have wagered had been Billie Jack Given's favorite nesting spot with his stripper-seamstresses. The brothers apparently shared the space. The furniture was early cheap, and the office decorated with a two-month coat of dust. A side window looked onto a combination courtyard, weed patch, and junk pile at the edge of the property.

Bush pulled a silk handkerchief from his pocket and carefully wiped down his plastic chair before sitting.

"Sorry about the housekeeping," Givens stammered awkwardly.

"No problem, sir." I gave Bush the stink eye.

A window behind the desks fronted into a room where about ten women were seated at sewing or other machines. Most looked to be picture images of dissipated strippers turned biker girls each with 200,000 miles, being forced to work by their biker old men. Dance until 3:00 A.M., ingest a little meth, sew brassieres at 7:30.

Givens slumped in a desk chair. "How can I help you gentlemen?"

I said, "Your brother have any enemies angry enough to do him and family harm?"

"Yeah, them damned bikers. He hired their women from that puke joint down the street and another dive on Northwest Highway. Kicked me outta the office from time to time so he could play grab-ass with one or more of them." He glanced at the sofa, confirming my initial observation.

"That add up to trouble?"

"Well, he got crossways with that sorry Sonny Beeman over one of them chicks that dances nights down the street and works for us part time. That would be when she wasn't in here under Billy Jack's desk."

"You said trouble?"

"Beeman had a deal with Billie Jack for any money due the girl...Beaver they call her, to be paid to him and not her. She hadda habit and would blow the cash on dope. Y'all know Beeman pickin' up his ol' lady's cash ain't the only one whut does that."

"And?"

"Chick they called D.D. Originally, her old man was a big ugly sucker they called "Gut." I heard talk from the girls he'd been murdered...shot, I believe. Then she took up with that little guy with the limp. I think they called him "Shoots" or some such. He and Beeman are close as the thieves that they are."

"Got a name and address for this D.D.?" I asked.

He opened a worn folder. "I got Charlene West. Social Security is prolly counterfeit and if the address she gimmie is correct, it would be the first."

"She around?"

"Ain't seen nor heard of her in the last week or so. Ain't seen that little monkey with the bad foot, neither." Another glasses punch-up followed.

He was speaking of "Scoots" Garcia. "How do you know she's not with the guy who limps?"

"Cuz' she was one of the nicer ones of the whole crowd... and smarter. Beeman was in here last week with that little peckerwood Shoots or whatever. I ask him how was D.D. He sorta sneered and said, she'd left town. I wondered if the little rat mighta caved in her head or somethin' for not handing over her earnings."

"Did you see enough skin to recall if she had tattoos"

"Uh, yeah. Like most of those chicks, she'd come in in a halter top and shorts that showed half her ass. The A/C in the shop is not the best."

"Tattoos?"

"Uh, yeah, several, mostly on her left arm. I recall a rose vine winding around her left forearm. Two red roses were vivid on the top just before the elbow. Spider on the backs of both calves. Bunch more, but I see so many, I don't recall specifics."

I jotted down his comments and took notes from his file. D.D. was a lead worth pursuing. Dead, we already had a suspect—Scoots. Injured or wronged, she was a live witness.

"You think Beeman's beef with Billie Jack was enough to drum up a murder?"

"Look, I was and still am scared to death of that whole bunch, particularly that Beeman guy."

"What do you know about the boys' father. Any reason he'd want to hurt Billie Jack?" I asked.

"Lives in Florida, I think. No contact with the boys. They loved Billie Jack. Billie Jack and both boys were scared Linda's screwing around plus wantin' a divorce was gonna bust up the relationship."

"Divorce?"

"She never paid a lick of attention to those boys. Billie Jack had adopted them. I think the divorce chatter was just part of her mean assed way. Or for all I know, she really meant to divorce Billie Jack. If she did, it woulda been just to spite Billie Jack and the boys."

"Neglected?"

"She had plenty of activities that kept her out of pocket. Shopping all day and never showing up with a thing she'd bought."

"What do you know about Linda havin' a boyfriend?"

He confirmed what we already knew. "Or boyfriends, particularly that ass, Beeman. Linda was pretty loose with her relationships. I always figured she was sleeping around, but I didn't try to influence Billie Jack. That's why she didn't do much with Billie Jacks foolin' with strippers...at first."

"You sure Linda was hookin' up with Beeman?"

"Hell yes."

"You thinkin' Beeman mighta had a hand in your brother's murder?"

"He's certainly capable of it from what I seen. Billie Jack said he come home one evening and saw Beeman drive away in an old blue Ford pickup."

"Blue Ford pickup? Anything to make you think divorce talk was not just a threat?"

"She had a high dollar lawyer, Harless Androvski. Ask him."

Bush asked, "With your brother gone, do you inherit the whole business?"

"Naw. That trollop Linda gets his half. If you're suggesting I killed..."

"No," I said. "But did you?"

"Well hell no."

"Sorry, that's a required question. Did Linda come around here often?"

"Yeah, first time maybe two years ago. She got a gander of the ol' gals we had workin' back there and nearly dropped dead. One of our girls later told me Linda had been a stripper before Billie Jack pulled her outta the gutter. Linda jes' come around to hit on Billie Jack for cash or just to bitch because she is one."

"Raise hell about what?"

"Everything and nothing. Billie Jack would dodge her on the phone and she drive down here from Lakewood in her damned black Honda and make a scene."

"Could Linda have killed Billie Jack and the boys?"

He punched up the glasses. "Well, she once told me that if anything ever happened to Billie Jack, she and her lawyer, Mr. uh, Androvski, would find a way to kick me outta here on my butt even though I'm half owner."

"Meaning?"

"I took it to mean if she could get Billie Jack knocked off, I was next. Billie Jack told me once she'd slept on the couch for a year. I didn't tell him I figured she was sleeping in a bed somewhere, just not at home. Yeah, she was capable of killing him, based on what I saw."

We already had heard from Linda about the sleeping arrangements. It must have been common knowledge.

I asked, "Mr. Givens, we have a neighbor who says Billie Jack and some huge dude driving an old Ford pickup had a wild argument in Billie Jack's front yard a day or so before the fire. Gotta clue who that might be?"

He punched up the glasses while his face broadcast "lie" before he opened his mouth. "No." Norvil was not shooting straight and I wondered why.

I held his gaze. "Neighbors also state that on the evening

before the fire, two biker types in an old blue Ford pickup sat down the block from the Givens' house drinking beer. Old Blue F150. Reckon that's the same guy who argued with Billie Jack?"

"I wouldn't know."

As we drove away, I said, "Norvil strikes me as lacking the *cahones* to stomp on a cockroach. Besides, with Billie Jack out, looks to me like he's out, too. I think he knows who the big guy who argued with Billie Jack is."

Bush squirmed on the vinyl seat. "He seems harmless, but abnormal psychology studies show mild men are often capable of heinous acts."

Somebody heinous had sure as hell killed Billie Jack and the two boys. It wasn't quite time to rule Norvil out of bounds.

"Bush, we need to try to figure out if the big guy who had the argument is one of the two who sat down the block before the fire."

He said, "And whether we have two old blue Ford pickups or one."

I worked my way through gathering afternoon traffic to the auto detail shop on the Central Expressway. The beat-up Ford they'd assigned him was parked in front, still appearing ready for the junkyard. Bush paid the bill with his *Visa*.

"Randall, be sure to voucher that expense."

"Oh, it's only eighty bucks, Kobok."

Traffic influenced me to call it a day. I called Tootie on the radio for any messages, found none, and started up the crappy journey up Central. I planned to grab a shower and call Lynn O'Hara. Maybe some pasts, a glass of wine, and a rematch on her sofa.

When I made my apartment complex at just past five, the swimming pool was jammed like a stuffed turkey. Tad, barefoot and soaked, came on the run.

We played catch until I was exhausted, only to be saved by Anne. Dresses…maybe undressed in a bikini small enough to fit in a cigarette package which covered about one percent of smooth flesh, she walked from the pool past me and started up the stairs to her apartment.

She stopped, a towel over her arm and said, "You look like

you could use a shower and a cold beer."

A man, to satisfy all his obligations, must prioritize. I'd call O'Hara another time. We had pasta all right, only it was Anne's recipe of string spaghetti. I called the answering service, left Anne's number and spent the evening playing monopoly with Tad. Thank God we weren't using real money. He cleaned me out.

Hooper answered his home phone on the second ring.

"Bull, any chance your lieutenant might change his mind about some extra bodies to help us cover the biker rally, Sunday?"

"Nope, he still says monitor and don't get involved."

"Can you meet me at the federal building in the morning. Maybe Short Cummins will detail a couple more ATF agents."

"I can be there by 8:30. I'll get a uniform to drop me so I don't have to fight parking down there."

"Okay, 8:30." I hung up and called Bush.

"Bush residence," answered a male voice.

"Randall Bush, please."

"Whom should I say is calling, sir?"

"Kobok."

"Sorry, sir, he's in the library speaking with his father."

"Tell him please. It will only take a second."

"Sorry, sir, he'll have to phone you back."

I ignored the cantankerous tone creeping into his voice and gave him Anne's number.

Tad was dozing on the sofa when Anne's phone rang. She answered and gave the receiver to me.

"Who was that who answered your telephone, Randall?"

"Oh that's Haskins. He's been my father's butler for several years."

"Sounds a bit testy."

"He was supposed to get off at seven, but he had several duties which kept him over."

"I usually send my butler home at six." I felt like I'd hooked a large mouth bass with the comment.

"His home is over the garage. Not far to go. Can you afford a butler on a government salary, Kobok?"

I ignored the question. To ponder butlers and government

salaries would give Randall some mental exercise. "Randall, we gotta meet with Hooper and Supervisor Klaster at 8:30. Be there."

"What kinda meeting?"

"To discuss the biker rally out in south Dallas County this Sunday."

"Oh, yeah, I remember. Are we gonna work this Sunday?"

"Yeah, we need to watch and see the fun and games. Maybe pick up some info on the Givens case."

"Half past eight. I'll see you then."

CHAPTER 17: Manpower, Insurance, Funerals:

All "Musts" for a Rainy Day

I crept over to my apartment in a towel at 5:30 A.M., grabbed a quick shower and shave, and with the aid of a large 7-11 caffeinated, made the office at 7:20. Bush was not five minutes behind. Hooper, having hopped a ride with a marked squad car walked in before I had coffee fully made.

I had drafted a supplemental report of the activity the day before and tossed it into Short Cummins' desk before he wandered in.

"Phew, it's gonna be hot out there today," he sighed. An astounding complaint from a guy who sat inside in air-conditioned comfort all day.

I explained the need for more manpower in the upcoming Sunday's Blood Lord sponsored biker rally.

"Where is this supposed to be held?" Short Cummins asked, his expression much like a man who was about to undergo hemorrhoid surgery with two aspirin as anesthetic. Decisions were not Short Cummins' long suit.

"Supposed to be?" Hooper rolled his cigar stub.

"No smoking in the federal building," Short Cummins said.

"Ain't smokin' it, I'm eatin' it."

I interceded. "As you know Cummins, ATF and the Dallas P.D. have been monitoring the shooting war between the Blood Lords and Diablos motorcycle gangs, the past two weeks. We've been unable to stay hitched with that the past couple of days because of the Givens murder investigation."

"When are we gonna indict the Givens woman?"

"When we have enough proof to support at least an arrest

and eventually a trial. We have a growing pile of circumstantial evidence, but we're not quite home yet. Now the biker rally…"

"What is a biker rally, exactly?"

Hooper, who appeared likely to throttle Short Cummins at any second, said, "It's a social affair where screwups get on motorcycles and ride around like idiots. Then they tend to get off them motorcycles and shoot the shit outta each other. We need a police presence out there this Sunday but we don't got enough manpower to watch the sun come up."

"Sun come up…?"

I said, "The DPD says they haven't got manpower to spare."

Short Cummins said, "There's a lot more cops than ATF agents. Boy, more manpower. I'll have to put in a request…in triplicate, to Washington. Probably take 'til next Tuesday to get authorization."

Hooper said, "The rally is Sunday. If we could muster the troops, we could catch some of those dirtbags doin' something dirty. There'll be enough guns and dope out there to fill a pickup truck bed."

"Sorry," Short Cummins mumbled. "Gotta go through channels."

As we got up to leave, Short Cummins said, "Kobok, a minute?"

I turned back. "Where and what time is this rally, Sunday? Washington might need more info."

"Starts around 10:00 A.M.." I drew him a diagram of the location and walked out, vaguely uncomfortable he'd asked.

Bush, Hooper, and I strategized in the elevator. "Okay," I said. "I'll take the Trojan van home tonight, make sure it's gassed and ready. We meet at the Kickstand Café on Industrial at say, 9:00 A.M. Sunday. Hooper and I will set up somewhere around the restroom—there's only one—in the Trojan Van. Bush, you'll have to establish surveillance from a car outside the place. I'll check out three or four radios to make sure at least two will work. We'll photograph hell outta things and see what happens."

Bush said, "I've never been in on anything were we used the Trojan van. Why not three of us inside?"

"Too hot for one, Randall. Slow death for three."

The vehicle of which I spoke was an old panel truck with "Trojan Plumbing" and a telephone number painted on both sides. A door between the front seats allowed access to the rear which was equipped with one-way glass in all four directions. Designed for surveillance, if anyone called the number displayed, a machine answered, "Trojan Plumbing, leave a number." No return call was ever made. A major malfunction was that the unit had no air conditioning and the restroom was a large Folger's can with a plastic, clamp-on lid.

Hooper said, "Take it from me, kid, do your part in an air-conditioned car parked nearby.

Bush said, "Kobok, I could work on foot, undercover."

Hooper chewed his cigar. "Kid, you'll have to shoot a few dirtbags. You don't look like no biker."

"I could tell then I'm a movie producer's representative, looking for very macho men for parts in an upcoming biker film."

I held Bush's gaze. "Hellfire, why not? Be sure and keep your pistol where you can get to it. We still meet up at the Kickstand Sunday morning, okay?"

Bush and Hooper nodded.

In the lobby, I filled Hooper in on the results of the bank inquiries, including the check written to the Garland insurance agent, the comments of Norvil Givens, and the story of Dr. Tolbert. "I'm thinking we need to drive out to Garland and see what the insurance deal is about."

"We gotta double shooting in East Dallas, Kobok. Can y'all handle this insurance man.?"

We drove Hooper back to the Police and Courts building. It was the sort of day that walking six-blocks in the heat could be fatal to old folks. Hooper squeezed out.

I said, "I'll call you tonight if there's any hot news. Otherwise see you Sunday morning."

As we drove away, Bush said, "What about the big guy in the old Ford truck who argued with Billie Jack in his front yard? Should we...?"

"Bush," I said. "First, we gotta see about cash paid to an

insurance man and then go to a funeral."

On the way to Garland, I swung through the apartment address Bush had garnered from DPS for the registered owner of the F150, Bruce Clarence Ligon. No such vehicle was spotted, and the management office was closed.

"Next week's business, Bush. Maybe I'll do a drive by tomorrow and see if the old truck is on the premises."

Bush thumbed through his Mapsco. "Turn left up here and get on Skillman. It leads right into Garland."

"I know, Randall, thank you." In addition to East Dallas, Randall had probably never been to Garland.

Just before Garland Road crossed the Dallas/Garland city limits, I turned into the residential area which had the misfortune of being the location of the Diablo house. All windows were boarded up with plywood. One panel showed several bullet holes. The latest Blood Lord attack had left some scars. No sign of cessation of hostilities was in sight, and Sunday loomed like a second Pearl Harbor.

The Thomas Grant Insurance Agency occupied what appeared to have been a gasoline station in an earlier life. Perched on a busy corner near downtown, the small building had been renovated extensively, and it's sizeable parking lot resurfaced with asphalt. The insurance business appeared healthy.

A smiling young lady with a gap between her gleaming white teeth sat behind a desk just inside the front door. Thomas Grant, easily identified by a pinned on name tag bearing the same name, sat at a desk inside his small office behind the receptionist.

I flashed my badge. Bush followed suit. "We're federal officers, investigating an arson/homicide, ma'am," I said. "We need to speak to Thomas Grant, please."

Grant, tall, fit, about 35, with enough cultivated hair to become a varsity TV evangelist, stood up behind his desk and motioned us in. "Tom Grant." He smiled through glittering, dentist assisted ivory as he examined our credentials, and said, "Did I rob a bank, gentlemen?"

"Mr. Grant, I don't know if you saw it on the news or in the papers, but Billie Jack Givens and his two sons were killed in an arson fire early Wednesday morning."

He sat back down and motioned us to two chairs opposite his desk. "Know about it. The widow Givens has called me several times, including midmorning Wednesday while she was still in Baylor Hospital. Her lawyer...uh," He shuffled papers on his desk. "Androvski, called me yesterday. Needless to say, they want that money?"

"Money?"

"Oh, A couple months ago, Mrs. Givens, blonde hair, chest and all walked in wanting to write a $100,000 life insurance policy on her husband, Billie Jack. I placed it with Dixon Mason over in Atlanta. He was young enough and they wrote the policy."

"Did he sign the application?"

"Yeah. Came in with the blonde, showed two forms of photo ID, and signed in my presence."

I was holding in my folder, a copy of Billie Jack's actual signature and Linda's forgery to Ajax S&L but thought it best not to share the info with this mope.

I pulled out the family photo I'd picked up in the boys' bedroom. "That Billie Jack Givens?"

"Yep. Clean cut, mustache, sharp clothes, nice looking man."

"Any discussion as to why the policy or why they came to you?"

"Well, after he signed the app, he said to his wife, 'Satisfied, now?' "

Somehow, I already knew the answer, but I asked, "Who is the beneficiary?"

"Linda Givens."

"No mention of the boys."

"No sir."

"You didn't know either Linda or Billie Jack before she came in?"

"Yeah, I wrote policies for other coverage. Hellfire, I was eligible for a Dixon Mason paid trip to Hawaii which is shot now because of this big loss so soon after policy inception."

"Did you write the coverage on his homeowners and car insurance?"

"Yes." He slid the fat folder across.

"How about his company hospitalization policy?" I shuffled through the folder.

"No, God no. He hired low rent help to do menial work. A group plan would have busted him."

Linda had either lied to us about Billie Jack telling her Leemis hospitalization didn't cover her breast surgery or she was out of the loop. Lying struck me as behind door number one.

"Can we get copies of the applications and policies?"

"Absolutely." He called the receptionist in and handed her the folder.

"Is Mrs. Givens the loss payee on the homeowners?"

"Yeah, $89,000 worth...and some change."

As we drove away, Bush asked, "What do you make of the life insurance situation?"

"No idea, but it seems to tilt the pile a little more toward Linda Marie Givens. Sounds like she browbeat him into taking out the policy on his life, then might have hurried his demise by thirty years or so."

I worked the Dodge through midday traffic down Northwest Highway and pulled through the parking lot of the Purple Parrott. The lot was nearly deserted. "Bush, ever interview a Russian Mafia tough guy and a bunch of strippers?"

"Huh-uh."

"They look a lot different in full light."

"Russians own that place?" He craned his neck backward.

"One Russian, a mean one. Remember, Linda Givens used to dance there. Billie Jack hung around the place. Just makes me curious about the relationships. But first I need food and we have to attend a funeral."

We stopped at a McDonald's and I downed two sausage biscuits and a coffee. Bush ate nearly all of a side salad and made no death-burger comments.

The Spillman—Preston Funeral Home was on Hillcrest north of the City of University Park limits. A uniformed rent-a-cop standing out in the street in the blazing sun motioned us into a sparsely occupied parking lot. Linda's black Honda was parked close in. Inside the funeral home, the cooled interior contained nearly as many hired funeral hands as attendees.

Linda, with her right forearm heavily bandaged, Norvil Givens, and a graying lady who I would later learn was the boy's paternal grandmother were alone and seated separately in the family section. Norvil and the old lady were in tears. Linda dabbed at her nose and eyes with a tissue, but I saw no tears. I about half expected the tissue to dissolve from contact when hydrochloric acid oozed out her nose.

The two dozen or so mourners seated behind the family were a smattering of men and women in black and a few, typically Texan, were dressed casually in blue jeans. Not surprisingly, no one identifiable as a biker was in attendance. A very large man in a suit two sizes too small sat several rows behind Linda. He was close, but outside the family section.

The preacher, whose pretty hair was at least ten points more coifed than insurance agent Grant's, rambled on for twenty minutes about the injustice of the loss of the Givens lives. It was apparent he was an in-house fill in who did not know the dearly departed. Then he gave another 20 minutes of boilerplate fire and brimstone extolling the wages of sin, handed off to an organist who turned out a doleful offering, and we were dismissed.

I had nudged Bush and I into a back-row seat which allowed us to exit first. We walked about a block from the sanctuary in the heat to a canopied, open grave. The elegantly haired preacher spoke briefly, then mumbled a few unintelligible condolences to the three family members. To have remained longer must have meant he went on overtime. He snapped his funeral-script notebook shut and hitched a ride on an employee operated golf cart back toward the sanctuary.

In the small gathering, Linda spotted us and glared with death ray intensity. Her expression was undoubtedly a precursor to shooting the finger, but for reasons known only to herself she did not. We hurried back to the Dodge on the edge of the parking lot.

"Bush, we shoulda brought your junker. We need to follow that big dude that sat behind Linda and Linda herself. I opt for Linda."

"Why the big guy?"

"Cuz he was crying. We can try for him later."

Linda, alone in the Honda, turned north on Hillcrest and sped away without looking back, simplifying tailing her in the heavy traffic. She drove to a low rent motel on Central, entered an outside entry first level room, and slammed the door. In five minutes, she came back out, dressed in shorts that revealed considerable backside, and swayed across the parking lot to a low rent bar next door.

I told Bush to sit tight, allowed time for her to order, then stepped inside the darkened interior.

Linda Marie Givens, grieving widow who'd just planted her two sons, was locked in a slobbering kissing embrace in a booth near the back with a fellow I knew well. Sonny Beeman's ugly mug came up for air and I split. If they saw me, they gave no indication.

I walked back out, slid in the Dodge, and dropped Bush at the GSA garage.

"Aren't you going to take the Trojan van?"

"Didn't get the keys. I'll drive down and pick it up tomorrow."

I phoned O'Hara, picked up a six pack, and drove to her place. I called the answering service with her number and after pizza delivery and thoroughly testing the sofa, set her alarm for 6:00 A.M. There was surveillance to be done in the morning.

CHAPTER 18: Saturday—A Fine Day to Sleep In

I rolled out at six, only moderately hung over from beer, pizza, and sofa. The trip down Central was relatively early before the regular Saturday traffic built up. Linda's black Honda was parked nose in to the motel room I'd seen her use the afternoon before. I figured reptiles wouldn't be up and around when I pulled up at 6:40. I'd bought a large 7-11 caffeinated and a pair of nutritious apple fritters down the street.

The beer joint where I'd seen Linda and Beeman in foreplay the afternoon before was separated from the motel by what had once been a hedge row. Although now in advanced stages of neglect and deterioration, the remaining bushes provided some cover. The joint wouldn't open for several hours. I parked the Dodge with a good view of Linda's room, and waited.

After twice using the hedge row for camouflage while I deposited used coffee, the motel door opened at 9:45. Wearing a light blue, semi-transparent robe, Linda walked to the rear of her Honda, raised the rear hatch, and dug a small package from the pile of clothing stacked against the rear seat. Nothing like a little grass for breakfast before venturing out into the heat.

In another half hour, Beeman, gentleman that he was, walked out ahead of Linda and slid into the Honda's front passenger side. Linda, in skimpy shorts and a yellow halter top, followed, taking the driver's seat.

She drove up Gaston into east Dallas. Was she headed to Lakeview and her devastated house? Traffic had picked up, making the Dodge less visible in the rear-view mirror. Based on previous history, it seemed highly likely that both Linda and Beeman were actually too dumb to pick up on a surveillance, no matter how obvious it was.

She turned north on Beacon, swung into a dingy apartment complex, then pulled back out into traffic. She had pulled through the address Bush had developed for Bruce Clarence Ligon, the registered owner of the old blue F150 who neighbors had reported arguing with Billie Jack. I followed at as much distance as experience had taught. Sitting in a rear parking lot was the old F150 with the license number matching Bush's find clearly visible on the rear bumper. What the hell was this?

In those pre-cellular days and with no dispatchers on duty in the ATF system on Saturday, calling for reinforcements was tricky. The Dodge was equipped with a Dallas P.D. multi-channel radio. I could have called the DPD dispatch office. I was in the channel 1 district. But trying to explain via radio to have someone call Hooper or Bush at home was a step too far since we were only guests on their system. I'd have to bide time and hope to find a friendly, functioning payphone.

I closed slightly on the Honda as she drove north to Live Oak Street, east to Skillman, and into the Garland city limits. She drove directly to the revitalized service station headquarters of Thomas Grant Insurance Agency. It seemed the not so sharp duo didn't figure the place was closed on Saturday. It wasn't.

Thomas Grant appeared in the front doorway high dollar haircut and the mouthful of ivory visible from a half block away. Linda parked nearby. She and Beeman exited the car. I wondered if they were going to throttle Grant for not delivering the proceeds of the $100,000 policy on Billie Jack's life. That was going to prove to be an incorrect assumption.

Linda rose on tiptoes, gave Grant a good ol' Texas hug and a peck on the cheek. Beeman shook Grant's hand and they all disappeared into the air-conditioned safety of the office.

I spotted a payphone, gambled that it worked, and dialed Hooper at home. Although he lived in Garland, but still some distance from our location, he was the best available in a stormy sea.

It seemed an hour after his wife answered when he picked up the instrument. "Hooper."

"Man, get saddled and meet me at the Thomas Grant

Insurance Agency where Garland Road crosses Avenue G. Hurry."

"You all right?"

"Yes, dammit, just come quick."

I waited twelve minutes across the busy street and had just decided to walk in on the little insurance meeting, when Hooper's GMC pickup swerved on Grant's parking lot. I goosed the Dodge across the traffic.

"What the hell?" Hooper unfolded from the truck cab.

I identified at least three citizens of interest who were inside, and that for all I knew the entire Blood Lords crew was in there having cookies and milk.

We barged in the front door. Grant was behind his desk. Linda and Beeman faced him across the desk in plastic chairs. The occasion was made more meaningful in that each was sipping a margarita. At a glance, no one else was inside.

All three sprang to their feet. More surprised than angry, Beeman spat, "Whut the hell, Kobok?" Grant stood with mouth agape, displaying the rows of white teeth. Linda sat back down.

Hooper, bull necked, old, worn, smiled. "Beeman, if in the history of the world there was ever a dumb sumbitch who oughta sit down, right about now would be the time to do just exactly that."

Beeman sat. Grant followed. I would have hoped they had an open folder on the desk. On the long held legal ruling that the eye couldn't trespass. We had entered a public premise when the door was unlocked, we could have confiscated the entire original file. A judge might have later ruled the seized material inadmissible, but then again, he or she may not have. But, it didn't really matter, because we had copies voluntarily given us by Grant. Billie Jack's signature had to be a forgery, machine copy or original.

I pulled up a third plastic chair and sat at the end of the desk. From facial expressions, I rather expected any or all of the three to break for the door.

"My goodness, folks, if you flee you'll either be killed in six lanes of traffic or suffer a fatal heatstroke. It must be a hundred already out there."

Grant stammered, "Mrs. Givens just stopped by to check the status of her husband's life insurance policy."

"Curious, Grant, what is your cut of the take?"

"Now hold on, by God." He started to stand again.

Hooper, who had remained standing motioned him down like a third base coach telling a base runner to slide. Grant resumed his seat.

I continued. "Grant, here's the deal. Billie Jack Givens' signature on that insurance application is a hell of a lot better forgery than the one on the check for 76 grand Linda here wrote to her credit union. It's so good, you probably only get about ten to do in the Texas prison system's free hotel. Your hair is so pretty, some alpha con will make you his trophy bitch."

Grant looked like he might vomit. "I didn't...know."

"That would be before or after Billie Jack came in with Linda here, with her switchy ass, and signed the app in your presence. I forget, did your receptionist witness the forgery. She was sort of homely. She'll probably have to play the husband's role in the women's prison unit."

"Dammit, that's my wife you're maligning."

"Oh, sorry. Maybe not homely, just plain."

Hooper pointed at Beeman. "But for you, Sonny, it's the three-needle cocktail. They wheel you in on a gurney which raises up like a cross, so spectators can see. Then they slip you the juice and your eyeballs pop out—one down each cheek."

Hooper didn't much like Beeman. The eyeball part was pure fiction, but I liked the story telling.

Hooper looked at me. "Bust 'um now. Maybe Beeman will resist."

I motioned Hooper to head for the door. "We'll go to the grand jury first thing Monday," I cheerily called out as we walked out. The threat was more bluff than a plan. We had the evidence and could file whatever insurance fraud charges necessary after we'd unraveled the Given's murder case.

I followed Hooper a few blocks where we talked over a McDonald's soft drink. I explained the visit Bush and I had made to the Grant insurance guy the day before and added the surveillance of the funeral and Linda's temporary place of residence. He was as surprised as me at the idea that Linda drove through the apartment complex where the big guy who argued with Billie Jack probably lived.

"Kobok, maybe we should go back down there today?"

"Damn, man, it's Saturday. Let Bruce wait until Monday."

"Suits me." He stepped back and eyeballed my Dodge. "Thought you were gonna check out that plumbing van. This mean we don't gotta go to that damned rally tomorrow?"

"I'd drive down and get the van today. We still meet at the Kickstand at nine in the A.M., okay?"

I didn't swing back through the apartment unit where the old F150 had been sitting. Too much temptation to knock on the door, get into a hassle, and not get the Trojan van up and running.

The van battery was dead. I jumped it off cables from my Dodge trunk, drove to Sears, bought a battery, waited an hour for installation and started home. The government system would repay me for the battery when I filed my month's end voucher. I stopped, gassed the old bus, and was playing catch with Tad at four o'clock. I had four or five beers, spaghetti, and Anne in that order.

When I got around to calling the answering service the lady said, "Call Sonny Beesom at 555-1935". Beesom was pronunciation close enough to decipher.

I called and after several rings, a drunk answered, probably a wino. "This is a damned payphone and I cain't sleep with it ringing."

"Where is this telephone, sir?"

"On Gaston Ave, dumbass." He hung up.

Sonny Beeman, in all probability, had borrowed or stolen Linda's car and was trying to snitch his way out a death penalty. Now how in six kinds of hell was I going to make contact? As it turned out, seeing Beeman again was not going to be difficult at all.

CHAPTER 19: THE WINDS OF WAR

At just before nine on an already blistering hot Sunday morning, I herded the van into the Kickstand parking lot. Hooper's pickup and Bush's rusty Ford were parked around back.

Inside, Hooper devouring an enormous plate of eggs, grease and cholesterol. Bush picked at toast and tea. Hooper was dressed in walking shorts and a fanny pack which I knew to contain a pistol, a badge, and some God-awful cigars. Bush was adorned in silk walking shorts and a monogrammed white knit shirt. He looked like a movie producer to me.

"You look like you didn't get much sleep," Hooper declared through a mouthful of carbs.

"Stayed up late reading the bible." I ordered coffee and a scrambled egg and sausage sandwich to go from a large lady with larger hair.

I briefed Bush on Linda's motel location and the meeting I'd stumbled across the day before in Thomas Grant's Insurance Agency.

"I played golf with father Saturday, Kobok. Sounds like your day was more exciting."

I didn't tell him about the van's dead battery and the trip to Sears.

"What's your take on filing murder charges against Linda?" Hooper asked.

"Well, it's definitely not a case we could run through federal court. We've got plenty to indict her in Dallas County on state charges of murder...plus forgery of the $76,000 check, plus that forged life insurance app, plus she had a wad of gold jewelry in her pocket when the fire started. We need to trace that wad."

"Grand jury don't meet until Tuesday."

"Problem is," I said. "it's all circumstantial. We can show the forgeries but putting the pen in her hand is gonna be tricky. We could use some direct testimony. I think Sonny Beeman tried to call me late yesterday and I missed him."

Bush looked up. "Beeman called? Why?"

"Tryin' to snitch his way out of the deal. Not sure how to make contact again."

"Bet we see Beeman today," Hooper said through a mouthful of hash browns and carbs.

"Alive, I hope, if we're gonna have any luck with makin' him a witness and not a defendant. I still see him as a major player and a co-defendant with Linda."

Bush said. "I still think she shoulda got her kids outta harm's way first. What a piece of work."

Hooper and I shrugged again. We'd both seen worse.

With Hooper and me in the van, Bush followed in his rusty Ford. When we rolled into the old theatre at just past nine thirty, the place was largely deserted. Bush parked near the entrance, then exited the Ford with a clipboard in hand and a camera around his neck.

Hooper asked, "Did you ask him if he's got his pistol?"

"If it's not in his right front shorts pocket, he's gonna get hi-jacked for the camera."

I had no problem finding a parking place near a restroom that appeared to have survived abandonment. Only the few women present would use it. The men, half animal to begin with, would use the plentiful weed patches dominating the landscape. We both slipped through the small door to the rear compartment where we had 360 vision and two comfortable, swivel chairs. I stashed my scrambled egg sandwich on a window ledge. Yeah, we were undermanned, but we were only just gonna watch—so we thought.

By just past 10:30, the temperature in the metal, mobile oven was flirting with suffocation mode. The rig of course had standard, dashboard air conditioning. But to allow the vehicle to run would have quickly overheated it and told any passerby it was occupied. Besides, a conventional A/C unit would not reach the enclosed rear.

It was equipped with a large, battery powered fan. Before ten, the rolling theatre grounds were filling rapidly with motorcycles, most with ugly women sitting behind ugly men, plus considerable traffic of old pickups and an occasional junkyard ready car. Although we saw several bikers we didn't recognize, the ones we identified were all Blood Lords. Diablos had to show eventually as sure as gravity.

By eleven, the rising heat had kicked the fan's butt and we were both ringing wet. We both had drunk heavily from the five-gallon water cooler and had made judicial use of the Folger's can. For male plumbing, the procedure was simple: Pop off the plastic lid, do what needed to be done, and snap the lid back on.

Shortly, the one gallon can had risen precipitously toward the brim. Dump time was imminent. The rear compartment had a side pedestrian door. Hooper put forth a suggestion.

"Call in a napalm strike and I'll dump it out the door," he said.

At that instant, a beat-up old Buick convertible parked adjacent to the van side door, in the partial shade we provided. Incredibly, amidst an accumulation of the least attractive humans imaginable, the female passenger, a clone of Mighty Joe Young, quickly began making passionate love to the zombie driver. A crowd of enthusiastic spectators gathered.

Hooper studying the distant crowd with binoculars pointed out a second couple in the throes of delegacy in bushes near the rest room fifty feet away. Hooper flipped open the outlaw biker mug shot book.

"Don't recognize the pair in the convertible." He studied the couple in the bushes through binoculars. "By cracky, that's Dog Ass Mulvaney, head knocker of the Diablos, Kobok. And if I'm seeing right, that chick he's with is Big Rat Kowolski's ol' lady. Kowalski's a big noise in the Diablos. I ain't sure we're watching a consensual act."

"How did Mulvaney get in there without us seeing him?"

"He's a rat. Maybe he was hiding in the bushes and that ugly woman slithered off and raped him."

"Kobok, Bush is standing about fifty feet the other direction from us, surrounded by a group of bikers. Christ, he got them lined up to take photographs."

"He's a movie producer rep, remember. Looks like he's gettin' an updated list of addresses and telephone numbers of photo-identified outlaw bikers. Hope they're all Blood Lords so there's no killin' in the line."

We turned our attention back to the couple in the bushes near the restroom.

"Kobok, if that chick Dog Ass Mulvaney is rollin' in the bushes with is Big Rat Kowalski's old lady, we're about to see some serious violence."

"The way, these guys pass their ol lady's around for general use, I can't see how the hell it makes any difference. Just raise the price."

Then, although not quite the Second Coming, I saw the next best thing right below me. Transfixed amidst the glut of about twenty-five spectators cheering on the couple in the convertible, stood the damnedest thing on earth.

In white sneakers, black socks, orange walking shorts, and a potbellied *Dallas Cowboys* tee shirt stood ATF Bomb and Arson squad supervisor Cummins Klaster. Some damned fools just never seem to figure when to drop out of the race.

"That peckerwood is out here slow-trailing us," Hooper snorted through his cigar stub.

"Right now, he's watching a free freakshow, Bull."

All said and done, I should have slid back into the driver's seat and beat it to hell out of there. Short Cummins was so enraptured with the convertible scene, he shouldn't have missed us for an hour.

But that wasn't to be. Big Rat Kowalski, a scrawny little man with a black mohawk and a full black beard, had apparently wondered why his true love had not returned from the restroom. He strolled down to investigate. The scene was reminiscent of a Crocodile approaching a herd of hippos.

Big Rat, seeing the rape of his woman, thereupon, as the report would read, withdrew a .38 revolver from a rear blue jeans pocket and put two in Dog Ass Mulvaney's chest at close range. According to the manual, such wounds were invariably fatal—only the manual doesn't specify a time frame.

Dog Ass, having not read the rule book, and definitely not yet out of action, sprang to his feet, drew a twelve-inch hunting knife from his belt, and drove it far enough into Big Rat Kowalski's gut to reach solid matter near the spine.

Big Rat had designated another Blood Lord, the now familiar Sonny Beeman as "good eye" to slow trail his every step. Beeman lunged at the entangled pair.

Big Rat Kowalski was instantly down, and dead of the stab wound in ten seconds. In the Nano fragment of the last second of his miserable existence, Mulvaney pulled the trigger of the .38 again. The round shot off Beeman's left little finger, although we didn't realize the exact nature of the wound at the time. It wasn't fatal, but Beeman was definitely on injured reserve. From where we sat as executive seat spectators, Beeman, flopping around like a fresh caught carp, looked somewhere between almost dead and deader n' hell.

"Hooper, I'm afraid we just lost our witness against Linda."

"Or co-defendant."

Dog Ass Mulvaney, nearing, but not yet arrived at the time limit on remaining life, fumbled a .32 revolver from another pocket. In the last, desperate dance of death, he staggered randomly toward the Trojan van. Directly in his path was the convertible spectator crowd, each of which had the good sense to run like hell—except the aforementioned Short Cummins Klaster.

Short Cummins, in blind terror, whirled and ran directly into the side of the van, rebounding flat on his back in the dust. Clambering to his feet, squealing like a failed ball bearing, he waddled a few steps, which unfortunately carried him directly in front of the damned near dead Dog Ass Mulvaney. Mulvaney raised the .32 and busted a cap at Short Cummins, aiming at the biggest target, a wide ass.

Bullseye! Short Cummins went down in the dirt a second time, still wailing at 10,000 decibels. I assumed he was dead. I was instantly glad that I'd put aside a quarter for his flowers. Then, sporadic gunfire erupted around us, almost instantly exploding to massive.

From the opposite side of the van, Bush, discontinued his movie casting duties and burst around the old vehicle. He drew his .357 magnum from his front shorts pocket, raised the firearm and shouted, "Federal Officer, halt."

Now anyone with a dime's knowledge of Dog Ass Mulvaney could have offered testimony that Dog Ass had not a cussed idea what the hell "halt" even meant. The move saved Short Cummins' life. Dog Ass, ready to deliver the Coup de gras to the downed Short Cummins, turned slightly toward Bush. Revolver in both hands, Bush cranked off two rounds, one taking Dog Ass in chest center, and the second taking off the top of his head. My tall tale to the bikers in front of the Fireplug topless joint just became shorter. Bush was a deadly pistol shot.

With bullets working over the sides of the plumbing van, Hooper and I drug Short Cummins into the van. Bush clambered in and locked the door. In the frenzy, my scrambled egg sandwich had fallen to the floor where it formed an unthinkable soup with the spilled contents of the Folger's can.

"Stay on the floor, Cummins," I shouted. The other three of us took window positions, hunkering low to repel any boarders, to include about thirty bikers firing weapons.

Cummins flopped on the floor in the nasty, scrambled egg based gruel like a dog who'd peed on an electric fence, shrieking, "Oh my god, I'm shot in the ass." Later, It would occur to me that a more accurate description of Short Cummins could not have been invented beyond the fence comparison. In a whole larger sense, the boy was definitely shot in the ass.

Unbelievably, at the apex of gunfire, a black Honda pulled in the main gate, the blonde driver looking about. Then, she whipped the Honda next to the restroom. In the confusion, I recognized Linda Givens driving and Sonny Beeman diving through an open passenger side window. He was far from finished. The Honda roared back out the entrance. I wondered if I'd really seen the action, or a mirage.

Uniformed officers began arriving in blocks of five. Most shooters escaped. The toll was three dead, plus two wounded who would later die in hospitals, and four wounded who would survive. Beeman was not among the dead or wounded. He'd just escaped in a black Honda.

The young EMT who treated Short Cummins' wound told our leader the bullet had hit his billfold and although painful, the damage would only be a bruise. Nonetheless, he would ride out his days with the rep he'd been shot in the ass while running for his useless life.

If the day had a hint of anything good, it was when the EMT asked Short Cummins if he'd been eating scrambled eggs when he pissed his pants.

Until well into the afternoon, we gave written statements to three unhappy Dallas P.D. homicide dicks who'd been called out on a hot Sunday. Short Cummins, although in great pain, and greater humiliation, drove his brand new, taxpayer funded Chevrolet home.

No way Sonny Beeman would return to the cheap motel with Linda. It seemed more than a small problem to try locating him amidst several million people. It would not be.

I dropped the van back at the GSA garage, and found Spring Valley around five. I endured the mandatory game of catch with Tad, drank at least six beers, and was a weaselly weak performer at bedtime.

CHAPTER 20: Rat Faced Ralph

From long habit of self-abuse and with a pretty severe hangover, I was trapped on the Central Expressway along with half of north Dallas by 6:25 A.M. I had bundled the insurance forgery evidence in an envelope the evening before. The Institute of Forensic Sciences was not yet open when I dropped it through the night deposit slot in the front door.

Aside from a couple of agents at desks in the far back of the squad room, the office was empty when I staggered in at 7:30. By 8:00 A.M. Bush had wandered in and most of the desks across the room were occupied with agents typing on manual typewriters. Computers had not found their way onto our desks in 1986.

Bush answered his phone, jotted on a notepad and hung up. "DPS, Austin, says no record of Linda Marie Givens having applied for a lost, duplicate driver's license."

I said, "Somehow, the lost driver's license claim was part of some kinda scam she was trying to work. Probably mixed up somehow in the bank forgery. I dunno, really."

"We gonna file that forgery against her?"

"The lab out at the morgue is working on it...and Jason's journal. We'll see."

Normal procedure in those days required agents to rough out reports on those manual typewriters, then the group clerk would re-type them on one of the original typewriters equipped with a readable, correctable screen. I finished several pages on the Saturday surveillance of Linda and Beeman and the Sunday biker rally disaster. The rally would require considerably more paperwork later on. The insurance office encounter would probably blossom into a grand jury appearance.

Tootie sent me a telephone call. It was Kelly, of storage room fame.

"Hey, mister," she said in her best Marilyn Monroe. "Lab sent down reports on a handwriting analysis you requested and uh…an evidence bag with a diary and a little diamond shaped ball thingy."

"What's the news?"

"Uh, unable to match forged signature of suspect or suspects. Check is forged, signer is probably Linda Marie Givens but unverifiable. That bad?"

"Yep, what else."

"They can't make head nor tails of the diary and the ball thingy…it's a long name starts with 'dode…'"

"Okay, I'll drop by and pick up the stuff. I need to give you back the evidence on Richard Scharf. I dropped some forgery evidence in the slot earlier this morning." It meant Linda could be charged with forgery and a jury might buy the story, but the case was iffy. Circumstances would change all that.

She whispered, "I sent the evidence envelope you left up to the lab squints. I'll look forward to seeing you."

"Kelly, how about a telephone number so we don't get jail time for fooling around in closets? Richard's heart won't take much more trauma."

"Can't come to my place. I live with my mom."

"Oh hell." After we broke the connection, I realized I should have asked if her mama ever took a night off.

I told Bush the bad, but not unexpected news. We could still easily file forgery charges on Linda and Jason's journal seemed of little value, anyway.

His telephone rang. He spoke briefly and hung up.

"ATF, San Antonio says Beeman's alibi witness checks out, but figure the guy is lying like hell, quote. They'll go at him again if need be."

"Bush, I think we need to drive out and see who the big boy who argued with Billie Jack before the fire."

I called Bull Hooper. He agreed Bruce Clarence Ligon needed interviewing. He said he'd wait on the Commerce Street side of the Police and Courts Building."

In fifteen minutes, Hooper was stuffed in the back seat. Passing through pedestrian traffic heavy with derelicts, junkyards, hostility, and prostitutes trying their luck before lunch, I made Beacon Street in fifteen more.

The address we had, the same I'd followed Linda's detour through, was on an old, twelve-unit apartment unit which bore the faded, lopsided sign declaring the place was called the "Victoria Gardens". The exterior had seen no paint in twenty years and the only garden that had grown within five miles in many years was weeds stubborn enough to peek through sidewalk cracks, fertilized with wine bottles and trash.

I stopped near a door bearing a "manager" sign. We stepped out into the heat, both Hooper and I sweating like cold beer at an August picnic. Bush, in a gray pinstriped suit, appeared display window ready. He looked like the almost-lawyer he was.

The manager sat in an un-airconditioned office, a small fan doing its best to keep him alive. Not thinking about the fan in the plumbing van was impossible. He was a smallish white man of about fifty with a cue ball head and so skinny he could have stood beneath a clothesline to stay dry in a downpour. He peered over gold half glasses, his expression plainly reflecting we were not the first cops who'd visited, or the fourth, or the tenth. His desk name tag said his name was "Ralph Rubinstein". With rodent-like movement, Ralph nervously and sporadically tugged on his left ear lobe.

"What's the problem officers?" he began with a negative conclusion. He probably smelled cops coming when we were a block away.

We all flashed badges. I said, "We need to talk with Bruce Clarence Ligon?"

Rat Faced Ralph asked, "Whut's that goofy bastard Clarence done this time?" Apparently, Bruce was known as Clarence.

I said, "We'll ask the questions. What unit is he in?"

"Clarence is in 3A. That's downstairs in the rear."

"How long has he been a resident?" I asked.

"Oh, six, eight months."

Hooper asked, "What's he do for a living?"

"Some kinda railroad pension. Damned if I know what.

Pays his rent in cash first of the month like a cash register. Wish some o' the rest of the riffraff I got in here got a railroad check. Some of 'um might learn to pay the rent on time."

"He have problems... trouble?" I asked.

"Only all the damned time. Clarence is as crazy as a fruit orchard boar."

Hooper asked, "He dangerous?"

"Well... yeah as a matter of fact. Most the time he stays on his medication and he's quiet. Miss a damned pill or two and he's liable to eat the furniture."

"He a biker?" I asked.

"A whut?"

"A biker. Like does he have a motorcycle?"

"Clarence ain't got enough sense to ride no motorcycle."

Hooper asked. "He got any friends who ride motorcycles?"

"Clarence ain't got no friends, and I never seen nobody back there, 'cept maybe a whore when he's got money." He ran his right hand over his bald head and tugged the left earlobe with the other.

Hooper leaned close. "We go back there and you call him, I'll come back over here and pull off both your damned ears."

Ralph appeared near to bolting for the door at the comment. "Cain't call the dumb ass, cuz he ain't back there. Drove out about a half hour ago. Sides, he ain't got no phone."

"Driving what?" I asked.

"That old blue Ford F150. He'll be back sooner or later. No idea when."

"Look, dude," I said. "You are hereby deputized to write down the tag numbers of any cars that go back there until we come back."

"Yessir, I'll start right now." He grabbed a pen and sat, leaning forward over a notepad. The resemblance to a sewer rat was incredible. "They's six apartments on the rear. I ain't got no way of tellin' who goes to Clarence's. I can tell y'all right now if anybody goes to Clarence's place, it would be the first damn visitor he ever had...cept' the girls he hauls in in that old Ford." He gave the left ear a tug.

I tossed my card on his desk. We drove to *Pepe's*, an all you can eat Mexican Restaurant on Gaston, a plan with inherent dietary overtones. I called Tootie with the location. I ate too much, and Hooper did his damnedest to clean them out. Bush ate a salad while watching with amazement the quantity of food Hooper could consume.

Hooper and I were munching honey drenched tortillas when the big haired lady cashier held up a telephone receiver and shouted, "Anybody name Kobox in here?"

Tootie said, "Some dummy named Ralph said to tell you Clarence is back."

CHAPTER 21: THE EXPLOSIVE RABBIT

The stalwart Rat Faced Ralph was standing guard in his office. He smelled like a wet goat.

"I ain't had no car come in cept' Clarence." He was still bent intently over his desk, pen in the "ready" position.

"You done good, Ralph."

"Yessir, ain't no problem, that. Allays glad to help the laws. Clarence is crazy as hell and I ain't about to get involved in his bidness. He gave the left ear one last tug. It appeared that if Ralph lived long enough, his left earlobe would reach his collar.

"Nervous tic," Bush said as I got back into the car.

"What?"

"That apartment manager, Mr. Rubinstein. He has a neurotic tic which compels him to tug on his left earlobe."

"Yeah, Randall, and he smells like a litterbox."

I considered the medical possibilities. "Randall, could he undergo shock treatment to cause him to tug on one ear, then the other, so they'd come out even at shoulder length. Christ, Bush, if the cops come too many times, Ralph is gonna pull off his left ear."

"My father's a psychiatrist. I could ask him."

"Randall, I know about your dad who lives in a house with nineteen bathrooms. I don't care if Ralph works on that ear until it reaches his waist."

Apartment 3A was equally as shabby as the whole place, except for the pipe bomb laying on a table by the front window, fully visible to anyone walking past.

Like a dog with a trained nose, Clarence opened the door before I managed to knock. He was somewhere around six-five and 300 pounds with shoulder length brown hair that hadn't seen shampoo in a year and a half. He lacked the motor function to focus both eyes behind coke bottle lens glasses. I'd seen him before.

"Ain't did shit."

"Saw you at Billie Jack and the boys' funerals the other day. Didn't get a chance to talk."

"They was dead."

"Yep, Clarence, wouldn't be right to bury them if they weren't. We need to come in and talk with you."

"Uh, I don't think that would be a good idea." He partially closed the door.

I caught it with a foot. Hooper stepped up and added a shoulder.

"We're cops, Clarence. We have to come in," Hooper said. We both waved badges.

"You'll violate the erroneous zones." The wandering eyes partially focused.

"Life's a bitch." I started to push past him, causing him to squeal like a rusty hinge.

Bush stepped up. "Mr. Ligon, we understand the importance of erroneous zones. Please mark them for us."

Clarence, obviously elated at finding the first kindred soul since being sprung from the nervous hospital, waved his hand carefully back and forth below door knob level.

Bush carefully stepped in. Hooper and I followed. The smell was a combination of rabbit droppings, burned meat, and the city landfill. When I saw the very large white rabbit in a cage near the pipe bomb, plus something frying in a pan on a small burner at the rear of the one room place, I brilliantly deduced the source of the stink.

A white sheet of paper taped to the rabbit cage had the word's "Caution, Explosive Rabbit" in magic marker across it. It appeared the rabbit might be the brains of the outfit.

"I was just fixin' lunch," Clarence said. "Want some?"

Somehow the idea didn't seem practical. "No thank you, Clarence, we just had lunch."

I moved across the room and shut the burner off beneath something I didn't examine close enough to classify. A commode was visible in a closet sized room in a corner. Bathing was probably a matter of finding a garden hose outside. Hygiene didn't seem to register on Clarence's radar.

I said, "Clarence, we need to have a talk." I probably should have directed the comment to the rabbit.

"Okay, fellers, how can I help the law today?" Suddenly, the only two human occupants of the apartment complex we'd met so far were anxious to be deputized.

He calmly took a seat on a plastic milk crate at room center. I sat on a battered sofa. Bush did too, after he'd carefully brushed off a spot to shield his pinstripes. Hooper stood.

The explosive rabbit, poised atop a strait back chair eyed me warily, nose twitching suspiciously. I tensed, ready for a savage rabbit attack. I hadn't forgotten Jimmy Carter's ordeal.

Hooper stepped over and bent to look at the bomb.

I asked, "Clarence, why do you have a bomb in your front window?"

"Holocaust."

Hooper slapped a knee. "Hell, I knew that."

"Do you know that bomb is against the law, Clarence?" I asked.

"Man's law."

"Yeah, state and federal law both." I looked up at Hooper.

"It's time for Armageddon," Clarence looked up, cow eyed.

"That the same as the holocaust?"

"Basically. I have a direct connection to the Outer Boundary. Time is short."

Hooper stepped closer. We were both tense, expecting the huge man to explode or crash out a window. Clarence wasn't the first nutball we'd interviewed.

Hooper asked, "Outer Boundary? How short is time, dude?"

"Closer than you think. And officer, I'm no dude."

Hooper said, "Hope it's before next Tuesday. That's when my wife's car payment is due."

"Sir, it's not a laughing matter." Clarence eyed Hooper, trying to focus. "I've already written a letter to Satan."

"Did he answer it?" Bush asked.

"Well, hell no. There's no post office in Hell. Satan will tell me in another way."

I asked, "How?"

"Dunno yet."

I said, "Clarence, we need to see the letter."

Lower lip trembling, he said, "Are y'all gonna keep it. Satan will be angry."

"We can't have that, Clarence, you can keep it," I said.

From a greasy shirt pocket, he pulled an even greasier sheet of paper. On it, in longhand, with what would prove to be no mistakes, was his message to the Outer Boundary. It read:

Greetings, Satan, from Victoria Gardens, unit 3A:

Satan, I have debated for some time before putting pen to paper to report all this. I know if this was a letter to God, I shouldn't say "all this shit", but since you're Satan and must already know whatever I'm thinking, I'm confused. The old lady upstairs said saying words like all this shit in a letter to Satan would be okay because you're the head man in the evil part of the system. But I have grave concerns, anyway. Sorry for all the explaining 'cuz none of that is what I'm writing about.

Satan, I must warn you that you need to buy new furniture and stuff to make room for more people in Hell immediately, because I'm commencing Holocaust by the end of this week. I already have one bomb and have no idea how to get more. I'd hope you could send instructions and a few hundred bucks to get things started.

Satan, once I've eliminated the human race, and am the only man-servant remaining, I'll begin the Pentecost by building a tower 171 feet tall. I have not figured out how to bury all the bastards, yet, but will figure out something. That's partly why I'm writing. Could you mail me a bulldozer—a large one. Or send cash, or for that matter, just send a signal and I'll steal that damned bulldozer. Answer soon.

I remain your humble servant,

Bruce Clarence Ligon

Keeper of the Devine Pentecost and the Explosive Rabbit.

P.S.: Satan, they call me Clarence, but since you already know everything, I don't guess I have to tell you that.

Bush, who had sat quietly on the worn sofa, interjected,

"Mild schizophrenic and manic depressive with bipolar tendencies."

Clarence looked at him, astonished. "You friends with Satan, officer? Or maybe from the hospital. I'll go back if you say so."

"No, I'm a federal agent."

I said, "What the hell did you just say, Bush? Set him off and I'll shoot both of your asses."

"Clarence is schizophrenic of the process type—probably only a mild onset. That means he's had the disease for many years. Note, his symptoms show disheveled countenance with inability to concentrate or focus. I would guess his condition is exacerbated by a manic-depressive condition, more often called bipolar disorder. That means he wavers from deep, uncontrollable depression to equally uncontrollable periods of excessive euphoric behavior. The schizophrenia compounds his problems with what they call transient delusions. He sees and hears things that don't exist. I believe we caught him on route from high to low unless you get him revved up and send him into frenzy."

"Good God," I said.

"Great Satan," Clarence said.

The explosive rabbit wriggled its nose without comment but looked impressed.

Bush continued. "The doctors probably sent him home with instructions to take daily doses of a cocktail consisting of fluoxetine manufactured as Prozac, and maybe sertraline packaged as Zoloft. There are a half dozen or so more and I have no way of knowing exactly what drug and what combinations they've prescribed."

"I'll be damned," Hooper dropped his cigar stub.

Bush said, "I'd bet Clarence is off his medication. Right, Clarence?"

"Yessir, yessir, a big yellow one and a little white one ever day. I'll take 'um right now."

I expected him to fall at Bush's feet. Clarence sprang to his feet from his milk crate and in an instant was at a small kitchen counter where three large knives lay in open view. Hooper and I both drew pistols and held them at our sides.

Bush saw us and said, "Don't think that will be necessary."

Clarence reached into a drawer, fumbled open two brown RX bottles and downed a pill from each without benefit of water.

Bush said, "That will make him sleepy in a minute or two. He's big. They won't work quite as fast."

"Sit down, Clarence," I gestured to his milk crate. He complied quietly.

Hooper and I holstered our weapons.

"Clarence," I said. "You know we gotta take this bomb."

"Yessir. It ain't got no powder in it anyway. Jes' an empty pipe to scare off some of the riff raff in the neighborhood."

Hooper leaned down to stare the Explosive Rabbit in the eyes. "Clarence, you haven't been feeding this rabbit dynamite or something like it, have you?"

"No sir, that would upset her stomach. She only eats lettuce."

At that, he was back on his feet, amazingly agile for his size and at the counter where he picked up a very long knife. He raised the knife, looking over his shoulder at Bush. This time we actually pointed our pistols.

Bush said, "What are you gonna cut, Clarence."

"Lettuce," Clarence slammed the knife into a head of lettuce on the counter, sending vegetative shrapnel in all directions. He tossed the knife on the counter.

We again holstered our pistols.

"Clarence?" I asked. "What were you doing arguing with a man in Lakewood in his front yard last week?"

"Panhandling. Lots a' folks are willing to help out a feller in need."

"Why the argument?" Hooper asked.

"Don't remember. Lots o' people tell me to kiss off, but if you wanna see how much money I can collect…" He stood and stuffed a ham hand into his trouser's pocket. We all grabbed at weapons. He pulled a wad of cash from his pocket, and we relaxed.

"Put your stash away, Clarence," I ordered. "We wonder if you went back and burned down a house on Brookshore."

"When?"

"Last Tuesday night… actually early Wednesday morning." I said.

"I could never find that neighborhood in the dark."

We held a mini-psychiatric session in a corner.

Bush said, "Harmless. I don't think he'd hurt a fly. The Holocaust talk is drivel."

Hooper added, "And I don't think he could have gotten the Given's door open even if he had a key."

We conducted a quick, totally illegal search of the one room abode. No additional bombs, no guns, no more rabbits were discovered. I spent the entire time in the stink-chamber, never turning my back on the rabbit. It's damned difficult to tell what, exactly, an Explosive Rabbit might do if it got a chance at your back.

So, on Dr. Bush's psycho-analysis, we departed, leaving Clarence and the rabbit alone and bomb-less. He certainly seemed harmless. Not so, that sneaky rabbit.

As we pulled out into traffic, I said, "If ATF recruits ol' Clarence, he's a cinch to make group supervisor in months."

Hooper said he agreed. "Want I should drop the bomb off at the DPD bomb squad, down at the Central Sub Station. On South Hall?"

When we dropped off the bomb, Hooper strolled back to the car and announced Clarence had told the truth. The device contained no explosive.

Hooper said he had to be in court and we dropped him at the Police and Courts Building. I wondered if Rat Faced Ralph was still on point taking down license numbers. I wished I'd told him to sketch any pedestrians who walked by.

CHAPTER 22: Another Deadly Gamble

in the Dark Recesses of the Morgue

"Bush, the D.D., Charlene, uh…West thing bothers me. We need to find and squeeze Scoots Garcia. D.D. should be a connection to the little rat, except she hasn't been seen in several days. Hard to be a stripper when nobody can see you… dressed or not."

"Okay…what?"

"If Scoots beat her brains in or otherwise bumped her off, she might have turned up in the morgue. I had good luck on a murder last year by running records of Jane Does out there. Damned lawyer beat a hooker to death and left her in a dumpster."

"Morgue? Why not homicide records?"

"That would only cover the City of Dallas. The Southwest Institute does forensic work for the entire county and several other counties spreading over a wide area."

He looked slightly green. "Kobok, I'm not quite ready for another stint in the morgue? Any chance you could drop me at the office. I could get a supplemental report started on the Clarence episode this morning."

Well, he did volunteer. "Draft it, stuff it in my desk drawer, and do not show it to Short Cummins until I get a chance to see it, okay."

He literally appeared as though he might sing a refrain from "Happy days are here again."

"Yeah. Can you call if you need me after you've been to that God-awful place?"

"Okay. We need to drop by the Purple Parrott this afternoon

to visit with the owner and a few of the virgins who work there. I'll swing by and pick you up…if you can work late this afternoon."

"Sure."

I dropped him at the Cabell Federal Building and worked my way up Harry Hines Boulevard.

Lynn O'Hara, garbed in her surgical mask, green frock and rubber apron was carving on a piece of raw meat while Richard stood nearby, digging in the empty body cavity of a grossly obese white man with bleached blond hair. The cadaver's head was twisted at a severe angle.

"Hey, dude." She smiled through her gold glasses, again weirdly sexy in bloodstained apron while waving a huge, ugly knife.

"Heart failure?" I gestured to her "patient".

"Yeah, after driving a pickup off the Zangs Boulevard overpass. Surprised you hadn't heard. Hell of a mess."

Zangs Boulevard was a main route over the Trinity River to and from the Oak Cliff section of Dallas. Just south of the viaduct was the boarding house where Lee Harvey Oswald had fled to his temporary nest to pick up the pistol he used to murder Dallas Police Officer J.D. Tippet over twenty years earlier.

She leaned close. "Had a fine time when you dropped over the other night."

"Me, too, Doc," I whispered. "Are we gonna marry soon."

"Naw, screw that, Kobok. What brings you besides trying to seduce me?"

Richard partially overheard the comments and looked at us sharply.

"Still up to it on that Givens case. Need to see if you had a Jane Doe come in in the past five or six days. Stripper, tattoo of a rose vine and two red roses on her left forearm, spider tattoos on the backs of each calf."

"Damned sure did. Came in from Balch Springs. Richard and I did the examination. Kid had been stabbed ten or so times. Came in naked. Tattoos like you say. No sign of clothes. Got clean prints. Not sure they've run them yet."

Balch, pronounced "Box", Springs was a small, run down

community adjacent to the Pleasant Grove District of Southeast Dallas. The city limits were pistol distance from the Blood Lord House in Pleasant Grove inside the city of Dallas.

"Her name is Charlene West, called "D.D.", dancer about 22 or so. Biker chick."

She jotted the name on the edge of her clipboard. "We'll confirm via the fingerprints. Surely all strippers have some kind of arrest record?' She giggled. "You can ask Kelly up in my office about them. You know her, don't you?"

Oh hell. Was this a deadly trap? Was O'Hara sending me to my doom? Could Richard have spilled and Kelly cooperating to save her skin? I thought I might barf.

"What the hell's wrong with you Kobok? You look like you just encountered the Loch Ness Monster out in the hall."

"Uh, greasy spoon food for lunch. It's all the rookie will eat." I hoped that little white lie didn't draw much water in the count for Hell.

"See Kelly, dude. I'm up to my ears." She pointed her chin at three naked specimens on gurneys lined up behind her. Then she leaned close to my ear. "Call me, dude."

Aw heck, I'd like to say I trudged up the stairs like a man mounting the gallows. But you know, lust is a funny thing. It takes blood and thought-fluid directly from a man's brain.

Kelly was typing like sixty... or maybe eighty if we had been talking about typing speed. I sat the Richard "Gut" Scharff evidence on a table. "Returning some evidence."

"Hey, boy," she swiveled her chair around to face me. She was wearing a pale blue sweater, dark blue spike heels, and a cream-colored skirt that might have gotten her arrested a few years earlier. The smell of lavender filled the room to every corner. The fires began to consume me instantly.

"Uh, I need to see a Jane Doe file." I did stammer a bit. "And pick up the diary and handwriting samples you called me about."

"I did call your office." she smiled, confident the fly was already stuck by at least one foot. "But not about a Jane Doe."

She tossed two envelopes on the edge of her desk. "Here's the evidence from the lab."

"Er, uh, the Jane Doe came in in the past few days from the Balch Police Department. Young, dark hair, tattoo of roses on her left forearm."

She tapped computer keys. "Oh yeah, Kobok. That case iss typed and filed in the storeroom across the hall. Door's unlocked. Look in the fourth file cabinet from the door on the left. Jane Does' are in the bottom drawer."

Now, there is no real explanation as to why I felt a slight letdown when she didn't automatically include herself in the Jane Doe search adventure. Suspicious minds might offer nefarious reasons, but I like to think that as a dedicated professional, I needed to do my duty.

Naturally I couldn't find the damned file. Due to a bum knee from high school football, I never did well trying to kneel on a knee. I was leaned over, digging in the afore directed bottom drawer when the file room door clicked ominously shut behind me.

"Oh my," Kelly said, "I meant to say the bottom drawer of the third cabinet on the left." A likely story, skeptics might suggest.

The spike heels clacked the few steps from the door. Instantly, Kelly's lovely aroma surrounded me while I was still trapped and venerably bending down over the wrong cabinet. The lovely presence brushed against me, the heels still mapping her progress. But as I stood erect, I realized, in sinking, lustful realization, that between the door and the file cabinet, she'd dropped her entire ensemble, save the blue spikes. What a horror. Trapped again by a ravishingly beautiful, nude, blue heeled vixen.

In seconds, I was down to my socks, my pistol tossed beside my trousers in front of the open drawer. Like a soccer star, she kicked the drawer shut while flat on her back and in seconds we were rolling on the cold tile floor. In an instant I was nearly to third base, but had obviously only punched Kelly's low gear button, spooling her up for a couple more hour's effort.

But of course, the damned door opened. Would you have expected less? And it had to be him.

"Jesus Christ," exclaimed Richard.

"Jesus Christ," exclaimed Kelly.

"Jesus Christ," I added unnecessarily.

Richard disappeared, mumbling "Jesus Christ" on autopilot as he stumbled down the hall.

Kelly, if anything, beat her previous re-assuming of clothing by several seconds and even managed to get the shoes on the right feet.

I figured this time, if O'Hara rushed me with a lynch mob, I'd deny, deny, deny.

I opened the correct drawer, dug out the file on D.D. and walked down the hall to a common copying machine. The file contained several duplicate death photos. I settled for one showing a nude, horribly mutilated woman, her body perforated by numerous stab wounds. Defensive wounds were prominent on the rose tattooed forearm. Taped on a 3X5 card were several short, gray hairs with the morgue case number written across the top. I thought they might be animal hairs. Does Scoots have a dog?

Someone had inflicted an unspeakable atrocity on a young person who could have enjoyed many more years of life. Why would Scoots, assuming he was the perp, do this to a woman with whom he had to have been intimately associated with before the crime?

I replaced the original file, closed the file drawer, and walked softly back to the office O'Hara and Kelly shared. Thumbing the copies I'd just run, I noticed a single bloody scrap of paper, which had been taped on a larger sheet to avoid losing it. On the scrap was scribbled, "3A-rear".

I stepped in behind Kelly, once again typing like she'd never stopped. I slipped my card into her purse sitting on the floor beside her and said, "My home number is there and I do not have a mother living with me. Do you drink wine?"

The blue eyes alight, she looked up. "Only in large quantities."

It occurred to me she might likely break my main spring with too much exposure. I'd die with a smile on my mug.

I showed her the copy of the scrap. "What is this?"

"Oh, there was probably another sheet attached." She looked

through my pile of copies. "Yes, here it is. That little snippet taped on was stuck on her back by blood when they found the body in a field in Balch Springs...wherever that is." •

I was nearly clear. The main door was only a few steps away. I'd touched the self-destruct button and survived once again. Then, a commotion as several people burst from the elevator right next to me. O'Hara's voice was prominent in the confusion. I turned. With luck I could escape through the emergency door at the end of the hallway.

"Kobok, come here, now," O'Hara commanded. Busted, I turned back.

Incredibly, four male employees from the basement morgue were carrying Richard strapped to a stretcher. "Oh, Sweet Jesus," Richard mumbled over and over.

O'Hara looked flummoxed. "Richard has lost it, Kobok. Totally twisted off. I sent him up to the file room and somehow it was the final straw. He's been acting like a frightened polecat for several days. Suddenly, he's in total collapse. Some kinda latent horror of closets. We're gonna carry him over to Parkland Psychiatric. God, now I have to find another Diener."

Kelly, hearing the sounds, had stepped out into the hallway. She looked on, angelic and innocent.

O'Hara and her posse disappeared out the back door toward Parkland.

I thumbed the D.D. file. No semen discovered. I started to ask Kelly, typing nearby about the lack of sexual assault evidence, but decided to avoid any talk of such intimate matters. She might trap me again. God I felt used—well, sort of.

I used Kelly's phone to call Bush at the office. I told him we needed to drive through Lakewood late enough in the afternoon to see if we could find additional witnesses to confirm events and circumstances at the Given's house. Then we needed to drop by the Purple Parrott and see what the mad Russian had to say and try to interview as many strippers as we could corral who were not too stoned to stay awake during the interview.

"Do we have to have the owner's permission to interview strippers?"

"Nope, but we'll try catching flies with honey first. If that doesn't work, we'll bring on the fly-swatter."

I picked up my two envelopes of evidence, stuffed them into my folder with the copies I'd just made of the Jane Doe, and walked to my Dodge.

I picked Bush up on the Jackson Street side of the Cabell Building. He looked across and said, "You okay, Kobok? You look a little tired."

"All's cool, Randall." I probably appeared a mite thoughtful because I was trying to figure a way to come and go in the morgue without passing "Go See Kelly."

In an hour we had found additional neighbors in the 4800 block of Brookshore who ID Clarence from his mug photo could as being the large man seen arguing with Billie Jack. All could testify that Billie Jack and Linda fought often, and of greatest importance, could verify that the dog barked at anything and everything.

"Bush, Linda looks guilty as hell."

"Are we going to charge her with murder?"

"Probably, but if we don't sort out the biker connection, her lawyer, whatsie...?"

"Harless Androvski," he said.

"Yeah, Androvski, will muddle the case by creating the image that bikers killed Billie Jack and that his loving wife is innocent."

CHAPTER 23: STRIPPERS AND ROCKET SCIENTISTS

RARELY OCCUPY THE SAME SPACE

It was past five when we parked in the rear lot of the Purple Parrott. The hard hats and hard noses were getting off work. The parking lot was about half full. Blaring music from inside rivaled the racket of the Fireplug Club. Admission was by front door only, guarded by a guy bigger than Clarence. At 6-6 and three hundred, he wore dark hair in a mohawk and showed his muscles via a sleeveless shirt with a logo, "Babes Welcome" across the front. A plastic tag on his chest said he was "Carlo".

"Two bucks cover," he said. The Russian was trying to compensate for slow drinkers.

I flashed my badge. Bush fumbled his out of his pocket.

"Still two bucks and no free drinks, boys."

I said, "We need to see Dimitri."

He stepped back into the darkened doorway and dialed a wall phone. "Couple a' feds wanna see you. Yeah, they got ID." He covered the phone. "Whut's yer names?"

"Kobok and Bush," I said.

He came back out. "Boss says come on back. Office is at the rear left, behind the men's john."

As we walked in, a brunette with fired egg cloned breasts was working the pole on a horseshoe shaped bar similar to the one at the Fireplug. Two girls were dancing on rickety tables. The one across the room was too far away to see in the smoky, strobe-lighted room. Near us, the table was decorated by a tall, long haired blonde with a tattoo of a snake circling her right leg below the knee. She appeared to be very attractive. Experience told me she wouldn't look so hot in bright light.

Dimitri stood in the open doorway of his cramped office. His stocky girth fully filled the doorway.

"Special Agent Kobok, it's good to see you again. I hope you're bringing news of the terrorist who blew up a good customer's car in our parking lot last year?" His accent was faint, but still distantly Eastern European. "And it's nice to meet you Mr. Bush." He nodded to the Rook.

"No, Dimitri," I replied. "We're looking at the arson murder of a customer of yours...and his two sons. Also need info regarding a girl named Charlene West, a dancer here who is currently in the morgue."

Bush gasped. "D.D. is dead?"

I shushed him. Dimitri had not reacted. He said, "Great God, D.D. I didn't recognize the name Charlene West. What a tragedy."

We took seats in the small, stuffy office. In the light, the sweat on his face and soaking his clothes was vivid. Was he afraid of us? It was the normal reaction to guilt.

"Two things, Dimitri. I would like to talk with some of your dancers and I'd like to ask you about your relationship to the dead man, Billie Jack Givens."

"Givens?" He scratched his nose in feigned memory failure.

"Brassiere man, operated a business down on Industrial a half block from the Fireplug Topless Club."

"Oh, yes of course. Billie Jack. His wife, whose name I forget, danced here at one time. Pretty girl, poor dancer. She's the one whose boob job ended up lopsided."

"We hear you were in some kind of business deal with him?" I mostly bluffed for effect.

His stolid expression showed a Nano second of concern.

"Dimitri, no law against business deals...as long as you give the IRS their cut."

"I owe the IRS nothing."

"Figure of speech, dude." I was more of a mind that Billie Jack might have been laundering sex slave traffic cash through Leemis Fashions. In the absence of a little thing called evidence, that sleeping dog needed to be left at rest. "Dimitri, we need to interview as many of your dancers as we can. Maybe get a line on what kind of lunatic mighta gotten cozy with D.D. and murdered her."

"Of course, you may, Kobok. Use my office. We have about eight girls on duty now and about sixteen all told. You already know, my friend, many are too spaced out from sucking poison up their noses to make much sense."

I could have corrected him about being my friend, but again, it was the old honey versus fly swatter syndrome.

He struggled out of his seat and said, "Anyone who'd strangle a girl like D.D. needs nuts ripped off."

Dimitri walked out. "I didn't say anything about cause of death, Randall. Dimitri knows more than he'd like to."

"I noticed that."

In a minute or so, a bleached blonde of about twenty, with genuine add on boobs walked in in a G string, a see-through white T shirt and red spike heels. I thought of Kelly and the closet. We introduced ourselves.

"Hey, guys, I'm Amber." She slouched in a chair. Then, staring Bush boldly in the face, she leaned up, removed the T shirt, and showed us a sizeable quantity of surgical miracle. "Warmish in here." She smiled, obviously proud of her assets, then lit a filter tip.

"Amber who?" I asked,

"How about Smith." She smiled. This was no Beaver from the Fireplug.

"Amber, a good customer here, Billie Jack Givens, was murdered along with his two sons in a fire in their residence early last Wednesday morning. A dancer here, D.D., real name Charlene West, was found murdered about the same time. We're investigating, hoping to see if there's any connections."

"D.D., oh my God. She was obsessed with those damned bikers. She went through at least three in the three or so months she worked here. They were fat, greasy, and that little limping rat, 'Soot" or whatever he was called made me wanna barf."

"Enemies, violence, creeps who might have abducted her?"

"All three. Both that fat one, 'Gut' I think he was called and the little gimpy one pimped her out. Guys, we all get off on something or other, but D.D. genuinely enjoyed random sex with Johns."

I asked, "You said three bikers?"

"Yeah, before Gut, there was that guy with all the red hair and beard. Called him Red Fred. That goof with his head on sideways was in the picture at one time."

She was referring to Red Fred and Richard "Bent Dick" Sullivan, but I didn't identify them.

"That's four," I said.

"Whatever. D.D. was pretty flexible."

"You're not into bikers?" Bush asked.

"God no. I'm in pre-law at the Community College. This job just pays pretty good if you can overlook some of the negative crap." She exhaled. She expanded her chest, if that was possible. "Personally, I get off on tender young cops, especially feds."

Bush, blushing, appeared ready to burst to tell this heavily chested beauty he was a lawyer. I helped.

"Bush is a lawyer, Amber."

"Really?" She smiled.

I wrote in bold across a yellow pad, "Is this room bugged?"

She shook her head, no. "Management is too tight."

"Do you have any girls with middle or eastern European accents dancing here?" I asked softly.

"Yeah, quite a few."

I asked, "Could the dead man, Billie Jack, be involved with Dimitri in smuggling girls into the country?"

"Hey, guys, life is full of could-be's, but I don't know shit about Dimitri's business."

"Nothing at all?" Bush asked.

She stubbed out her cigarette. "Well, handsome, I'm his great niece, actually. Granddaughter of his sister. And no problem, cops come in undercover and ask me crap like that all the time. I won't tell Dimitri you asked. However, Dimitri is a class asshole and y'all are on the mark about the girl smuggling thing. And I remember that Billie Jack guy. He and Dimitri were pretty tight. They were back here in the office together some."

"Talking business?" Bush asked.

"When they weren't having a little private nude girly party...

always with two or three of the girls with the accents you asked about. Sorta like they owned them."

I handed her a business card which she slipped into her G string. She turned to better squarely face Bush, her chest two feet from his face. "Call me sometime and we'll talk legality." She smiled and walked out, still minus the T shirt. "I'll send you Elga," she called over a bare shoulder. "She speaks a little English."

"Bush, you reckon uncle Dimitri paid for that boob job?"

Elga was tall with dark hair and eyes, had no add-on anatomy, and was noticeably nervous. She was dressed in jean shorts and a red T shirt. We got from her that she was from Belarus and that she was too afraid of Demitri to talk to us.

Third, we got Marta, a shorter version of Elga in both appearance and dress. In limited English, Marta stated she was from Bulgaria and acknowledged Dimitri had helped her into the country, but then dummied up like a discarded ventriloquist's mannequin.

I asked, "Marta, do you recall Billie Jack Givens?" I laid the family photo of the Givens' on Dimitri's desk.

"No," she said. The lie and fear were equally plain.

"Thank you, Marta." She walked out.

"Randall, Billie Jack had some connection around here, but I believe we're goin' nowhere fast like this. All the girls have been warned…threatened is more like it. Let's talk to one more."

In walked the tall blonde with the snake tattoo winding around one leg who I'd seen as red hot in the dim, stuttering strobe lights. She was topless in dirty white shorts, and barefoot. In the brighter light of the office, she was twenty, going on sixty. Her sunken, watery blue eyes were a classic demo of "street eyes". You can hide much with makeup, but eyes are hard to camouflage. This kid was well on the highway to destroying herself with too many late hours, too much substance abuse, too many girly parties where the cocaine was piled on the table like stacks of white gold.

I asked, "What's your name, please?" I motioned her to Dimitri's desk chair.

"Huh?" she responded from deep in the well.

"Your name, kid?"

"Dynamite, dude, Dynamite." She had a pretty good buzz on but could still walk and talk in a limited way.

"What's your real name, the one your mama gave you?"

"Sarah Whitaker and I ain't holdin'. Y'all can search my locker, mister."

I asked, "How old are you, Dynamite?"

"Uh, nineteen, man."

I said, "We're investigating the death of one of your better customers…"

"Hey, look, baby, I don't turn no tricks outta here. Dimitri would…"

"I meant the Parrot's customers. Guy named Billie Jack Givens. Burned to death in his home last Tuesday night. It's a murder."

"Fuckin' awesome, dude. Billie Jack?" She squinted her tired eyes. "Billie Jack's dead? Shit, I gave him head while I was settin' in this same damned chair while he sat on the desk. Big tipper. Who the hell would wanna murder Billie Jack?"

I tossed the photo back on the desk.

She struggled to focus. "Yeah, Billie Jack. Dunno the rest of them in the picture."

"Do you know D.D.?"

"Yeah, sweet chick. She loved to party in this little office with Billie Jack and some other dudes. I don't remember their names."

"She like bikers?"

"Yeah. Ain't seen D.D. lately. She was from like frickin' Lousianna. Musta gone home, man."

I didn't bother trying to insert a business card somewhere on her. If she happened to read it, she wouldn't recall it's origin. "Thanks Dynamite, you can go."

"Bush, the walls, have ears in a place like this. Let me thank Dimitri for his "cooperation" and we can beat it. It's past seven."

I thanked Dimitri and herded the old Dodge through inbound traffic toward downtown where Bush could pick up his Ford at the GSA Garage. As I entered the high-rise caverns of downtown Dallas, the fires consumed me. I whipped a left onto one-way East Commerce, found a curbside parking spot and stopped. Bush looked over expectantly.

"Randall, you ever been to Adair's?"

"Yeah. Who hasn't? When I was home from law school, I went in there with guys several times. Great burgers and ambiance."

Ambiance? Adair's saloon, arguably the oldest tavern in Dallas, on Commerce Street at the eastern edge of downtown, was a famous gathering spot for cops and others careless about fancy décor. Texas, among other inconveniences, is a dry state, wet by precincts. Voters in Houston, for instance, had wisely voted nearly every precinct in Harris County wet. Dallas at the time, was limited to a diamond shaped wet precinct, seven or so miles on a side, which basically overlaid Central Dallas. Adair's was inside the Southeast boundary line.

Entrepreneurs had seized the opportunity to convert a stretch of East Elm parallel to East Commerce Street into an area called "Deep Ellum". Most bars in Deep Ellum proper catered to a slightly different clientele who would not be comfortable in a basically country and western, redneck atmosphere such as Adair's. On the edge of Deep Ellum, Adair's was the most popular outfit of the bunch.

Bush didn't flinch when the bartender greeted, "Hey, Kobok, what goes?"

We ordered tall draw beers and a half pound burger apiece. Adair's was semi-famous for their burgers. By the time the burgers hit the bar, I re-ordered my beer. By the time we'd finished the burgers, I was on my fourth beer which I downed before paying the tab. No sense in wasting solid health food.

"Randall, can you walk over to that payphone and call the answering service while I hit the head?"

When I came out of the john, he was writing in his notebook. He caught my eye and motioned me over. Covering the phone, he said, "It's Amber from the Purple Parrot. She wants to talk to you."

"What's up, Amber."

"I need to talk to you guys. Can you meet me somewhere? Wait, where are y'all? I hear country music in the background.?

"Adair's, you probably never heard of the place. We can come…"

"Adair's? I live in Uptown, not far from Adair's. I already told Dimitri I was sick and had to go home. Give me thirty minutes and I'll join y'all."

We had another tall one. When Amber walked in wearing a very expensive silk red blouse, white short shorts, and knee length red boots, a near riot ensued. Guys knocked over tables and each other vying for a view. She waved, swayed majestically through the crowd, and joined us.

After we'd all three downed another beer and Amber's hamburger arrived, some measure of order was restored. But she remained the center of attention. Six or eight cops found reason to come over and ask me about some case I'd forgotten or had never existed.

"You wanted to talk to us, kiddo?" I asked.

"Look, Dimitri is a total prick. You damned right he smuggles these European girls in through customs. Hides them in those sealed metal containers they carry on ships. A few he uses as dancers, but I don't know where the rest go."

I asked, "Who picks them up at Customs?"

"Dunno. They got a big assed truck…big enough to carry one of those containers as big as a minivan. Someway, they get that container into or onto a truck and divvy up the girls somewhere. I heard that from some of the girls at the Parrot."

I asked, "Was Billie Jack Givens involved?"

"I think he was, but only in the money part somehow. Billie Jack wasn't the type to do heavy lifting or to haul chicks in a container on a truck. I heard that toad Dimitri talk money with Billie Jack, though."

"Think some girls went to the Fireplug?" Bush asked.

"I don't know anything else, but I by God do know that little biker punk Spoot, or whatever they call him, came by the Parrot about a week or so ago with the biggest, dumbest looking loser you ever saw. Thick glasses, cross eyed. It was a pimp deal. I saw D.D. get into an old Ford pickup with that ape. She hasn't been seen…at least anywhere I know, since."

I said, "Scoot drives an old F150."

"D.D. was the passenger and the big dumbass was driving. I think the gimpy guy was in a separate old blue truck."

I asked, "Why are you telling us this, Amber?"

She leaned forward so we could hear her better over the music. "Because that sonofabitch Carlo raped me. I worked late and that animal barged into the dressing room and used me like a common whore. I went to Dimitri and he told me I was little more than a common whore and that if I went around half dressed, I should expect to be molested."

Bush asked, "When did this…"

"Two weeks ago. No worry, I went to Baylor, had the aids and EC tests plus an antibiotic. I'm okay."

I said, "EC as in emergency contraceptive?"

She nodded.

Bush asked, "Why do you still work there?"

She smiled. "I have a severance plan in mind."

"Christ," I said. "Dimitri is a bastard."

"Bummer," Bush added.

Later, we stood drunkenly on the sidewalk, cops staggering out of the bar on varying pretenses, all of which included getting a gander at Amber's assets.

Amber impaled Bush's chest with a bear-hugg and declared, "Bush, I need protection. As a taxpayer, I demand you accompany me home and stand guard at my door while I shower and get dolled up."

I figured with those boobs, she needed help drying her back. That was exactly the way Adam got his business in a wreck with Eve and all of history. Who on earth could have refused that call to duty? Bush looked at me in the dim streetlight.

"Bush, you're full grown and it's past ten p.m. Will your parents ask where their child is?"

Bush rode away in a red Mustang. I realized I should have told him to stop by the garage, get his take home ride and follow her to whatever fate awaited. Sure as taxes, she was either going to have to drive him to the federal building in the morning or put him in a taxi. Oh well.

I let myself into my Spring Valley not so luxurious apartment at just before eleven. My phone rang in one minute. "I have a couple of beers and a snack if you have a minute," Anne said.

Hey, I had several minutes.

Then, while mostly asleep at around two A.M., I bolted upright in her bed. "Big, dopey guy in an old Ford pickup! Thick glasses! Note stuck in blood on D.D.'s body that read "3A—rear." Was it possible that little dork Scoots some perverted, convoluted way had pimped D.D. out to Clarence? Who, exactly the hell was Clarence Ligon?

CHAPTER 24: JUST ANOTHER BORING DAY IN THE LIFE

Around six A.M., I staggered across the courtyard wrapped in a towel, carrying my clothes under my arm. Yeah, yeah, I had a too-many-beer headache, but I'd survived much worse. By six thirty I'd shaved, showered, and was in the Central Expressway road race with countless others who could not afford a helicopter.

I found Bush's draft of the Clarence confrontation of the day before, walked over to the shredder, and eliminated it. Clarence, it seemed, might not be exactly the harmless character we thought he was.

I spent nearly an hour on the telephone before locating the Givens boys' father, Jason Francis in his office in Florida. He advised Linda was a slut, that Billie Jack Givens was a philandering thug, and after a symphony of profanity, told me that he hadn't had time to come to Dallas for the boy's funerals. I re-used the ever useful line of advising him that if the opportunity arose, I'd run my foot in his ass and walk halfway back to Florida. A worn line, but always effective, it caused him to hang up on me. I eliminated Francis as a suspect in any violence against his sons or their adopted father.

Bush showed up at around 8:30. Although he was wearing the same silk shirt and tie from the day before, he was clean shaven and appeared fresh. Amber had apparently loaned him a razor, pressed his shirt, and given him a lift to the front door. He did, however, look a little goo-goo eyed from a gallon of Adair's beer, a short night's sleep, and whatever God-awful treatment Amber had subjected him to.

I explained the possible connection of Clarence Ligon and

Scoots and the relevance of the snippet of paper stuck to D.D.'s body.

Hooper called. I told him what we'd learned from strippers about the Purple Parrot and what appeared to be a connection between Billie Jack and Dimitri Bastovic. I told him Bush and I would go re-interview Norvil Givens if he would start a search warrant for Clarence's apartment on Beacon. He knew to file his probable cause affidavit before a State District judge instead of one of the Justice of the Peace courts in the courthouse. The J.P. courts were not what was called a court of record. If we obtained a warrant from a District Judge, who was a court of record, meaning a clerk wrote and recorded all proceedings, any evidence obtained would be fully admissible in federal court in case we ended up filing federal charges.

"I'll have it by ten A.M.," he promised. Typing the forms, finding a parking place six blocks away, and getting a judge to read and approve in two hours was a full load. Hooper could do it and would.

Short Cummins wandered in. In line with a well-established practice of being certain that the less the management knew of my activities, the better, I did my best to give him the cold shoulder.

He strolled over to my desk which was next to Bush's. "Any progress on the Given's murders?"

I explained the possible connection of Dimitri to Billie Jack.

"From reports you guys have submitted, we need to arrest Mrs. Givens for murder and get on with other business, Kobok. She looks guilty as hell. If other suspects develop later, we can worry about them then."

I stalled him by saying Clarence Ligon needed some additional investigation before we busted Linda and that I had no idea where she was presently holed up. He retreated to his little glass enclosed man cave, pissed, but ignorant of what we were doing, or what we intended to do. We were going to lock Clarence up for D.D.'s murder if possible. Short Cummins could learn later.

I drove the Dodge to the Kickstand Café, Bush managed to get a scrambled egg and half a cup of coffee down. His color improved considerably.

The air conditioning in Leemis was as puny as the business itself appeared to be. When I asked the receptionist-door-guard-secretary we needed to speak with Norvil Givens, he appeared from around a corner.

He looked more hungover than either Bush or I and I doubted he consumed adult beverages. We sat in his little office overlooking the beat-up cadre of ladies sewing brassieres.

"Gotta clue where Linda is staying, Mr. Givens?" I asked.

"Naw, the bitch and that lawyer Androvski have both told me I'm gonna get kicked out here," he said glumly.

Bush asked, "If she called, did she leave a telephone number?"

"Yeah, matter of fact, she did. Y'all gonna call her?" He punched up his glasses with a thumb.

"No," I said. "Just wanna know where she is."

He nodded, not fully understanding we could trace the telephone number and would as soon as I got back to the Dodge. I then explained Title 18, Section 1001, United States Code, often misrepresented by the press as "lying to an FBI agent." The statute actually states that a crime against the United States has occurred if and when a suspect, witness, or citizen makes a false statement to a federal officer. There was no law specifically titled, "Lying to an FBI Agent".

"And, Mr. Givens, that said, we asked you the other day about the large man driving an old blue Ford pickup who argued with Billie Jack Givens a day or so before the fatal fire. You said you didn't know him. Would you like to re-think that answer, sir?"

That little speech normally scared the hell out of the average citizen, particularly a nervous type like Norvil Givens.

He gave the glasses a pair of double punches. "Awright, awright, I'm afraid we're talkin' about that goofy damned brother of Linda's. Name's Ligon and they call him Clarence although that ain't his first name. He's nuts but harmless. I just didn't want to cause the poor dumb ass any more grief. He just did a stint in Terrell. Linda's maiden name was Ligon, you know."

No, I hadn't known. "Tell us more about him," I prodded.

Clarence had apparently been one of the last, if not the last person to see D.D. alive. "Mr. Givens why was Clarence all up in Billie Jack's face?"

Norvil punched the glasses so hard I was surprised he didn't cut the bridge of his nose. "He tell y'all about a railroad pension?"

"No, sir, somebody else did, though."

"Okay." He sighed deeply. "Clarence used to show up down here panhandling for money. Linda browbeat Billie Jack into paying him a grand or so every month. I hadn't heard about any confrontation at Billie Jack's house. That's the God's honest truth. But Billie jack had told Clarence to stop coming down here and he'd mail him a money order the first of every month. Some damned way, Clarence either worked for a railroad, or more likely got run over by a train. Whatever transpired, Clarence told anybody who would listen he got a railroad pension."

"So, Billie Jack missed a payment?" I asked.

"Hell, I dunno. Clarence probably hasn't got enough sense to cash the order or maybe just lost one. I'm surprised Clarence could actually find the Given's house. Hell, I can't believe they give a guy that goofy a driver's license. I didn't volunteer that info the other day, 'cuz I sorta thought it sounded like Clarence's antics, but I wasn't sure. I'm thinkin' with Linda and all the divorce poison she was spreading, Billie Jack mighta cut Clarence off. That woulda caused a stink."

"We need to go have a talk with him. You think he could murder somebody?"

"Hard to say. He's nuts and excitable, but I never saw him do more than have a hissy fit. Clarence is such an oddball. A real pain in the ass. A freeloader of the helpless kind. Smile at the dumb clod and he'd stay for two weeks, understand?"

"Clarence work at the brassiere factory?"

"Clarence is too brain dead to do any real work. He might eat a brassiere, but to make one...?"

"Eat a brassiere?" I asked. "Did he have any sexual deviation problems?"

"Could not by God leave the chicks we got workin' here

alone. Not violent or even aggressive, just like a silly pup who'd had two beers."

"Could Clarence have climbed the back fence, entered the garage, returned to the kitchen, then leave without the Doberman going nuts?"

"Doubt he could get over the fence. The dog, I dunno. Prolly not. Be a damned fool to try. 'Course Clarence is a damned fool."

I didn't feel the need to caution him not to call Clarence and warn him we were coming because Clarence had no phone.

I called Hooper. He was standing by with the warrant and two uniformed officers.

We'd soon learn if Clarence was in a hissy fit, what, exactly, followed.

CHAPTER 25:

JUST ANOTHER BORING, ROUTINE DAY AT THE OFFICE

We met in the strip shopping center lot across the street from the Victorian Gardens: My Dodge, Hooper in an unmarked small yellow Plymouth, and two uniforms in two cars. That many cops in a glut in that neighborhood probably caused a mass exodus of perps for a twelve square block area. I asked the uniforms to wait until Hooper, Bush, and I got inside the apartment then to approach slowly, park out of view of Clarence's window, then enter.

Rat Faced Ralph was visible through the office window at rigid attention at his desk. He was either monitoring traffic come and go or he had died sitting up. Clarence's truck was parked adjacent to his door. We didn't bother to stop and talk to Ralph.

No one was actually surprised that fully visible in Clarence's window was another pipe bomb.

As before, Clarence, now confirmed to be in direct contact with Satan, opened the door before we knocked.

"Remember us, Clarence?" Hooper asked.

The eyes tried, unsuccessfully, to focus. "Uh, I'm sure I do."

Hooper tried again. "We were here yesterday. Picked up your pipe bomb?"

"Oh yes, now I recall. As you now know, sir, I should be called Mr. Ligon."

I said, "Sorry, but we gotta come in again, Mr. Ligon."

He carefully marked the erroneous zones, and the three of us went through the matrix. The apartment was outright hot and smelled like dead rabbit and maybe a dead rat tossed in for flavor. But the Explosive Rabbit was alive in her cage, eyeing me with contemptuous disdain. I entered right behind Hooper and motioned for Bush to leave the door ajar. No need for the two uniformed officers who were due momentarily to have to kick down the door.

"Sit Clarence," Hooper gestured to the milk crate at room center.

Clarence sat meekly. "Mr. Ligon, please."

I asked, "We aren't gonna call you Mr. Ligon until you tell us the truth. We know you killed Billie Jack Givens."

"Naw. I ain't killed nobody, yet. But the holocaust…."

"Screw the holocaust, Clarence," I snapped. "You argued with Billie Jack because he didn't pony up your so-called railroad pension. You got somebody to let you in the front door because they recognized you, you rummaged around and found a front door key, then got the gasoline and torched the place."

"Nope, ain't kilt Billie Jack. Ain't set no fire."

"Are you gonna tell us Linda Marie Givens is not your sister?"

"Yes, she takes care of me."

"And a day or two before you killed Billie Jack and his boys, you murdered D.D., the dancer from the Purple Parrot."

He looked up at the three of us but didn't speak.

I showed him my badge and credential case. "Clarence, we're federal officers. Don't you know the federal government knows everything you've ever done since you were born?"

"Y'all know about the time I pissed in that old mean Mrs. Kennedy's gas tank. It was a Buick with the gas cap behind the rear license plate. I had to sorta kneel down to make the connection. Like to amputated my Johnson."

"Absolutely, we know about it, Clarence." I said.

The sad eyes haltingly scanned the three of us standing in a rough circle around him.

"I didn't mean to do it," he said with childlike innocence, his eyes brimming with tears.

"Piss in Mrs. Kennedy's gas tank?" Hooper asked.

"No, to kill nobody."

"What?" I asked.

"I didn't have enough money."

Hooper asked, "So Billie Jack was gonna cut off your money?"

"Naw, he talked some about that, but it was an accident. Linda wouldn't let him. I'd paid the rent and bought some groceries with the money Billie Jack gimme and then I didn't have enough money."

I asked, "What was an accident?"

"Billie Jack not givin' me the money. I went down to the brassiere place and Billie Jack wasn't there. I tol' that other guy, Norvis or whatever, that Billie Jack hadn't gimme my money. That little Mexican guy who limps, Spooks, was outside, waiting on some girl. He told me if I could get the money, and come to the Purple place with the money, I could do it to her. God, she was beautiful. That's the day, I drove over to Billie Jack's and had the argument. He'd sent me a money order in the mail. How the hell I'm gonna cash a money order?"

I said, "We need to hear the whole story from you, Clarence, just the way it went down." I tried not to show my surprise. Billie Jack and the boys' murders were about to be solved. Short Cummins wouldn't be able to bump me up to Butte, Montana this year. "Did Linda help you kill Billie Jack and someway the boys got caught in the fire?"

"I tol' you guys I didn't do it."

"Wait," I said. "Didn't do what?"

"Hurt Billie Jack and the kids." He broke into sobbing. "With Billie Jack dead, I ain't got no money."

Bush said, "I believe he's trying to tell us about something else. Clarence, tell us more about not having enough money?"

"I drove my truck out to that Purple place… followed Spooks or whatever his name was."

"Purple Parrot?" Bush asked.

"Yeah, hadda buncha nekked girls."

"Bitch come all the way down here and then wanted more money than I had. I was five bucks short. She said she needed cab fare back to that Purple place…"

Bush asked. "The pretty girl, did she have flowers… roses tattooed on one arm?"

"Yeah, flowers, red."

I asked, "Did you write '3A-rear' on a piece of paper."

"No she did. She was hollerin' like hell. I tol' her I'd give her cab fare and she stopped screamin' for a minute. We didn't know how to spell Victorian Gardens. There's a payphone across Beacon there an' she said she could see the name of this place from the phone. She had the little paper in her hand when she walked over and called a cab. I guess she gave them directions to come around back. When she come back, I guess she still had it in her hand."

Bush asked, "Why didn't you drive her back to the Purple Parrot?"

"Cuz I didn't have no gas in my truck. I give her twenty-five dollars and then I didn't have no money left. Tol' her she'd hafta pay the cab from the twenty-five bucks."

"Why give her all your money if she didn't...?"

"She showed me her tits and said I hadda give her twenty-five bucks. When I tried to touch them, she started up again."

"Screaming?" I asked.

"Uh, yeah. Bitch started screaming again. Said I was a stinking damned freak. I didn't want Ralph to hear and throw me out. He said he'd throw me out if I caused any trouble. He lives next door. I didn't wanta get throwed out and I tol' her over and over to shut the fuck up."

Hooper asked, "We're talkin' about D.D. here from the Purple Parrot?"

"Yeah. Bitch kept screamin' and I choked her some, then I drug her in the commode there and stabbed her."

"Then you took off her clothes and dumped her in Balch Springs?" I asked. "Did you have sex with her after you'd murdered her."

"No, no sex. And it wasn't no murder. It was a accident."

That explained the lack of evidence of sexual assault. I asked, "Why Balch Springs?"

"Where?"

"The body was found in Balch Springs. It's a suburb."

"Dunno where that is. I got lost."

Bush asked, "What did you do with her clothes?"

"Washed them in the sink an' put 'um in my drawer over there."

Hooper opened a kitchen drawer and held up a wad of clothes which showed dark, residual blood stains. He stuffed them in his coat pocket. Yeah, in those day, plain clothes cops wore suit-type coats.

"Where is the knife, Clarence?" I asked.

With astounding agility, he was on his feet and had reached the kitchen cabinet in the small room in one step. He had the knife in about the time it took the three of us to draw revolvers. Bush opened the door and motioned in the two uniforms who were standing just outside.

"Lay it back on the counter, Clarence," I said as calmly as I could. I turned my left side to him, holding my revolver, which he hadn't seen, out of his sight against my right leg. It was impossible to tell if he intended us harm or if he was just going to hand over the knife. It was not a time to gamble.

"What are you fellas gonna do with me?" He held the knife in front of him at waist level, his unstable eyes expressionless, but with his gaze fixed on the knife.

"Clarence, you're gonna have to come downtown with us." I cocked the hammer of the pistol, still holding it against my leg, out of his sight. The question was, would the pistol stop this huge man six feet away. The magnum would kill him but would it do so soon enough to prevent him from running the knife through one of the now five cops in the room. We'd just witnessed the Big Rat Kowalski/Dog Ass Mulvany disaster.

"Lay it on the counter, Clarence," I repeated, weighing the possibility that if shots were fired by five pistols, how many would hit somebody besides Clarence. I wondered if Butte or Detroit would have been a better option than Hell, which was standing two steps and three hundred pounds away. I expected my life to race in front of my eyes at any second. The only thing racing was my heart.

Clarence stood, granite still and silent, holding the knife in front of him. He appeared to be measuring the options, of which he had three and two were very bad. He'd made no gesture with the knife, but again, he hadn't offered to cut up birthday cake. The expressionless face was morphing to moronic confusion. But Clarence wasn't a moron, just a little nuts and a little stupid.

His suddenly focused eyes shot from the knife to my face, then back to the knife.

Bush, also hiding his pistol, said in a calm voice, "Clarence, recall, my father is a psychiatrist. I spoke to him about you." Clarence, whose attention had been primarily fixed on me, found Bush to his side. "He reminded me to tell you how important it is to take your medications every day."

"Been takin' them ever since y'all was here before."

"What is your daily dosage?" Bush slid his pistol back into the holster.

"One big one ever morning, one little one ever night." He moved closer to Clarence.

"Don't get between us," I whispered.

Bush asked, "Where are your pills?"

"Right here." The giant turned toward the cabinet.

"My father said for me to be sure and check them to make sure you have the correct medications."

"They're right here." Clarence laid the knife on the counter and pulled two vials from a drawer.

Bush casually picked up the knife and handed it to me behind his back. Bush carefully examined the bottles. "This looks exactly right, Mr. Ligon, exactly what my father said you needed. You're being a very good person." He sat the bottle back on the cabinet.

"Thank Satan." Clarence leaned on the cabinet, surrendering—assuming he was resisting in the first place.

"Good God," I said.

"Good God," Hooper said.

Bush, on a roll, said, "Mr. Ligon, it's a rule. We have to put these handcuffs on you. My father says they won't violate the erroneous zones." He pulled the shiny manacles from his rear waist.

Clarence meekly complied as Bush helped him fold his massive arms behind him. He snapped a cuff on each wrist, each catching in the first rachet. The cuffs barely girthed the huge wrists. It appeared he could snap them with a shrug and probably give all five cops a hell of a fight. He probably could have, but he was as limp and docile as a warm bath.

I walked over to the office and told Ralph to desist surveillance. He tugged his earlobe and sighed, obviously glad to be relieved of hazardous duty. Hooper walked in and used Ralph's phone to call the Crime Scene Search Unit to the scene. They would be able to isolate and preserve enough of D.D.'s blood samples from the apartment and the commode to implicate Clarence.

I unscrewed the metal galvanized cap from the pipe bomb. Once again, no powder. I tossed it in a dumpster out back. No sense making another trip to the Dallas P.D. Bomb Squad and causing them extra paper work over an empty piece of pipe.

We spooned Clarence into the back seat of my Dodge.

"I'm hungry," he said, childlike.

"We'll stop and get you a cheeseburger and malt," I said.

D.D.'s murder was strictly under the jurisdiction of the State of Texas. They'd sentence him to the State Hospital for the Criminally Insane at Rusk, Texas. This time, there'd be no thirty days hold and release. Clarence would never get out. Although unsaid, we all felt a certain empathy with the big dude. If the system had provided for the help he needed to begin with, he would have been incarcerated long ago and D.D. would be gyrating on a stage somewhere. Clarence would no longer have to worry about his railroad pension.

"Bull, did anyone make the death notification for D.D...uh, Charlene West?"

"Closest kin we could find is an aunt in Waco. Waco P.D. made the notification yesterday."

His comment was a relief. Death notification was tough business. I leaned in to speak to Clarence.

"Got any idea where we can find Scoots, the little guy who hooked you up with D.D.?"

"I didn't even know him or how to say his name right."

I tested the water. "Clarence, it sure seems you had something to do with the murder of Billie Jack."

He teared right up again. "Dammit, I didn't do that."

"Did Scoots or Beeman?"

"I dunno, but I don't think so, mister."

"Who do you think did it?"

"Did you ask my sister? She was mean as all get out."

We held a mini conference in the sun. General agreement was that Clarence was a mess who had killed D.D. in a sudden fit of frustrated rage but had not been involved in the Givens' deaths. I leaned back into the Dodge. "What do you want us to do about the Explosive Rabbit, Clarence?"

"Oh, could you take her back to the pet shop on Mockingbird Lane, please. That's where I stoled her from. Please tell 'um she ain't had no lettuce today."

If we carried Clarence to jail now, in late midmorning, he'd miss the toast and black coffee served at the Sterret Center around ten A.M. for "breakfast". Docile as he seemed, we still couldn't chance un-cuffing him. If that huge man lost it in my back seat, the three of us would have had a hell of a time trying to subdue him. We left Hooper's city car at the Victorian Gardens and as I'd promised, drove to a nearby eat-in-the-car drive in. Bush, who declined to consume such garbage, hand fed Clarence a large burger and fries. Hooper and I pigged out.

We dropped Hooper back at his Plymouth. Bush and I transported Clarence to the Sterret Center and booked him in. Hooper would carry the explosive rabbit back to the pet shop from whence she'd been purloined, then drop by his office for the endless task of updating reports. Bush and Hooper argued that Linda was a lone murderer. Something niggled at me that we needed to look further.

The deputy in charge of the turnkey desk spotted me and walked over. "Kobok, I was just gonna call your office. Inmate upstairs, guy named Roscoe, wants to talk to you and Bush." He looked at Bush. "That you?"

Bush nodded. "Roscoe?"

"Red Fred", Randall, your half-lawyer buddy from the Fireplug joint. Same guy Amber named as a possible associate of D.D. at the Purple Parrot."

CHAPTER 26: SNITCHES: A KEY TO MANY, MANY DOORS

BUT NOT ALWAYS THE CORRECT ONE

When jailers brought Cletus "Red Fred" Roscoe down, he had already acquired the normal jail house stink of stale sweat, a result of limited air conditioning, while wearing an orange canvas coverall. He was tall, slender, with a full head of shoulder length red hair and an unruly red beard. I was surprised the jailers hadn't sent him to the barber.

"Either one o' you gotta smoke," he said as he took a battered metal chair across a metal table from where Bush and I sat on similar battered metal chairs.

Neither Bush nor I smoked and the physical process of getting a pack of smokes to him was an hour's labor.

"Red," I said, "I'll leave ten bucks with the desk in your name when we leave. If we possibly can, we'll bootleg you a pack up this afternoon."

He seemed reasonably mollified. I dug his sheet out of my folder.

"You have prior arrests for assault, and burglary. This shows you to still be on parole for the burglary for two more years. That what got you in jail, Fred?"

"That snitchin' little prick Scoots dropped a dime on me. I come outta the Fireplug last night and the narcs were waiting. Busted me for two dime bags of California Brown I was holdin'. Got word inside here from a buddy, it was Scoots snitched me off."

"Why? Bush asked.

"We hadda beef over a chick they call D.D."

"We thought she bounced back between Gut Sharf and

Scoots," I said. I had heard Red Fred was a distant contender. "How the hell did you get in the mix?"

"She was my ol' lady before Gut ever got in the picture. I heard Scoots threatened to kill her if she didn't get back in his bed."

I didn't tell him that D.D.'s devastated body was still in the cooler at the morgue, and that we had just booked Clarence Ligon into the same jail where we now sat, for her murder. Problem with dirtbags was that although Fred's story would probably have some truth to it, his word was questionable. His trouble with Scoots, a fellow Blood Lord, in the middle of the biker war, was probably unusual, but information is information. There was no handbook of interpersonal relationships in that area.

I leaned forward. "So why call us?"

"Scoots put me in here, lookin' at two more years to serve on the parole violation. I can't get out to kill the little bastard, but y'all gotta know he's got a murder warrant floating around."

I said, "Yeah, he's also on parole, and you're right, he's wanted for the murder of a Diablo he shot in one of those bars on South Lamar. We need to talk to him about the murders of Billie Jack Givens and his sons. We haven't found him so far, but we will."

"He's hidin' out in his brother's place in Pleasant Grove." He was referring to the sprawling Pleasant Grove District which encompassed much of Southeast Dallas.

"Got an address?" I asked.

"On Gaspard, first block north of Lawson on your left as you go north. Green paint. Bushes in front makes the house hard to see."

"How sure are you he'd be there?"

"His brother deals grass like a damned burger drive through window. You just pull in the center of them bushes, and ol' Juan will bring out the grass like a car hop."

We stopped at the turnkey desk and I left $10.00 in Fred's name.

"Aren't you gonna try to get him a pack upstairs today?" Bush asked.

"Let's see how reliable his info is. We need to interrupt

Hooper's report writing, check out the Trojan Van, and drive down there and ask Juan if his reptile brother Scoots is available. It had to have been Scoots, who drives an old blue Ford pickup similar to Clarence's, who was parked down the block from the Given's house before the fire. And Beeman was probably with him.

I called Hooper at his office from a jailhouse telephone and explained the situation.

"Kobok, how do you know this guy will sell to us?"

"We don't exactly, but if we can get inside those bushes, as you know, probable cause increases as circumstances change. It's all outside, plain daylight. No harm in asking. I'll hang back and cover."

"We gonna have Bush go with me in the van. I don't like the idea of puttin' a rookie in the trick box on a shaky undercover deal."

"We don't have anyone else, Bull. You drive the van with Bush as shotgun and I'll hang back for backup."

"Don't like it, but you're right. We need to try."

I double-parked behind the Cabell Building and sent Bush up to sign out whatever undercover surveillance devices he could find. He came back with the body recorder, but with an expression of a kid who'd missed Christmas. He'd been unable to find the remote transmitter which broadcast on the ATF channel one radio frequency. We'd be able to record what was said, and listen to the tape later, but would not be able to hear the conversation live via my car radio.

Bush and I pulled the Trojan van onto the rear parking lot of the Kickstand Café at just past noon. We needed to form a plan to get onto Juan's property. We had no grounds for a search warrant. Scoots had a warrant floating around for his arrest for murder, which would allow us to kick down the door if we had reasonable cause to think Scoots was there. We still were legally limited in exactly what we could look for under authority of an arrest warrant.

Hooper arrived in the same little yellow Plymouth he'd driven to the Victorian Gardens. For an undercover disguise, he'd found an old t shirt in his DPD locker. In it, he appeared to me to be a fat policeman in a T shirt chewing a cigar stub. He stated that since it was broad daylight he would pull into Juan's front yard with Bush as a passenger, make conversation, advertise plumbing services, and casually hit on Juan to buy some sort of narcotics.

We opted to tape the recorder to Bush's chest under his shirt. Bad business, we'd soon learn. In the absence of the transmitter, the deal was for Hooper to pull on the emergency and remove his foot from the brake. If there was any distress or problem of any sort, he would tap the brake twice. If I saw the brake light flash twice, I would charge—one man cavalry to the rescue. Easy as cake, because pie wasn't going to quite fit.

What we didn't know, was that Red Fred had given us the wrong address. Well, not exactly the wrong address, just out of date. Juan Garcia, Scoot's older brother, had rented the house until three months earlier. He sold smack carelessly to too many drive-in customers. A Dallas P.D. undercover cop had sat in the drive-through line and bought enough scag to make Juan eligible to do five in the joint. Juan, retired from the dope sales business, was sitting in the Sterret Center one floor above Red Fred, awaiting trial. We didn't know that.

The occupant at the address where we were headed was now a two-time ex-con named Norwood Sneed. Sneed had been released from the Texas Department of Criminal Justice four months before after serving six years in the aforementioned Rusk State Hospital for the Criminally Insane. Doctors had erred, it appeared, when they figured they'd fed him enough smart pills to put him back on the street. Ol' Norwood was still crazier than a drunk, Arkansas goat. To compound the problem, neighborhood kids had been hazing and tormenting him. Norwood rented the unkempt place with his mother and a very large dog which Norwood had acquired to help repel vandals. But we needed info and we needed it now. Norwood didn't need to sell dope. He lived on his mother's welfare check. We should have done due diligence on Norwood, but time being what it was, we gambled.

With me following in the Dodge at about a block's distance, I watched as Hooper pulled between the bushes. The plan started sideways when he never took his foot off the brake. The stop lights couldn't blink, because Hooper was not playing by the rules. He had good reason.

I'd quickly learn, Norwood, who in addition to being nuts, was seriously hard of hearing. The plan, as is often the case, went to hell as soon as the curtain rose.

When Hooper pulled through the bushes, Norwood was on the front porch, on standby surveillance, waiting to blow a kid or two away. Then a damned plumbing truck intruded. Holding his .45 semi-auto pistol at his side, he approached the passenger door, where Bush sat in his version of undercover garb. He'd removed his necktie.

Norwood stuck the .45 through the window, about a foot from the side of Bush's hundred-dollar haircut.

Hooper, never inclined to lose his cool, did not, but he did mis-speak his next line. "Hell, we was lookin' for Juan Garcia. We was hopin' to score a baggie of grass." Hooper should have skipped line one and gone to line two which was: "We thought you hadda plumbing problem."

Norwood was not in the dope business, but he did have, we'd learn, a stopped-up commode. Too late. "I'm a gonna shoot both you two dope fiends," he spat. "Gimme your damned money, first."

Bush reached into his trouser pocket and handed Norwood a wad of bills. Norwood looked at the handful of wealth—bad business when Bull Hooper is about.

Hooper reached, as if giving up cash, but pulled his magnum from his rear waist, leaned across, and discharged the weapon twice about fifteen inches in front of Bush's face. The rounds carried the top of Norwood's head all over the front yard, while carrying Norwood out of this world to whatever the hell happens to the lunatic Norwood's of the realm.

Down the street I sat in professional surveillance. As an illustration of how finely-honed minds worked, I heard the two shots, muffled inside the van cab and thought, "What the hell. We're trying to work an undercover deal and they're down there shooting off fireworks." Then in horrified realization, I said aloud, "They're not shooting fireworks, they're shooting bullets, in all probability at each other."

I gunned the Dodge and skidded to a stop behind the van. The elapsed time from first blast to arrival was less than five seconds. I pushed through the shrubbery to see Hooper, cigar stub still in place, had bailed out of the van, circled the front, and was leaning down to see if Norwood continued to be a threat. Minus the upper half of his head, Norwood had been rendered harmless.

A pudgy, dirty, bald clone of Norwood came around the house, an axe raised above his head, charging Hooper. Hooper leveled his weapon and the man stumbled and partly turned but kept coming. Hooper fired, the bullet catching the man in the side of his ass cheek. He went down screaming.

Twenty-five feet away, a skinny, disheveled woman in a dirty housedress with stringy gray hair emerged from the front door, waving a rifle. She raised the weapon. Hooper busted two more caps at her. She fell from the porch and rolled under it, holding her foot. A huge black dog emerged from beneath the porch and charged Hooper. He raised his weapon and fired one round into the snarling animal's maw. The dog, yelping like shot dogs might, retreated beneath the porch with the wounded or dead woman.

Hooper whirled at my approach. I held out both hands. "Whoa, Wild Bill, I'm on your side. Reload and keep shooting. You've already wiped out half the damned neighborhood. Keep 'um pinned down and I'll go for more ammo." I hid behind the van in mock terror.

"Ain't damned funny, Kobok. We need to check the house for Scoots."

A ten-minute search disclosed that the home was void of humans and the back door was locked from inside. Scoots Garcia could not have escaped out the back. He wasn't there.

From beneath the porch the gray-haired woman moaned over and over again, "Oh, Goddamn, whud ya' shoot me fer?"

With my magnum in one hand, I drug her out by the unwounded foot. Hooper had apparently only scored one hit— in her foot. The dog, uninjured—Hooper had missed—whined piteously, refusing to come out. "I sorta know how you feel, partner," I consoled. The pudgy guy was rolling around in the yard dust holding his back side, shouting, "I'm shot in the ass. Call the cops."

Hooper re-loaded his pistol while I ran back to my car and called for assistance and an ambulance on the DPD radio. I could almost instantly hear sirens spooling up in the distance as I clawed back through the shrubs.

"Hooper, where is Bush?"

"My God, that toad musta shot him." Hooper spat out his cigar stub.

Bush was sitting starry-eyed upright and motionless in the passenger seat of the van. In the background both the wounded man and woman continued to wail. The dog was too shell-shocked to even attempt to bark.

I opened the door and Bush never moved. Eyes open, he appeared dead, except he was still breathing.

When I put a hand on his shoulder he jerked away involuntarily.

"Oh, no! he shouted at top volume.

"No, what, Randall?

"My God, Kobok, did they kill you too!" he shouted.

"No," I shook my head.

"Kobok, can you hear me!"

"Yeah, me and everyone else within four blocks."

"Are we in Hell?"

I looked around. "Close. Maybe if you didn't talk quite so loud."

"Kobok, you sayin' I'm not dead?" His expression changed from midnight to high noon.

"Nope," I shook my head again.

He climbed out of the van and did a little dance, shouting, "I'm not dead," repeatedly.

"What the hell y'all shoutin' about," said the man Hooper had shot in the ass. The woman lying next to the porch shrieked, "I'm shot in the damned foot over here."

Marked Dallas squad cars began arriving in numbers. Through the shrubs, an ambulance could be seen screeching to a halt.

It took a while to realize that when Hooper had fired his pistol, twice, within inches of Bush's ears in the closed quarters of the van cab, Bush was stricken instantly stone deaf. He'd seen Hooper bail out, fire several shots and turn to speak to me, but heard no sound. He concluded he'd been shot dead by Norwood.

"My goodness," he'd declared. "I'm killed." He felt a certain twinge that he would never know if he'd passed the bar exam. Otherwise, he'd seen in movies that upon death, the deceased could see their surroundings, but couldn't hear because they were dead. He sat, self-deceased, waiting for some sign from the next world, hopefully heavenly music. Whatever would be, would be and would do so automatically. He sat, waiting for the next step. Since he was already dead, there was no point in trying to move around, because he now belonged to the spirit world. Surely instructions would follow.

Being young and full of vinegar, he'd soon begin recovering his hearing, but was still speaking in a semi-shout twenty minutes later.

I walked out to the Dodge, called Tootie, and dictated a report for Washington D.C. I stated that neither ATF, nor Bush and I had fired any shots, that all shots fired by a Dallas police officer were justified, that one assailant had been shot and killed, and two more shot and wounded. I did not mention the dog, nor that the guy shot in the side of the ass had four full bullet holes as the round passed through. Man, that had to hurt.

Washington, as usual, was not concerned with injuries to Bush or I or to the local cops. Their concern was bad press.

Short Cummins showed up at the scene, but wanting no part of the action, soon went back to his man-cave.

By 2:00 P.M. ambulances, the Trojan van, cops, and us were all gone from the scene. The dog was still beneath the porch when I drove away. We checked in the van and had coffee and late snack and coffee at the Kickstand. The waitress, with hair as big as a beach ball, fell in love with Bush again. Her ardor was unfazed even when she discovered he could only hear a portion of what she said. But his hearing was rapidly returning.

CHAPTER 27: ELIMINATING FRUCTUS

Hooper had already been summoned to DPD Headquarters to explain to a shooting board of Internal Affairs rats that the death of Norwood and the wounding of the other two was a good shoot. I doubted he'd mention the missed shot at the dog. Bush and I dropped by the DPD and wrote out detailed statements, supporting Hooper.

Short Cummins, intimidated by Washington D.C. inquiry, demanded by radio, Bush and I report to the office to further explain what had transpired. I'd already sent a report via Tootie, so I played dead and declined to answer the radio. We could tailor our alibis just as well another time. Before long, Bush's hearing had improved measurably.

I drove us to Leemis Fashions. Norvil Givens was his normal bundle of nerves. When I asked him about financial records, he immediately took cover behind the "all records are at our accountant's office." Leemis wasn't a large enough outfit to have too many records.

"Mr. Givens, I can have a grand jury subpoena your bank records in an hour or so. We have information that Dimitri Bastovic, owner of the Purple Parrot smuggles middle and Eastern European girls into the country using metal shipping containers to conceal them. Sir, we can find some of those girls easily."

"I got nothing to do with that."

"Glad to hear that, but we know Billie Jack was mixed up in that racket. I know from experience, those water tight containers come in through Houston, then are off loaded onto trucks and distributed. Dimitri sends his own truck. We have no evidence that Billie Jack or Leemis or you did any actual smuggling. Mr.

Givens, Billie Jack was laundering cash Dimitri ginned up from the sex trade. He received a free girl or two frequently. Billie Jack is out of reach, but you could be looking at twenty-five years."

From a desk drawer, he drew out a thin ledger and tossed it onto his desk. "It was all Billie Jack. I always suspected, but I found this after y'all were in here that first time. Cash from some unknown source was keeping Leemis afloat. I guess Linda can have this damned place, now. Am I under arrest?"

"Not yet." I picked up the ledger and we walked out.

As we merged into traffic, Bush said, "We can show Leemis got extra cash well beyond their regular sales but proving where it came from is gonna be a load."

"I know, Randall. But I just wanna let that dork Dimitri know what we know, but pretend we know a lot more. Money laundering is not our focus here. Whether Dimitri felt inclined to send that mope Carlo or some other thug to murder Billie Jack is the issue... before we have nobody left to arrest but Linda Marie."

"You really think Dimitri murdered the Givens'?"

"No, but we need to eliminate him before the defense lawyer throws him into the trial of whoever we manage to arrest as a distraction. Common lawyer tactic. You oughta know that."

Suddenly, a lot more Dimitri news came via the radio from Tootie. "'Thirteen—thirteen' have Bush call Amber at 555-5432." I didn't answer because we were dodging Short Cummins and he could be listening.

We found a payphone, Bush borrowed a quarter from me, and spent several minutes on the phone. I figured he was organizing his love life. He popped back into the seat.

"Amber says those two middle European girls we interviewed, uh..." He peered at his notebook. "Both are missing."

"Missing? Hey, Randall, strippers are notorious for lack of punctuality."

"I don't think so in this case. Amber says she came to work at three o'clock and heard Carlo telling Dimitri 'it was taken care of '. Carlo and Dimitri then tore out and Amber sneaked into Dimitri's office and called the home phone number on file for the girls. They lived together. When Amber called their apartment, Carlo answered. She's convinced Dimitri and Carlo have done something with the girls."

"Did she have an address?"

"Yeah." He read off an address on Webb Chapel Extension. "Amber says she's quitting the Parrot today."

The apartment complex Amber had identified as the girls' was stashed amidst several shabby, similarly run down, units within blocks of the Purple Parrot. I considered calling Hooper out, but it seemed the less witnesses we had to an end-around run illegal search, the better.

My concerns of lack of cooperation were unfounded. The apartment manager, whose brightly red dyed hair made her a candidate in the Wicked Witch of the Zombie Galaxy lookalike contest, handed over the file folder with minimum comment. The girls had lived in apartment 23 for six months. Neither had registered by the names they had given us at the Purple Parrot. Both listed relatives in Philadelphia and former residences in Boston. All would be fictitious. She handed us a passkey to apartment 23 and we were in. Legality increased slightly by the management providing a key.

Bush made a cursory search of the premises. "Kobok, take a look," he called from the bathroom. "somebody washed blood off their hands in the sink."

The sink and bathtub both showed considerable blood splatter. Someone had met a violent end there.

Then, a eureka moment. Whoever had been busy washing off blood had not looked at the floor. A half sheet of notebook paper against the baseboard read "INS 214-555-5789". A logical mind would assume the two dancers were interrupted while dropping a dime on Dimitri.

I called Hooper on the apartment telephone. Information indicating a crime had been discovered, altering the limits of the illegal search we'd just conducted. In minutes a pair of uniformed officers showed up. We met them outside and told them Hooper from Homicide was on the way out with a search warrant. I gave each my business card and we headed for the Purple Parrot a few blocks away.

We went through the Carlo door blocker route. Dimitri stood outside his office, smiling broadly. I had cautioned Bush to say nothing about the blood we'd discovered in the European girls' apartment. We would leave that to Homicide and speak only of smuggled girls and money laundering.

Ten minutes of quiet interrogation regarding sex slave smuggling and money laundering and Dimitri picked up the phone to dial his lawyer. We walked out. We didn't have squat, but we did have Dimitri's attention. Maybe he'd murder Carlo.

It was past five and I dropped Bush a half block from the GSA Garage. Any closer ran the risk of encountering Short Cummins who parked his brand-new management car in the same garage. I drove up Commerce to Adair's and had finished my first tall one when it occurred to me to call the answering service.

"Call Thomas Grant and Kelly." The young lady read me off two numbers. After an eeny meeny, I called the insurance man, Grant, first.

"Kobok?" He pled into the telephone. "I don't want to go to the joint over this Given's deal. Dammit, it was all Linda. First she asked me to meet her at an address to discuss pending insurance matters. It turned out to be a motel on Garland Road. My wife and I had not been sleeping together. Linda met me at the door nekked. Hell man, you know how it is?"

"Yessir." I really did know and felt some sympathy, but I had a murder to clear, or Detroit to bear.

"First thing you knew, we became regulars. When she brought that damned life insurance application in with her husband's signature, I honestly believed it was valid. Man, I'll take a polygraph or testify or whatever it takes. He didn't sign in my presence."

I figured the insurance regulators were his main problem, but he'd learn that soon enough. "Sounds like a plan to me, Mr. Grant. Especially if you can tell me where she's staying."

"Uh, Swifty Motel on LBJ Freeway. She called me today and asked me over. Screw that. You just know that damned Beeman is shacked up there with her, jes' waitin' to murder my ass."

"I'll make a full report to the prosecutor and get back to you,

Mr. Grant." I didn't tell him our case against Linda was subject to attack by a good defense lawyer and that I still thought if Linda was responsible, she could easily have had some help. Grant could testify to sleeping with Linda and being a party to insurance fraud, but he could only guess at exactly who had murdered Billie Jack and the boys.

I dialed the number for Kelly, mindful she might pop out of the receiver and have her way with me. A more mature female voice answered that was not Kelly. Assuming I'd stumbled onto her mother. I went into an impromptu line of bull. "Uh, yes, ma'am, this is Special Agent Stephen Kobok, ATF. I need to ask Kelly a question about a case we conferred on down at the Institute."

"Oh, hell, dude, you're the stud Kelly has been telling me about. We were hoping you could drop by for a nightcap one evening soon." I realized after a complete sentence, she had already been working on that night cap. I'd guess about three martinis' worth.

I intended to drive by the Swifty Motel to see what I could see, but life can't be all business. "Uh, and you'd be...?"

"I'm Ginger, her mama."

The idea of dropping by, meeting mama Ginger, and managing any time with Kelly seemed highly unlikely. "Well, Ginger, I have a pretty full schedule the next couple of days. Maybe...?"

Kelly came on the line. "Dammit, Kobok, come by for a drink. Mama wants to see you, too, if you follow my drift." She gave me an address in what I estimated to be the north Dallas high rent district.

Man, I had not telephoned the Walton's. "Do you keep beer on hand, Kelly?"

"Yes, silly, and plenty of it."

"I've got something to check on. It would probably be after eight."

"I'll tell mama we're expecting you."

"How late is too late?"

"Kobok, just call when you grow tired of pursuing that damned job."

If I didn't pursue that job, Kelly and mama Ginger might have to move to Butte or Detroit to share that drink with me.

CHAPTER 28: Tough Guy in the Hole

I hung up and worked the Dodge through slowly dwindling traffic to the Swifty motel. Linda's black Honda was parked in front of room 221. No other cars were parked close. In all probability, Linda and whoever else was in room 221. I found a payphone and dialed the number prominent on the front of the place and asked for room 221.

I recognized Linda's voice answering. Speaking through my sleeve, I said, "Tell Sonny the cops are on the way with a warrant," then hung up.

I had barely made the block back to the place when Linda, flashy in her short shorts and bright colored top hurried out the door, followed by Beeman. Sonny had not yet made the first team, because Linda slid behind the wheel. She drove Southeast on LBJ for several miles in the slow traffic before exiting into the Pleasant Grove District of Dallas. I thought they were heading for the Blood Lord House.

Suddenly, she whipped the Honda into the gravel driveway of an older frame house still in the City of Dallas, near the extreme western edge of the City of Mesquite. Beeman got out, walked to the front door, and on receiving no answer to his knock walked back to the driver's side of the Honda. Linda exited, stood beside him and looked at her wrist, which at distance I figured to be equipped with a watch.

I was assigned the standard, inexpensive and expendable agent proof camera which had no lens focus feature. It didn't do well outside twenty or thirty feet. I snapped several shots, pulled closer and snapped more. I tossed the camera on the seat and jumped the curb to position the Dodge sideways across the rear of the Honda. Linda could either back into me or wait and see what I wanted. She chose the latter.

Beeman stormed up to my driver's side, puffed up like a birthday balloon, a bandage on his left hand. Only then did I learn the bullet I had seen him take at the rally had only taken off a finger. I got out to face him.

"Kobok, you sumbitch, you're harassing us," he roared.

"That's good thinking, Sonny. You're a lot smarter than I thought. Now step back or I promise to kick the dog shit outta you right here in front of who the hell ever lives in this house. Cops show up, I promise you'll get ten to do for assaulting a federal officer. Have at it, tough guy."

With Linda still standing beside the Honda, Beeman leaned close and whispered, "Dammit, Kobok, I ain't wantin' no part of this bitch. I think she murdered her old man and her sons. I didn't have no part in settin' that damned fire and I ain't involved in that insurance scam crap she's trying to run on Billie Jack's life insurance."

"She's no longer trying, Sonny. Tried is as far as it went."

He leaned forward slightly, as if considering throwing a punch.

By the bad luck of losers, a panel truck turned into a driveway almost directly across the street. I could see the driver's feet as he got out, walked past the truck and around the side of his house, probably arriving home for the evening. Beeman, concentrating on me, didn't see the van or the driver's movement.

"Damnation, Sonny, the SWAT boys have been talking all afternoon about how those new .243 magnum rifles they just got issued will blow up a man's head like a busted watermelon. They were following me and just pulled in across the street. A wrong move will be your last."

I stepped in front of him and waved frantically at the van. "You're probably safe for now, dude, but don't do some crazy thing. As salty as those two guys in the back of that surveillance van are, they might just plunk off your left ear for practice."

I faced the evil van, placed my left hand over my left ear and waved off the non-existent sniper. Beeman grew ten percent smaller.

"Jesus, Kobok, I'm trying to distance my ass from this, not get by balls shot off by some damned cop who don't like my looks."

"Just don't make any sudden moves. I hate it when I get blood splatter on my clothes. Get in on the passenger side. Shout something about false arrest for Linda's sake."

"Bum damned collar again, baby," he called out to Linda as he plopped into the seat.

As I took the seat behind the wheel, Linda screamed, "Kobok, you're gonna hear from my lawyer." Her anger cut the air like a razor.

I stuck my head out the window. "You may hear from mine, Mrs. Givens. Except he's a prosecutor who will ask for the death penalty."

"You can't prove nothin' you bastard. You can't even prove Sonny and me was together. Your word against ours."

I picked up the Cannon and waved it. "Guess again, ma'am." I didn't see the need to tell her the quality of photos might not be magazine quality.

I tossed the camera into the back seat and backed out. In a few blocks, the Dodge, short on looks, but long on engine, had lost Linda who was trying to follow.

"Dammit, Kobok, I was in San Antonio. Me and Scoot did do Beaver before we left. There was a third guy who got some of Beaver, too. He'll back me up."

"What third guy?"

"Bent Dick Sullivan. Fact o' bidness is, this is his mom's house. Some sucker called the motel back there and tol' us the cops was comin'. Now I'm thinkin' that was you."

I didn't reply.

"Look, I ain't gonna take the needle for this bitch. She's a low rent nut job."

I exited and pulled behind a large home improvement store. "Okay, Sonny, spill all of it."

"Awright. We, me n' Scoots, had this picture of Billie Jack screwin' D.D. She was in on it. Got him to drive her out by Lake Lavon, find some bushes, and did it right on the car hood. We got a Polaroid, not a very good one, but you could tell it was him.

"Blackmail?"

"Yeah, sorta. We wanted him to keep D.D. and Beaver on the payroll for a few weeks without them havin' to go there and work."

"Well, I'd say that's sort of blackmail."

"Didn't work. He told us to stick the picture up our asses. Didn't care who knew he was hosing D.D. or anybody else."

"Plan failed, huh? So you killed him. Did Norvil, his brother hear any of this talk?"

"Godammit, I didn't kill Billie Jack. And no, Norvil didn't hear. We sent him outside to talk. And the plan didn't fail, not exactly. Linda gimme $300 for the picture. Said she'd use it in a divorce or to get Billie Jack to give her boob surgery money."

"How many times were you in her bedroom?"

"Uh, three. She said she wanted more for 300 bucks than a picture of Billie Jack's bare ass."

"Where were the boys?"

"At some kinda sissy day camp. She wouldn' lemme drive Scoot's old truck out to her house. The first two times, we got finished and she drove me back to the Grove. Third time, she'd gotten carried away and bit me on the nipple. We was in a hollarin' squabble and both boys walked in. We was both buck nekked. That was the day I left my damned colors."

"The boys saw you getting it on with their mother?"

"No they jes' seen us nekked. She screamed at 'um and called 'um bastards. That day, when she hauled me back to Pleasant Grove, she said she wanted to divorce Billie Jack and give the kids to their real father over in Florida. Said she wished they'd never been borned. Said if their real father wouldn't take them, she'd leave 'um in a bus station. Yeah, an' no matter what, she hated Billie Jack so much for not giving her money to straighten her boobs out, no way he was ever gonna get custody of the little bastards."

We sat for an hour while Beeman wrote out on a yellow pad in a childish scrawl, allegedly disclosing all he claimed he knew. As bad as he smelled, I was genuinely curious how Linda managed to stay next to him. His statement would be lead weight on Linda's slender ankles when they hanged her, so to speak. Her lifestyle and attitude had undoubtedly driven her to the destruction of her children.

Beeman signed his statement.

"To corroborate this, Sonny, I need to talk to Scoots."

"Don't think he'll talk to y'all."

"Where is he?"

"Christ, the Diablos are tryin' to kill him, half a dozen Blood Lords are pissed cuz' thay blame him for Guts gettin' it, and the cops want him on a murder rap."

"Where?"

"He's been stayin' days at Bent Dick's mama's place where you picked me up and night's at a cousin's junkyard in West Dallas. Man if you tell him...?"

"We're in the business of collecting information, slick, not handing it out. Name of the junkyard?"

"*Valdez Salvage,* on Bernal off Singleton. He parks his old F150 by the little office shack. Place's gotta TV and a half assed air conditioner. He's gotta key to the front gate. Gets over there around dark. If y'all walk in on him, he's gotta double barreled shotgun. He's double fucked up 'cuz his connection got busted and he ain't been able to score."

"One more thing, Beeman. Tell me the truth. It was you in the old F150 sitting down the street from the Givens place before the fire?"

"Yeah, we was waitin' on Linda to sneak out and take care of both of us in the truck bed. Got tired of waitin', picked up Beaver at the Fireplug and went out to the Blood Lord House to party. Took a couple tabs of meth, went to San Antonio and you know the rest."

"Scoots was with you in his truck?"

"Yeah."

"Where do you want me to drop you?"

"Back at that motel. Bitch will be there. I'm gonna tell her we're through and I ain't by God afraid to testify against her."

It was past nine. I debated making the relatively short trip to the address Kelly and mama had given me. Sins of the flesh overcame the need for sleep. I hoped they had some snacks to go with the beer.

The house was a fifteen-bathroom mansion. Mama apparently had done well—probably swindled an ex-husband out of his fortune. The ten second symphony provided by punching the door bell was answered by a Kelly Clone who looked no more than ten years older than Kelly herself. "Kobok." Her face showed too much booze and God knew what else. Her gleaming smile was lost by the magnetic effect of a light blue, see through nightgown.

"Who is it, Mother?," I heard Kelly call from above. The thought of Bela Lugosi standing in the mansion doorway suddenly blocked out any carnal thoughts. Man, even I wasn't ready for this. I turned, found the Dodge and went home. Anne called and I had the usual. I spent the night over there, dreaming of Dracula's Castle. Later, I'd be reminded that I had forgotten to leave Anne's number with the answering service.

CHAPTER 29: Rodent Extermination

I wanted to get the journal from Leemis in front of one of our auditors as early as possible. I needed to type a supplement and include Beeman's statement. And all that needed to be completed before we knocked on Bent Dick's mother's door. That all went to hell when I dialed the answering service just as I staarted to leave at 6:30 A.M.

"Dr. O'Hara has called you four times. She says she knows you were out screwing off all night or you would have answered your telephone. Also, Detective Hooper has called twice. Says to call his office."

I was too bombed to face O'Hara first up, so I dialed Homicide. The desk sergeant said, "Kobok, Hooper is at the morgue and wonders where the hell you been all night."

Good news. People were worried about my welfare?

I dialed the direct line in the basement morgue. A strange male voice answered. "Hector."

"Uh, I'm Kobok. Are you new, Hector?"

"I'm Dr. O'Hara's new diener, sir and she needs to talk with you."

O'Hara came on the line. "Dammit, Kobok, you have work to do. Get up off your dead butt and get down here, now."

Hooper took the phone. "Kobok, she's got her hands full. We have three new guests on gurney's awaiting your inspection."

"Who?"

"Sonny Beeman, Dimitri Bostovic, and his bodyguard, Carlo Esconti."

"How, when?"

"Beeman came in around midnight. O'Hara has finished

him. Two .25 slugs in his left ear. Found him on a motel parking lot on LBJ."

"Dimitri?"

"Both found by the cleaning crew at the Purple Parrot. Each got one to the heart and one between the eyes. Double tap with a .45. Looks like a professional hit."

"On the way, Bull."

Christ, there went my best witness against Linda and a possible witness backup in Dimitri in case we needed to squeeze him to testify. I wondered if winters were colder in Butte or in Detroit. I dialed Bush's residence.

"Bush residence," answered the crisp English accent.

"Hawkins, this is Kobok. Need to talk to Randall right away."

"It's Haskins, sir. I'll see if he's available."

"You know, Hopkins you got a smart mouth. Next time I'm in the neighborhood, I might take time to stop by and slap hell outta you."

"Yes, sir, and when you do sir, I'd remind you to come to the back door. Only social equals are allowed in the front."

After a minute or so, Bush came on the line. "Good morning, Kobok. What's up?"

I briefed him on the mass murder of local no goods and told him we were needed at the morgue pronto.

"Just going out the door. Thanks for the call."

"Hey Randall, your butler is a class smartass. How the hell did he ever get a job as a butler, a live in one at that?"

"Oh, he's only been a butler for five years or so. Dad met him in England. He's sort of the night watchman around here, too. He accompanies my father to the golf course and to several social clubs he belongs to."

"What did he do before your father found him?"

"He was the British Isles light heavyweight boxing champion for fourteen years. Lives over the garage. I hear barbells clanking up there all the time. He's pretty buff."

"Oh. Well meet me at the morgue." I decided to give ol' Hopkins a break on that slapping around.

As soon as I cleared the door of the morgue, the gruesome

odor instantly overcame any other thought. When I got close to another human being the rest of the day, I'd see them discreetly sniff the air. What the hell do they know?

Hooper stood watching O'Hara and her new diener dig inside the naked cadaver of a very fat, very dead Dimitri Bastovic. The body of Carlo, Dimitri's heavy lay sprawled on a gurney, next in line."

"Folks, I'd bet my pension that Linda Givens put Beeman out of his misery. Hooper, got any clue as to who would want to do harm to such fine citizens as Dimitri and Carlo?"

"Yeah, the line stretches down the block."

I reminded Hooper that Bush and I had poked Dimitri's ribs with first an interview of several of his dancers at the Parrot and then by asking him about money connections to Billie Jack. I added that I had in my car trunk the Leemis Ledger which had Dimitri lived, might have been evidence not only of money laundering through Billie Jack, but also a motive for murder.

When I told the part about the two middle European girls missing, blood in their apartment and the scrap of paper with the phone number of the Immigration and Naturalization Service, Hooper said, "Hell, we already found 'um. Young, dark hair, slim like dancers?"

O'Hara said, "They're right over in the corner on gurneys. Damnation, last night was wholesale slaughter."

Bush wandered in, already appearing ill.

Hooper studied the blood splattered ceiling. "Dimitri was a real dick. Homicide considered him the prime suspect instantly when they found these two in a dumpster on Harry Hines last night. Someway, somebody either made the connection between that ledger you mentioned or took mighty offense at the murder of two girls who Dimitri had surely smuggled in illegally."

I added, "Or maybe that somebody just figured Dimitri had screwed enough people and it was time to shut down the operation."

I called Bush aside. "Look, Randall, everyone can't be a morgue rat. It takes a while to get used to this place. Come. At least take a seat in that little office in the corner." He followed me and actually poured himself a half cup of coffee.

"Kid, you look beat. Did you hook up with Amber again last night?"

"Well, sorta. I dropped by her place. She ran me off around midnight. Said she had something to do. Figured a chick that looks that good would have plenty to do after midnight. Hope she's not turning tricks."

Or driving out to the Parrot to square up with her sadistic uncle, whom she hated, for murdering two girls who were obviously better friends than I'd thought. Could somebody who looked that good have offed two hard-nosed characters like Dimitri and Carlo with a double tap—forehead and heart? Stranger things had happened.

"Bush, we need to talk to her today. See if she knows anything more about the two girls lying dead over there on gurneys."

Obviously stunned and horrified at the death of the two girls, he said, "Can't talk to her, Kobok, she caught an early morning flight to Italy. Said she had relatives there and was gonna take a vacation before the fall semester classes began here."

Dimitri's great niece might just also have the combination to the big safe in the Purple Parrot office which would provide plenty of traveling cash. Especially if she capped Dimitri and Carlo first.

I declined to share the obvious theory with anyone. If Amber had done what I strongly suspected, she certainly didn't wipe out any boy scout camp. Besides, someday I might need a lawyer with a forty-inch bustline. Homicide wouldn't spend an abundance of time on the murders of Dimitri and his thug. It was pretty apparent who had murdered the two strippers. Dimitri and Carlo had received the ultimate punishment.

I walked out to the Dodge and retrieved the Leemis ledger. I handed it to Bush, still in hiding in the morgue office, then rejoined the merry band now circling the body of the girl I recalled being named Elga.

In thirty minutes, Bush scurried out of the office. "Kobok, this is a coded ledger, and a poorly done one at that. Looks to me like Billie Jack was receiving thousands of dollars in cash from an unstated source. No way to tell where it originated. Definite appearance of money laundering."

I said, "Which may or may not have contributed to the Given's murders. We put Linda on trial and the defense learns of this, they're gonna put Dimitri on trial to cloud the issue."

Bush looked up from the ledger. "Probably exculpatory anyway. Prosecution might have to give it up before trial...if Linda's case goes to trial."

"We're still a distance from a murder trial, Randall."

Hooper rolled his cigar stub across his lips. "If Billie Jack was rolling in cash, wonder why he wouldn't pony up to have Linda's boobs adjusted?"

O'Hara looked over her glasses. "Typical damned male tightwad. Love 'um and ignore them." She snapped her gaze to me. I could testify she didn't need a boob adjustment.

I made O'Hara a promise of everlasting fidelity and we left, Bush following me to the GSA Garage.

Short Cummins, still walking on a cane as a result of being shot in the billfold, was on point.

"Kobok, we gotta file murder charges on Linda Givens. We have other fish to fry." His weak chin created the illusion he was going to cry.

When I explained the deaths of Beeman, Dimitri, and his goon, he lacked the mental capacity to understand the evidentiary problems that the defense could formulate with two possible accomplices dead. Like a damned fool, I explained that I didn't think either Beeman or Dimitri were involved.

"All the more reason to strike while the iron is hot," he contended.

Iron is hot? Short Cummins had been reading somebody's stash of clichés.

"We have a couple of leads to pursue, Cummins. Then we'll appear before a Dallas County Grand Jury and request Linda's indictment for capital murder. No federal case here."

"Capital?"

"Death penalty, Cummins. The three-needle cocktail."

Cummins retreated to his man cave, forgetting to limp the first few steps. He recovered and barely made the door. I called Hooper and ran the Bent Dick Story past him. I explained that Sullivan was, according to Beeman, a witness, to Beeman's alibi that he'd been third in line for Beaver's favors at the time the Given's house went up. Bush and I picked him up on the Commerce Street side of the Police and Courts Building. We then embarked on another venture that seemed to happen only to cops- or maybe just to Bush.

CHAPTER 30: For the Life of Him

We made one pass by the address where I'd confronted Linda and Beeman the afternoon before. Hooper used the the DPD. radio in the Dodge to call for two uniforms to assist. If Scoots was inside and armed, no harm in arriving with a numerical superiority.

Bush dug through my folder. "Richard Delmar Sullivan is 28. He's on parole from the Texas Department of Criminal Justice after doing four of a ten-year sentence for burglary. Several arrests for dope, assault, public drunk. Did only county jail time on all except the burglary."

I reminded him of Bent Dick's physical impairment caused by the collision with the bus which left his neck turned about a third to the left.

"I remember, Kobok."

We'd parked a block away for several minutes waiting for the cover squads, when down the block, a marked car, red lights flashing skidded into the driveway of Bent Dick Sullivan's mom. Then another, then another bounced into the yard.

"Good God," Hooper growled. "Somebody got a signal crossed. Better get down there."

As I approached, a fourth marked car swerved into the driveway ahead of us. "Damn," Hooper spat. "I musta got hold of a new dispatcher."

The three of us piled out waving badges. No sense getting shot by an over-anxious rookie who thought Hooper too ugly or Bush too pristine to be the law.

The neighborhood resembled many in Southeast Dallas. Run down and in disrepair, it was built on a larger than normal parcel of land, with some distance between houses. Several disassembled motorcycles or piles of metal that appeared to be motorcycle parts were strewn on the porch and front yard.

The front door of the Sullivan house burst open and a girl rushed toward us. She was white, mid twentyish, looked hard as hell, with shoulder length dirty blonde hair and numerous tattoos including a dog urinating on a fireplug on her left buttocks. All tattoos were fully visible because the girl was nude.

"Rape, they raped me, rape!" she screamed with sufficient volume to be heard in downtown Dallas. She shot a terrified glance over one shoulder, causing her to partially trip, colliding head on with the innocent and unready Bush, and bowling him over like Niagara Falls. They landed in a heap in the dirt, creating a brief dust storm. She bounced up and broke toward the house next door.

The nearly sideways, wild eyed face of Bent Dick Sullivan appeared in the doorway in pursuit, brandishing a machete. Skinny, pale-skinned to the color of milk white, he too displayed an array of tattoos on both arms, both legs, his chest, his back, and both ass cheeks. An ink artist would have been hard-pressed to find a bare spot. The Tats were visible because, Bent Dick also was as naked as a jaybird.

On seeing a yard load of cops and flashing lights, Bent Dick also ran for the house next door. The girl had continued around the house, disappearing in tall grass, uncut for at least a year. Bent Dick barged through the front door into the neighboring, equally shabby residence.

"Holy Jesus Christ!" shrieked a female voice from inside.

A greying officer in dark rimmed glasses with sergeant's stripes on his shoulders sauntered over to us. "What gives, Paul?" Hooper asked him.

"The naked chick claims somebody, probably that biker, Bent Dick Sullivan, raped her."

The sergeant wiped his brow with a handkerchief. "What we have here is a failure to agree on terms of a business agreement. This is the third time this girl, her name is Ruby Dent, has come out here, made some kinda deal for dope, cash and God knows what else in return for sex. It's also the third time she's run all over hell screaming rape. Once she made it all the way to the Mesquite City Limits. Caused a two-mile traffic jam. If she had bigger boobs, Bull, the jam woulda been three miles."

Ruby appeared on the opposite side of the Sullivan house, having circled the place around the rear. "Ruby," the sergeant bellowed. "Get your ass over here."

When Ruby got close enough, she was outwardly so stoned, it seemed standing upright would not be possible. A patrolman handed her his yellow raincoat which she folded over an arm and continued to stand naked and glassy eyed in the hot sun.

A female officer arrived. Her name tag read Sanders. She approached the naked girl and said, "Dammit, Ruby, I've told you to keep your nekked ass outta this neighborhood. Now get yourself covered up. We're gonna have to arrest Bent Dick again. Ever consider marrying that loser so rape is harder to make noise about?"

Ruby hung the raincoat over her shoulders. "He promised me he'd pay me this time. All I got was a couple of damned pills."

The sergeant said calmly, "Ruby's a whore. She catches a taxi out here, makes it with some of these bikers, gets stoned on their crank, then decides it was a pay for play deal and shouts rape."

A fat lady in a purple housecoat crashed out the door we'd seen Bent Dick's bare ass disappear into. She stumbled across the front yard into the Sullivan yard where we were clustered. Visibly intoxicated, she caught Bush square in the back while waddling full bore. Down went both. Bush's silk britches would never survive. Now zero for two in collisions with physically impaired women, he stood back up, assuming a half crouch, ready for attack number three.

The fat lady bounded up. "Bastard's got my damned husband!" she screamed.

"Got him with what?" Hooper asked.

"A Goddamned sword. He's a' holdin' my Sylvester in the commode."

Ruby asked, "Anybody gotta smoke?" The sergeant offered her a Winston, then lit it with a cigarette lighter.

I approached the hysterical fat lady. She blurted, "If that mope murders Sylvester, I'm gonna starve. He's the only one who gets a welfare check."

"Lady, you gotta phone in that house?"

"Well hell yes."

I walked into the Sullivan house, gambling that all other occupants had fled out the back. I dialed the number the fat lady had provided. After several rings, a man answered.

"Is this Bent Dick Sullivan?"

"Who's callin'" He was rasping for air.

"I'm Kobok, the fed working on the Billie Jack Givens murder. You know me, Richard."

"I ain't did none o' that shit that skank is babbling and I ain't had nothin' to do with that brassiere guy's killin'. You the one with the kid-cop who is also a lawyer? He was a nice kid." His breath rate increased.

"You need to calm down, Dick. Everyone knows you didn't kill Billie Jack Givens and that this chick out here screaming rape is just stoned. Don't make this worse than it is."

"Man, I'd just shot up when the bitch showed up. Then I took a couple of new pills. Besides that, I'm scared."

"Screw that, dude. C'mon out, now."

"Y'all murdered Sonny Beeman and now you're gonna do me."

"Come out right now or they might just shoot your ass if you don't."

"Lemme talk to that kid lawyer. I'll surrender to him. Nobody else."

"Lady out here says you're holding her husband prisoner. Send him out first."

"Man, she jes' run out the door when I come in nekked and high. This is jes' ol' Sylvester in here with me and he's takin' a dump. Soon as he finishes, I'll send him out. Don't shoot him." Bent Dick was breathing like he'd just finished a marathon.

I walked back out and found Bush, covered in dirt and dust from two collisions with out of control females. "Bush, Bent Dick says you talked nice to him at the Fireplug. He say's if you come up on the porch so we can't shoot him, he'll come out.

First, Sylvester, this lady's husband is on the throne. When he come out, you go up and cuff Bent Dick."

The old lady, hearing the conversations, shouted, "Damn that Sylvester. Gets that welfare check and spends all day drinking that damned cut-rate beer. Then he sits on the pot all the next day and we ain't got no more money."

Sylvester, sixtyish, graying and stooped, with one of the galluses of his overalls hitched up, appeared on the front porch. As he limped off the porch, the old lady shouted, "Shithouse bastard."

Bush, dirty and disheveled, bravely marched to the front porch. One of the uniforms laid across the hood of his squad car, aiming his AR 15 rifle at the doorway just in case.

"Hold your fire," directed the sergeant, his voice showing the edges of deadly urgency.

A machete sailed out the doorway into the dusty yard. Bent Dick Sullivan wobbled through the doorway. Still naked, he passed Bush, uneasily stepped down from the porch, turned his eyes skyward, and pitched facedown into the dirt. His body lay beside his machete, twitched violently a few times, then ceased moving. We rushed forward.

Body, it was. Bent Dick Sullivan was deader than good manners.

Hooper lit a fresh stogie. "Damned good work, Bush. You scared him to death."

Officer Sanders, an attractive blonde, said, "Bush, I gotta couple of mopes over in my district who are bad news. Suppose you could come over and scare 'um to death?"

"Never touched him." Bush looked searchingly from face to face.

I said, "Bush, that guy was so doped up, he woulda been hard to touch off with a .12 gauge. It's just your terrifying demeanor."

"I didn't do anything."

I said, "Bush, if you'll just give me the recipes to your super man-killer elixir, I'll be your butler while Hopkins goes on vacation."

Hooper said, "It was easy. Bush just whispered his lawyer

fee for rescuing winos off the toilet and it was more than Dick's heart could stand."

We hung around in the heat until the field agent for the Medical Examiner's Office—that was O'Hara's department—showed up. He declared Sullivan had had suffered cardiac arrest from the combined causes of degenerative lifestyle, poor health, and an overdose of a mixed recipe of drugs ingested that only laboratory tests could ascertain.

At just before four p.m., Hooper, Bush, and I stopped at an all you can eat Mexican food restaurant on Samuel Boulevard. Hooper tried to put them out of business. I downed enchiladas until my headache cleared up somewhat. Bush even ate three tacos with salsa, mild.

I picked up the tab, and said, "Guys, I know you're beat. But Short Cummins is up in my face to file murder charges on Linda."

Hooper said, "My lieutenant is in the same mood. They've probably been talking."

"Well, Beeman told me last night, Scoots, if he isn't here at Bent Dick's, he'll be hold up in the office of Valdez Salvage on Bernal, just off Singleton. We set up tonight, grab the little dork, and we've either killed or captured every pertinent witness I know of. It's gonna be late, but tomorrow is Thursday. Whether or not we bag Scoots tonight, we go to the grand jury tomorrow, arrest Linda, and get drunk on Friday."

Both reluctantly agreed with the plan.

CHAPTER 31: RAT IN A TRAP

Scoots, an active parolee, was more vulnerable than the average criminal. If we could catch him holding a firearm, it was parole violation straight back to the joint—no trial necessary. To back that, an arrest warrant, charging murder had been issued for him. A weasel facing hard prison time might be persuaded to clarify Beeman's relationship to Linda Givens and confirm Beeman's excuse for being parked near the Givens home just before the fire. The effect would again be to short circuit a defense attorney's attempt to cloud Linda's involvement in Billie Jack's demise by putting the dead Sonny Beeman on trial.

Hooper, Bush, and I met at the Kickstand at 9:00 P.M. Hooper had checked out a hand radio set, or walkie for Bush. Both the city Plymouth he picked up from the motor pool and my Dodge had Dallas P.D. radios.

Valdez Salvage stretched a block along Bernal Avenue in far West Dallas, surrounded by an eight-foot, concertina wire topped, chain link fence. Like many big cities, Dallas was informally divided into districts, or neighborhoods. North Dallas, well out toward the LBJ Freeway, Near North Dallas, just north of downtown, East Dallas, South Dallas, Oak Cliff, and Pleasant Grove were all neighborhoods which were part of the City of Dallas. West Dallas was a run down, heavily industrial area, cursed further by being "dry". West Dallas residents who wanted to quench their urge for an adult beverage, had to cross the Continental Street Viaduct to find liquor along Industrial Boulevard. Logic said Scoots left his junkyard haven daily to escape prying eyes of employees of his cousin and to make a beer run. He then spent time at Bent Dick's place. Beeman had said Scoots was hurting because his dope provider was in jail.

The camper trailer used as an office, was perched near the back fence as Beeman had said. Scoots' old dark blue, Ford F150 pickup, nearly identical to Clarence's ride, was parked next to the camper, barely visible in a salvage yard jammed with dead cars. This would be the vehicle parked near the Givens' house on the fateful night.

Protocol required we advise Short Cummins that we needed to watch the place and bag Two Scoots if possible.

We sat up in as close to a triangle as possible at around nine thirty.

The plan was, if Two Scoots didn't come out by midnight, we'd cut the padlock with bolt cutters and kick in the camper door, using the parole violation warrant as probable cause.

I parked on Bernal. Hooper, parked a block down in the alley behind. I called him. "Have you noticed this junkyard ain't got no junkyard dog?," Hooper said on the radio.

I had and said so. Maybe Two Scoots, stuffed in the little camper beneath a laboring air conditioner, was afraid of dogs.

At just past ten, the light went out inside the camper, although the glow of a TV in service was obvious. By midnight or sooner, we'd have the little rat.

However, several mitigating factors were about to enter stage left. Orville Wilson "Scoots" Garcia, 24, was well known for his odd hop-walk which had earned him his nickname. But part of the story wasn't in our files. We'd wondered why he'd paroled out after serving so little time of his original sentence. There was ample reason, which they'd learn only after they'd dealt with him in a West Dallas junkyard.

Orville Wilson Garcia had been locked up in the Jester II Unit of the TDC, near Sugarland, Texas, an hour's drive southwest of Houston. The Texas prison system is self-sustaining in that the 59 prison units grow and prepare all food consumed by inmates. All labor was also by inmates. Jester II raised tons of potatoes, onions and related truck-farming crops. For a small hourly wage, inmates toiled in the hot Texas sun. Tennis lessons and color television were still far in the future. Far from slave labor, no inmate was forced to work, although not to do so meant a lot of time spent in a six by eight trying to stare a hole in the wall.

Prison farm labor in Texas, while far removed from the old stereotype chain gangs, was still not a gig that folks line up to join. An inmate who wants to improve his lot, must show a work ethic and some self-discipline working in open farm fields, or they'd put him back in a cell block. Orville Wilson Garcia, in his quest for a new and better life, decided to improve himself by escaping. After all, Clyde Barrow with Bonnie Parker as chauffeur, had busted a buddy out of the same place thirty-five years before.

TDC guards were almost always country men from the widespread areas where most units were located. They tended to be far more proficient with firearms than with their respective levels of intellectual capability. Usually on horseback, armed with a shotgun and a revolver, they were issued standing orders to shoot any inmate who attempted escape. Usually, they hit what they shot at.

On a sweltering hot day in Fort Bend County, Texas, a lone guard supervised 18 men laboring in the sun hoeing onions. The onion field was bounded on both sides by cotton fields. Scoots slid into the knee-high cotton and crawled the half mile to the edge of the field, adjacent to a passing road. Things were going fine until the guard saw the scrawny prisoner scaling the wire. He galloped his mount to well within .12 gauge range and blew Scoots off the fence.

The attempted escape didn't end in the usual way because Scoots wasn't killed instantly, probably because the horse made a misstep as the guard fired. More surprising, Scoots didn't die of shock and blood loss. Scoots spent the next ten months in the prison hospital at the Goree Unit in Huntsville. The blast had blown off his left foot. TDC had neither space nor medical staff to handle a seriously ill patient any longer than they had to. Scoots was paroled to Dallas County as soon as he was able to walk on the ill-fitting appliance, hewn by an inmate. His infirmity was probably known to his parole officer, but no space on the form was dedicated to prison injuries received. Nor did his parole officer see a need to inform the Dallas County Records System that Scoots Garcia moved about on a wooden foot.

As Scoots watched TV in his little metal box in West Dallas, a variable was about to alter the plan. Two residents of the area, Fredrico Gonzales and Nathaniel Washington, both 19, both convicted felons on youth early parole were prowling the neighborhood on foot, looking for something to steal. Valdez Salvage, while not as approachable as a Sears store, was next best in the neighborhood.

Hooper whispered into the radio. "Two males on foot just walked right in front of me. Must be too stoned to have heard my engine running."

Parked in front, with binoculars I studied movement in the alley through broken cars and a front fence. Two figures were trying to climb the rear, eight-foot, razor wire topped barricade. One, who would turn out to be Gonzales, stood on the shoulders of the other and tossed an old blanket over the wire. He slid over and using the fence for leverage, landed feet first inside.

"They're climbing over the fence," Bush whispered into the radio. Parked in the alley east of the junkyard, the intruders had stopped to try their luck with the fence before they reached Bush's position.

Washington nimbly climbed the fence, twisted his feet over the blanket and dropped beside Gonzales.

Two Scoots, out of dope and booze, expecting to be murdered by any one of several potential assailants, was alert for strange sounds. When Gonzales hit ground, he made contact with a piece of scrap metal. Ten feet away, Scoots heard the sound. Who the hell ever it was couldn't be good. He snapped off the T.V. and grabbed the double barreled, .12-gauge Winchester he'd stolen from a pickup at a barbecue two blocks away the night before. He peered out into the poorly lighted, but not totally dark junkyard. To a hunted man, Fredrico Morales Gonzales standing ten feet away, looked enough like a biker, a uniformed cop, or the boogey man to be fair game.

Carefully opening the camper door just as Gonzales was reaching for the handle, Two Scoots gave the intruder one barrel—nine double ought buckshot in the chest at three feet. The blast blew Fredrico Morales Gonzales some distance. The young burglar's criminal career and life ended in a heap in the dust of a Bernal Avenue junkyard.

Washington, as agile leaving as he was arriving, clambered back up the fence, twisted over the blanket and dropped back into the alley. Scoots let fly with his second barrel just as Washington let go. The result: Scoots missed center mass, the .00 buck tearing into Washington upper left shoulder and chest above the heart. The shot was fatal, and the young man was destined to end his life in the dust behind a junkyard that contained not a dime in cash. However, like a biker I'd seen shot dead the Sunday before, death was not quite instantaneous. Washington staggered east in the alley, directly toward Bush who had exited his Ford and drawn his revolver

The shot that blew Gonzales away, lit the darkness with a millisecond of daylight. I radioed the Dallas Police switchboard and advised them of shots fired, officers involved, and gave them the address. The emergency services operator asked me to repeat and confirm the address. I had my mic open when Scoots shot Washington. She said, "Oh my God." I shouted out the Dodge window for Hooper to bring the bolt cutters.

After the Bent Dick dust up, Bush had found a clean white shirt. It stood out like a railroad semaphore in my headlights as I skidded into the alley. Hooper's car blocked my way. He had bailed out and was pursuing the wounded burglar as fast as forty years of enchiladas and degeneracy would allow. Washington was on a direct collision course with Bush. Bush raised his left hand like the Statue of Liberty, pointed his revolver at Washington, and shouted, "Halt, federal officer". Of course, Washington, eternity whispering in his ear, didn't hear. He crashed headlong into Bush, the pair landing in a dusty heap at mid alley. For the third time in a single day, Bush had been knocked on his ass by a fleeing, impaired citizen. Washing shuddered and died.

In the dim light, Scoots, incredibly active for a man missing a foot, climbed onto the roof of the Ford pickup, then onto the roof of the camper, then over the fence. He ran east, toward Hooper, on foot, and Bush, on his butt in the dust.

"Bull, the shooter is in the alley with you. He's gotta shotgun and he's behind you." I shouted.

Scoots stopped, started to turn back toward me, thought

better of it, and bolted on East past Hooper, then around Bush, still tangled on the ground. He tossed the shotgun and straddle hopped into the darkness out of range of my headlights. We had no way of knowing that when he had pilfered the shotgun from the trunk of a car, it was loaded, but the two shells were all the ammo he had.

Bush gained his feet and in seconds he and Hooper had disappeared in pursuit of Scoots. I figured I was way too far out of the chase to join.

In minutes, an ambulance, and a half dozen marked squad cars arrived, along with a totally unexpected visitor. Short Cummins Klaster rolled up in his shiny new taxpayer owned Chevrolet. Clearly, he was slow trailing the three of us, ostensibly to monitor what the hell ever he thought we were doing. Short Cummins wasn't smart enough to recall that when crap explodes, fructus spreads in all directions. Unfortunately for him, in his dim, paranoid mind, he'd forgotten that as ranking officer at the scene, any flak would find him first.

I advised both him and patrol units that the shooter was a biker, Orville Wilson Garcia, a Blood Lord outlaw biker and that Bush and Hooper would catch him and return in one more minute.

We'd soon learn Bush caught him all right and then Hooper caught him also.

By the end of the next block, Scoots was winded, terrified, and painfully aware his prosthetic foot was not designed for track and field. In blind panic, he sprang on a chain link fence and incredibly, was astraddle the top just as Bush caught hold of his left foot.

Then the horror. Inside the fence was a 113-pound Rottweiler who had waited until Scoots reached the apex before lunging at the little man, intent on a late dinner. Scoots, competing in hysterical shrieks with the Rottweiler's savage barks and snarls could have compared himself to Daniel and the lion's den, if he'd known the story.

Hooper lumbered up, stogie still in place. He holstered his pistol and joined Bush in the deadly game of tug of war. Then, Scoots threw a shoe, so to speak. His foot came off in Hooper's hands. Bush managed to drag him to the non-dog side by the leg of his blue jeans.

Hooper stood, studying the prosthesis by flashlight. "Bush, this don't look so good."

"Gimme my damned foot," Scoots whined from the ground.

Bush examined the foot. "Prosthetic device."

"Damn right it's pathetic," Hooper noted.

Scoots snarled, still on the ground. "Damn cops ain't got no right to tear off a man's foot."

And not much more than the prescribed minute I'd predicted, Bush and Hooper appeared, Bush holding Scoots' detached foot, Hooper supporting the small biker who was hopping on the other. Bush, following his collision with the wounded, dying Washington was coated with blood, dirt, and gore.

Short Cummins, afraid of Ferris wheels, crying babies, clowns, cemeteries, and prone to panic, froze. His eyes were, as they say, as wide as golf balls.

"They tore off my damned foot," Scoots shouted.

"No problem, Cummins" Hooper called out. "It's a damned pathetic device."

Short Cummins could take no more. He sucked in a lung full of dusty, humid air and fainted, flat on his back in the dusty West Dallas alley, his cane-trophy from being shot in the billfold flopped beside him.

EMT.'s arrived along with half the Dallas Police Department. Scoots sat in the back seat of a squad car, his prosthetic foot on the seat beside him for nearly an hour while we labored to resurrect Group Supervisor Klaster.

Short Cummins revived sufficiently to plead the case for having been overcome by heat exhaustion, work exhaustion, and having forgotten to take his blood pressure medication. The ambulance driver jotted "Patient fainted" then listed all three of Short Cummins' excuses. He'd be marked in DPD and ATF folk lore as the "Turkey who fainted behind the junkyard." How prophetic. "Shot in the ass Short Cummins now had another foible to bear."

Two Scoots confirmed Beeman's "in bed with Beaver" alibi and Beeman's trip to San Antonio. He did admit with Beeman, they had parked down the street from the Given's house, waiting for Linda to get Billie Jack drunk so she could sneak out for a quickie with both of them. He insisted that they fled before any fire occurred. He stated several times he was willing to take the polygraph on the issue, possibly the only time in recorded history an outlaw biker volunteered for the test.

We jailed him for the parole violation and conferred in the book-in area of the Sterrett Center.

Hooper said disgustedly, "Even if the little dork would actually take a poly, I'd bet my cigar case neither he nor Beeman had a damn thing to do with the murder of Billie Jack Givens."

I agreed. Beeman was capable of murder, but he seemed at this point, to be clear in the Billie Jack Givens case. Linda was in trouble.

CHAPTER 32: JUST THE FACTS, MA'AM

It had been a long, difficult night. I'd gotten to bed at around four. By nine, I drug myself to the office. Neither Bush nor Cummins were present. I called Hooper's Office. The Desk sergeant told me he'd be in by ten. I asked if he could have Hooper catch a ride with a marked car and drop by our office.

I had concluded the report on the previous day's activity and just dug Jason's journal and the misshapen ball thingy from Jason Given's desk when Bush came in. Short Cummins limped in and then Hooper. By 11:00 A.M. we were all crammed in Short Cummin's office. I stuffed the diary and dice gadget in my coat pocket.

"Kobok," Cummins said. "I called. Dallas County Grand Jury meets today. They're expecting you...and Hooper if he wants to go, to appear and request an indictment for murder against Linda Marie Givens."

I sighed. "Cummins, Linda is probably...note probably, good for Billie Jacks' murder. The boys were collateral damage. I think there are two peripheral suspects, Dimitri Bastovic and Sonny Beeman, both dead, whom the defense will try to dredge up as smoke screens to use in her defense. Her mentally challenged brother is in jail for an unrelated murder. The defense might also try to use him as a shield. I don't see how we can avoid these limitations. I'll appear before the grand jury as soon as I can hitch a ride to the Crowley Courts Building. Our case is purely circumstantial without a shred of direct evidence against her."

I then enumerated facts as known: "We see no way the fire could have been ignited by someone not already inside the house. Linda had tried to steal $76,000 from Billie Jack's checking account the Tuesday before the fire occurred past midnight on

Wednesday morning. Linda appears to have forged Billie Jacks'
signature on the life insurance policy. She'd claimed her driver's
license was stolen when it had not been. She'd widely stated she
hated Billie Jack and the boys. Sonny Beeman was murdered
shortly after I dropped him at a hotel room they were sharing.
She was sleeping with Beeman and we found his biker colors
under her bed. When she was admitted to Baylor Hospital, she
had her car keys and a fortune in gold in her blue jeans pocket."
I looked from face to face. "And if she didn't kill Beeman last
night, who did?"

Bush said, "Uh, the extramarital affair might not
be admissible. Beeman is dead and not subject to cross
examination."

Cummins asked, "Who killed the Russian, Dimitri?"

Bush and I exchanged glances. "Not a clue," I said.

Hooper nodded. "Plenty of suspects. No evidence."

I had a suspect in mind also, but said nothing.

I said, "Bush, parking at the Crowley building is non-
existent. Can you drop Hooper and I and double park while we
present the case to a grand jury?"

"Sure."

Bush drove us as requested. As I got out of the car, I asked,
"What do you hear from Italy?"

"Amber says she'll come back in a couple of weeks. Kobok, I
really don't think she did what I think you're thinking."

"Okay," I said and got out into the heat. I damn sure did
believe Amber knocked off Dimitri and Carlo. Okay by me.

The assistant Dallas County district attorney in charge of
the grand jury pushed us to the head of the line and in twenty
minutes, I had in hand a bench warrant for the arrest of Linda
charging capital murder, code speak for a death penalty case.

"Know where to find her?" Hooper asked as we drove back
to the Cabell Building. Hooper plopped in a chair, his size
thirteens on my desk.

I said, "Yeah, call her lawyer. What's his name...Harless
Androvski."

Cummins was actually smiling. He'd get credit for a
supervisory arrest. Good news for a fat boy who'd been shot

in the ass and later fainted at a crime scene, all in a week. I was vaguely uncomfortable. It seemed too pat, too easy, and our evidence was subject to defense attack.

I called Androvski's office. We could spend a day or two looking for Linda and might or might not find her. Chances were good, Androvski, as her attorney, would know how to find her. Most attorney's would bring their client to an arraignment if for no other reason, to avoid getting called out of bed in the middle of the night when we did find her.

Androvski's secretary curtly advised he was unavailable and would call me back shortly.

"I'm hungry enough to eat Bush's shoes," Hooper declared.

I leaned over and examined Bush's imported footwear. "Bull Hooper, that would be a four-hundred-dollar lunch. Grab some coffee over there," I gestured, "and we'll find a place for you to forage as soon as Androvski calls me back."

Bush said, "Meanwhile, would you mind if we had another look at the journal you picked up at the Givens' fire scene."

From my pocket, I dug out the journal, the odd shaped dice looking gadget, and the several scribbled-on sheets that had been folded in the book.

The sheets of paper were obviously tally records of the progress of what appeared to be a game. The end of day scores were noted at the bottom of the dated page. The last entry in the journal was the Tuesday before Billie Jack was murdered the following Wednesday morning.

Bush said, "Whatever they were doing, it appears there were only two players, Jason and Trey."

Tootie wandered in from lunch just in time to answer an incoming call. "Kobok," She covered the receiver. "Some lawyer for you."

"Kobok, this is Harless Androvski. You called?"

"Your client has been indicted by the grand jury for capital murder."

"What client?"

He knew damned well who I meant. "Linda Marie Givens. If you'll bring her voluntarily to the Crowley Courts Building for arraignment, it will save us kicking in doors, handcuffs, and the like." Arraignment meant the judge would read her Miranda rights, set bail, and have her fingerprinted before he allowed a tiny bond amount. Arraignment was society's message that they didn't trust cops who had read the defendant their rights from the same card before bringing the defendant before a judge.

"I'll see if I can reach her." That meant he knew exactly where to call her. "Judge Wilcox is a friend of mine. Unless you hear otherwise, Kobok, I'll have her in his chambers at 2:30 P.M. He'll arraign her in chambers. Save as much publicity as possible."

"Okay," Hooper struggled his 240-pound carcass to his feet. "I need to reward this fine body with food. Is there a hamburger joint in one of those buildings across the street? Last time I ate food in this building, it was cardboard on toast."

Bush said, "There's a dandy Chinese place behind McDonalds across the street to the West. Ate there the other day. Cheap and pretty good."

I said, "Whoa, Randall. I've never eaten Chinese food and see no reason to start today. Don't they serve worms instead of hamburger?"

Bush snickered. "Man, earthworms cost ten times as much as beef. They couldn't afford worms."

Hooper chewed his cigar stub. "Order broccoli beef. It's sort of like beef stew, only spicier."

The *Golden Palace* was actually a block west on Jackson Street, squeezed between a crafts shop and a vacant storefront. A previous sign: *Louie's Deli* had been crudely painted over on the front door glass. The darkened interior was augmented by candles burning on each of about twelve tables.

The waiter, a slight, very proper young Asian man, brought water all around and slid three place mats onto the table. I was dumbfounded as Jason's journal leaped off the placemat. Twelve animals printed around the edges, snake, dragon, and nine more were recognizable as properly printed versions of the crude replicas in Jason's journal.

"What the hell is this?" I exclaimed, perhaps with too much vigor.

"Chinese Zodiac," Bush smiled. "They're standard in Chinese restaurants."

I'd probably actually had been to Chinese restaurants, but I didn't recall the occasion and I always ate with my eyes closed. I stood and said to the waiter, still standing nearby, "Can you look at this little book?" I pulled Jason's journal from my pocket.

"Oh, sir," the waiter said thumbing through the journal. "Someone has revived the ancient Chinese Zodiac Game. It is a simple game of play-war, a favorite of children many years ago."

"How does it work?"

"Children roll a twelve-sided die in turns. Each player selects an enemy. Two players each have one enemy, four players would have four, for example. Player roll, say rabbit side down and rabbit is not selected as enemy, then die passes to other player or players who rolls. He lands on snake, if snake is player's selected enemy, player wins two marks against the snake."

"How do you win?"

"Players roll six times, then game starts over. Player who is ahead after six rolls is winner, then new game."

"What does Dragon Marks Eight mean?"

"Oh, sir, eights marks on any character is impossible. A player must roll the same symbol four times in six rolls. Odds are thousands to one against."

"What happens to the symbol if a player achieves eight marks?"

"Symbolically, the character must die. But it is only a child's game. No one is actually killed."

"So the players don't have to use all twelve symbols of the zodiac?"

"No, as I said, sir, they may play with less. If rabbit, for example is not wanted, they simply leave rabbit off the score sheet."

I held up the odd dice. "Are you familiar with this?"

"Yessir, it is called a doo-deca...uh, sorry, I don't recall."

"Dodecahedron," Bush said from his chair, pronouncing it phonetically.

"Yes," said the waiter, looking curiously at Bush.

I asked, "How does the person or enemy as you say, die... after they receive eight marks?"

"By their own weapon. You said Dragon. Dragon must die by fire. But Sir, again it is make-believe child's game. No one really dies."

My limited mind didn't thrive on revelations, but I sensed the waiter had just provided exactly that. Had Linda gotten involved in the child games of her sons? Perhaps to a cold-blooded murderer, the method of death didn't have to fit the exact rule of the game?

I folded the placemat and stuffed it in my pocket. I bolted out the door. To my surprise, Bush and Hooper followed. We crossed Commerce Street amidst honking horns and screeching tires, as I rushed upstairs to Tooties' computer—the only one in the office in that era.

Hooper asked, "What are we doing, Kobok?"

"Billie Jack Givens must have been born in the year of the dragon. Linda slew the dragon with his own weapon: fire. Something is screwed up!"

In several minutes of pecking and cursing, I had accumulated a list:

Jason Givens: Born in the year of the Snake.

Trey Givens: Born in the year of the Monkey.

Billie Jack Givens: Born in the year of the Tiger.

Linda Marie Givens: Born in the year of the Dragon.

But Linda was the Dragon, born in that year. The waiter had said the symbol representing that character had to die by fire. What the hell was wrong here? Billie Jack would have had to die by the actions of a tiger, not by fire.

Hooper stood and said at last, "Games be damned, I'm gonna walk back to that Chinese place and have worms...about five pounds of them. He and Bush led, and I followed. The waiter I'd earlier accosted seemed as if no conversation had taken place. We sat for Chinese cuisine.

CHAPTER 33: IN THE END, IT'S EASY.

IF YOU WANT TO FIND DIRT, LOOK IN THE CRACKS

Still puzzled, I endured some dish I thought might be called *Moo Goo Rat Fish.* When we'd finished, we walked to the GSA garage which was closer to the restaurant than the federal building.

I had intended to leave Bush in the car while Hooper and I went before the grand jury. As I swung the Dodge into the county parking structure, I negotiated around an ambulance and a half dozen marked police cars. I parked in an end zone, tossed my "ATF" placard on the dash and we hurried on foot through basement security. A uniformed deputy told us a woman had committed suicide in the lady's room. Premonition was unavoidable.

We badged our way inside. "She's dead in a stall, guys," a uniformed sergeant pointed.

The body of Linda Marie Givens, her arm still heavily bandaged, lay wedged between a commode and the stall wall. A .25 automatic pistol lay near her left hand in a wide pool of crimson.

Bush said sagely, "Typical female suicide...shot herself in the heart and not the face.

Hooper squeezed in and performed the mandatory body search. He pulled a note from Linda's blouse pocket, slipped it into a plastic evidence binder and held it up for us to read.

Through the plastic, the words were visible:

I am a slut, damned to go to Hell. I did not kill my husband, but I did kill that scumbag Beeman. He came by the hospital and demanded money and sex. I forged that check on Billie Jack's account because I needed money to repair a defective boob job. The life insurance policy was Billie Jack's idea for protection of the boys. He said it would be all right if I signed his name to the application. Great God, my baby, Jason set the fire. Me and Billie Jack hadn't slept together in weeks. I used the sofa in the den and he kept the bed. The night of the fire, Billie Jack had passed out on the sofa and I used the bed. Mother of God, I heard Jason shout, 'Trey, tonight we've slain the Dragon' and then the explosion and fire. He meant to kill me, not Billie Jack. They'd been playing some stupid Zodiac game. Oh God, why have you abandoned me?

"Well," Bush said. "We thought the killer had initiated the fire from inside the house. We just guessed the wrong family member. Family fights and Linda's hatefulness and lifestyle drove the kid nuts."

I said, "The word 'guess' is wrong as hell in this situation. Madness, sheer madness. A tormented kid, fearful of losing contact with the one person solid in his life, his stepfather, let a kid's game drive him insane...except he used too much gasoline. I had doubts. I sent word to that lawyer she was charged with murder...forced her over the edge. This could have been prevented." I gestured to the toilet stall.

Bush said, "Look, partner, there's no way you can beat yourself up over this. All of us, including the brass were convinced she was guilty...and she did murder Beeman. That little .25 she just shot herself with is gonna match the ballistics on the slugs the morgue pulled out of Beeman. They can't bump you to Detroit. You get credit for busting Clarence and for clearing this Givens' fiasco, even though it didn't go like we expected. Find something positive for a change. If nothing else, my father will intercede, and they'll transfer Cummins to Detroit." He grinned.

The weight of Jason's journal was bulky in my pocket. If the news media got wind of that, another circus would follow. The kid would be famous. I vowed to shed it as soon as I made my way back to the office and disavow any knowledge no matter what the hell. If Short Cummins had enough sense to recall its existence, Hooper could toss him out a twelfth-floor window.

"Bush, you've been okay to work with. You'll be associated with a high dollar law firm shortly and out of this muck. Do it while you can."

"Uh, Kobok, I've been thinking. Sit all day reading legal briefs and leave this three-ring circus behind? Not a chance. I'm staying on the job right here."

I looked at him, surprised.

"Kobok, you look a little flummoxed."

"Yeah, Bush, I guess you're right. Musta been that batch of worms I just had for lunch."

ABOUT THE AUTHOR

Gary Clifton, forty years a cop, including a twenty-five-year career as an ATF Agent, has spent a lifetime squarely in a free front row seat to the damnedest show on Earth. Having been shot at, shot, stabbed, sued, lied to and about, and frequently misunderstood, there is no violent crime, vicious situation, nor clever criminal subterfuge he hasn't seen. Of the many tales he's written, each is based in some actual crime he's handled, with names changed only to protect the guilty. He has a master's in psychology, an invaluable tool in trying to unravel the violence human beings can inflict upon each other.

Clifton published a novel, *Burn Sugar Burn,* in national paperback in 1987. Since, he's found more fertile ground in short fiction pieces. The Toronto based magazine, *Bewildering Stories*, has published more than fifty of Clifton's stories. He has published upwards of sixty more in various venues, including *Broadkill Review, The Simone Press, Beat to a Pulp, Yellow Mama, Rusty Nail, Crack the Spine*, and numerous others.

Currently, he's retired to a dusty North Texas ranch where he doesn't much give a damn if school keeps or not.

A selection of Clifton's work is available on his blog at:

http://www.bareknucklethoughts.org.

Curious about other Crossroad Press books?
Stop by our site:
http://www.crossroadpress.com
We offer quality writing
in digital, audio, and print formats.

Made in the USA
Middletown, DE
19 September 2022

10201927R00130